For Kevin
1934 – 2021

War
Babies

A NOVEL BY

Rachel Billington

UNIVERSE

This edition first published by Universe in 2022
an imprint of Unicorn Publishing Group
Charleston Suite
Meadow Business Centre
Lewes
East Sussex BN8 5RW

www.unicornpublishing.org

A catalogue record for this book is available
from the British Library

5 4 3 2 1

ISBN 978-1-914414-52-7

Cover design illustration by Matt Wilson
Typeset by Vivian Head

Printed by Short Run Press, Exeter, UK

PRELUDE

A woman lies unconscious on the carpet of a smart Westminster apartment. She is not young but still pretty; one red high-heeled shoe has fallen off. Nearby is a small but solid statuette of a buddha.

A younger woman, not dissimilar in colouring or build, lies with her eyes closed, half-hidden under a drinks cabinet. Her fingers clutch an empty bottle.

An hour passes.

Outside it is night time, a cold wintry night. The street lighting is good and shines on the mansion block. A car is driven up and parked neatly. A tall woman gets out, her face pale, her hair dark, her eyes blue. She lets herself into the block, goes up to the fifth floor in a wood-panelled lift with elegant grill doors and lets herself into the apartment.

The older women still lies on the floor. At the sound of footsteps, she moves slightly, makes a small noise.

'Oh, no!' The tall woman gasps, rushes to her side, crouches down.

The older woman lifts her head fractionally, opens her eyes and mutters in an angry, distorted voice, 'Leave me alone! Don't be a bore!' Her head flops down again.

The new visitor sits back on her heels, flushed and breathing heavily. She rubs her face, then peers forward again. She touches the woman's face, a loving gesture. She sits back again. She hasn't seen the other woman under the cabinet.

She stands up and nearly trips over the buddha. Now she sees the other woman. She gives a small scream which awakens neither of the unconscious figures.

The tall woman's gaze swings from one fallen figure to the other.

She turns her back and walks quickly out of the room and out of the flat, closing the door behind her.

ⓍⓄ

After about half an hour, the young woman under the cabinet rolls over and, hanging on to the furniture, totters to her feet. She sees the unconscious woman and bends closely over her, pushing aside the abandoned shoe in the process. She retreats a little, stands, swaying slightly. Eventually, she picks up the bottle and takes it over to a large desk where she places it next to a large black telephone.

She lifts off the receiver and, with some difficulty, dials 999. As she talks, she glances back over her shoulder, as if suspecting the other woman might suddenly rise up again.

PART ONE

CLEO

Why did we hate her? Why did what happened happen? Why did we want to love her? Or perhaps we didn't. Was she the worst mother in the world? Was I the worst daughter in the world? This is the story of three sisters and their mother. Their story, not hers. My story by the end. The father comes in too. If I was writing the blurb, I'd use words like shocking, inexplicable, thought-provoking. But in the end it's probably quite a usual story, apart from a wild few moments.

I was born 100 yards from the only bomb that fell in Oxford. My mother went out to feed our chickens. So the unlikely family story went. Julie was never a chicken-feeder. I wonder how much of our doomy world is due to being conceived and born in the war. Think of all those Home Service bulletins on the progress of the fighting boring into peoples' psyche, 'Hull has suffered over seventy bombing raids... Life is carried on amid burnt and wrecked homes, churches and shops...'
I was born into a generation of warmongers or avoiders, anxious hysterics, always stressing about what happens next. Answer: communism, nuclear weapons – more wars.

My mother, Julie Flynn, was elected a Labour Member of Parliament in 1950, the second election after the war. Think fragile beauty but tough as Boudicca. Red hair too. I inherited a faded copy.

The only person with whom I can discuss the past is my sister Millie, although her memory is what's called by her long-suffering carers 'in and out'. Last time I visited the creepy home where she resides, she entertained herself recalling the afternoon we climbed up a tree and peed onto the grass below. We were hoping, of course, someone would pass. No one did. Quite a feat, all the same, for two girls, ten and not yet seven. We had to stand on a branch, knickers pulled down, legs apart. I guess that's when my penis envy kicked off. Not. That's Di's province. Sort of. Was. In fact peeing dangerously from a tree was more her thing altogether. Di was the brave, adventurous one. Now and again Millie floated the idea she was a feminist but for that you'd have to believe Mary, Mother of God was a feminist. Quite clearly, the only classic feminist in the family was our mother.

I grew up adoring doubt, irony, sarcasm. I enjoyed annoying people. Pointless point-scoring was one of my favourite occupations. So I became a writer. And this is our story. The sisterhood. Millicent, Diana and me, Cleopatra. Millie, Di and Cleo. As events confirmed, I was the bad one. *There was a little girl who had a little curl right in the middle of her forehead and when she was good she was very very good and when she was bad she was HORRID.*

My father Doctor Brendan Flynn arrived back from the war in 1946. I was four years old and we had never met. He gave Julie plenty of notice and we were all well prepared. Millie (named after Millicent Fawcett) was eight, Di six, both in their school uniforms, me in a green nursery pinafore.

Our mother stood looking out of the window. 'Here he comes!' We clustered round her. 'As carefree as ever.' Her face sharpened. She turned away and waited for the doorbell to ring.

How splendid it was to have his square face, his crinkly brown hair, to hug his heavy, masculine body in our house of girls!

He sat me astride his knees and, after staring into my face for a solemn moment, smiled, 'Hello, little girl. I can see you haven't missed your dada.'

Millie, bossy and jealous as always, interrupted this important bonding. 'How could she miss you when she's never met you? *I've* missed you.'

'Of course you have.' Brendan stood me down and drew Millie forward with his long arm and I noticed the thick fair hairs on the wrist. He stared at his eldest child admiringly. 'You're a fine girl now, aren't you.' Although born and brought up in England, he could sound Irish on occasions. Perhaps he did it on purpose to annoy Julie.

'I was four when you went away to the war,' continued Millie, seeing opportunity to show off her maths, 'same age as *her* now.' She pointed a disparaging finger at me.

Di stayed outside this family get-together. She could scarcely remember our father, although, unlike me, she had been alive when he left.

At this point Julie pressed forward. That summer's day she wore my favourite dress, soft grey, printed with doves, a gentler image that belied the reality. Not long after this home-coming, I gave up searching for it.

'Now, girls, if you leave your father alone he might be able to relax and tell us some of his stories.'

Thus cued, Brendan, who had seemed perfectly relaxed before but wanted to placate Julie, sat back in his wood-framed chair and pronounced ruminatively, 'Ho hum.'

'Off you go,' said Julie briskly.

'So off I went,' echoed Brendan, 'in my smart Royal Army Medical Corps uniform, part of Operation Torch, heading for Algiers. The waves glittered in the sunlight as our ship passed the great rock of Gibraltar but then out of the wide blue sky came the black-eyed Hun...'

'Do you see what a brave father you have!' interrupted our mother with glinting bitterness.

Ignoring this, Brendan moved on smoothly from tending the sick in the desert to working in a hospital in Italy.

'Your father is a Surgeon General,' interrupted Julie again. 'He's very clever. He cuts off legs.'

'I'm even cleverer than that,' said Brendan. He leant forward to a small case at his feet and took out a hairbrush. 'Look at this.' We girls crowded round. It was an ordinary man's brush but the wooden back was intricately carved. 'Look closer.'

'Royal Army Medical Corps,' spelled out Millie.

'1944,' mouthed Di.

'What is it, Dada?' I nudged him crossly because I couldn't read.

'A brush that two Partisans made for me. You see, Yugoslavia down one side, Italia the other and your dada's name at the top.'

'But why did they give you it?' asked Di suddenly. She had taken the brush and was turning it in her hand.

'That's the point, dear girl.' Smiling, my father took back the brush. 'I *didn't* cut off their legs.' He glanced at my mother.

She gave him a narrow look which I soon knew for myself from times when I'd failed in one way or another. 'Tell your daughters, darling, why you spent so long getting back from *Italia*.' In her view she could have stood as an MP in the '45 election if he had been there.

We three girls, with our expectant blue eyes, lined up to know the answer.

'Ah, there's a tale! A good friend of mine, Squadron Leader Razor Brown, who was due for a spot of leave, had a Mosquito handy – the aeroplane not the insect – and when D-Day came round, we took off for months, flying wherever we wanted, not to Asia, of course; the dear old Med mostly, island hopping – Mykonos, Paros, Sicily, poor sad Malta, bombed nearly to smithereens, that sort of thing, landing on sand or dirt and sometimes even grass...'

At this point, I stopped listening. Even then, I wanted to be the one who told the stories.

MILLIE

Of course Mummy always loved me best. It was just my hard luck that she saddled herself with Di and Cleo – called after a cat, although she believes it was Queen Cleopatra. I don't expect my darling mother wanted more children but birth control was still a pretty hit-and-miss affair in the forties, or I suppose it could have had something to do with Dada's Catholicism but I doubt it. Mummy once confided in me that I was the only good thing that came out of sex with Dada.

Poor old Dada. He didn't have a clue how to deal with Mummy. During the war we were so close, darling Mummy and me. For four happy years we slept in the same bed, we breathed the same air, we ate the same food. 'Lightly, always lightly, Millie,' that's what she would say, 'More butterfly than buffalo.' We looked at the world with the same eyes. We waved the same red flag of socialism.

Naturally, it was a shock when I was thrown out of her bed to be replaced by long-forgotten Dada. 'I still love you most of all, darling,' she whispered as she showed me to the box room.

How huge Dada seemed that first afternoon when he dropped in with his little case as if he'd been round the corner for four years! First the house shrank, then beautiful Mummy, then all of us, like those shrinky-dink toys.

'Well, what a fine big girl! Are you really and truly Millicent Flynn?'

'Yes, Dada. I am eight years old. My birthday is on September 15th, I was four when you went away to fight.'

'Sure you were.' He didn't really talk like an Irishman but he gave the impression of Irishness. 'But your dada didn't fight, my darling. He's a doctor. A healer. A surgeon. A man to save lives.'

This contradiction was annoying. A poor opening to our relationship. I knew he was a doctor. I was using 'fighting' in a far more general sense. I looked to Mummy for understanding but she launched him on war stories.

He recounted them with Cleo on his lap, sucking her sticky fingers and rolling her little eyes. As usual, Di was far away in her own world. I decided Dada was trying to woo us as Othello... *I spake of most disastrous chances/Of moving accidents by flood and fields*... Even at that age I loved Shakespeare and found it easy to remember lines. I didn't always know what they were saying but I knew it impressed Mummy.

After a bit I went over and tried to take Mummy's hand. She looked at me vaguely before whispering, 'It must be Cleo's bedtime,' so I knew she wasn't any keener on Dada's exploits than I was. We're kindred souls, we really are. Were. Even now I find that hard to write.

The morning after Dada's arrival, he walked Di and me to school. He put us on either mutton-chop hand and exclaimed, 'What a lucky man! Two gorgeous girls!'

I looked over my shoulder to see if Mummy was watching from the door but she'd gone inside with Cleo. Cleo only went to nursery in the afternoon. She was quite backward, although imaginative, by which I mean she made things up when she couldn't be bothered to work out the truth. I suppose that's why she wrote her first novel, although it doesn't explain its success. Which doesn't mean I don't love Cleo now.

It was just hard when Mummy had made me think she loved only me.

DI

Nobody noticed that I wanted to be a boy. Apart from my loathed and idiotic school uniform (the grey wool knickers were as thick as carpets and later made sanitary towels seem like liberty), I wore trousers or shorts all the time, hacked off my hair with kitchen scissors and took long strides, with a touch of swagger *à la* Scarlet Pimpernel. I recognised men led more interesting lives.

Of course I never liked our mother or I might have been more impressed by her stellar career. I happened to prefer Brendan, our father.

The day he came back from the war I felt my heart bursting with pride. He began to tell us about the bombing of the ship that carried him to Africa – the HMS *Avenger*. 516 men died. I was only six but I could picture it all, the men trapped down below, the men swimming to the shore which wasn't far away, the heroic Doctor Brendan Flynn towing one man to safety, tending to others

'I crouched on the shore, a red sun setting to the west, towards you girls in Oxford, England. I'd only left a few days earlier and now I was staring at a blazing ship, black figures, as small as beetles, arms and legs spread, jumping from the deck, and there were still men inside, heading fast to Davey Jones's Locker. The ship lurched, slipped and slid below the red-tinged waves...'

'Oh, Brendan! You'll frighten the girls with such horrors. Tell them about the desert, the camels. Aren't they called "ships of the sea"?'

Despite this annoying interruption by our mother, Julie, Brendan carried on, skipping over the seas to Italy.

'So up the hill we climbed, grappling with poisonous spiky thorns, ducking the bullets dancing down on us like little fiends. A yell here, a scream there, not enough stretchers, not enough men to carry the stretchers if there had been any and only the one medic – me!'

I was enthralled. But I was quiet, silent, no indications of what I felt. Nobody noticed my flushed cheeks and quick breaths. Millie was busy showing off – 'I know where Gibraltar is, Dada, and Tangiers and Cairo!' – like a schoolgirl jumping up and down to catch the teacher's attention.

Millie has been clever all her life, but oh so needy! After that first day, she never made a play for Brendan again. Poor Millie! Like the British with the Americans, always looking for a special relationship with Julie. Cleo was only a baby, a sharp-eyed little creature. Julie hated anyone else being the centre of attention, even her own husband back from the war. Particularly her own husband back from the war.

But I realised Brendan was a hero.

CLEO

Julie Flynn prided herself on being an intellectual, despite having no links with university. There was nothing fancy about Brendan's doctoring: he just happened to be a junior doctor at the Oxford Radcliffe Hospital. But, after they met, Julie, working in a glove shop, managed to infiltrate herself into lectures, talking groups and private musical parties, despite being tone deaf. In fact that's how they first met. Brendan's then girlfriend, who *was* a student at the university, had taken him to an event where her then-boyfriend, also at the university, had escorted her. Quick as a flash Julie swapped one for the other. She was always hooked on winning against the odds. It strikes me now that her admiration for mind over matter, for triumphing over adversity, was the reason she despised her daughters. We bored her. We had too much, 'everything a girl could want', as she informed us often.

Julie had an important friendship with Drusilla who had a small clever don for a husband, but loved my mother more. Lesbians were unremarked back then. Drusilla's voice was very oddly accented.

'Julie, dearest, you have to *accept* that the USSR has nothing to *do* with the Russians.' She was my mother's only friend who was not a committed fellow-traveller or socialist as they were called then.

Drusilla was witch-like, with oily grey curls, sharp nose and black eyes underlined by heavy bags. My mother, of course, was the prettiest woman in Oxford, petite with coiled dark-red hair, sapphire-blue eyes and a pale, delicately freckled skin. She only tolerated Drusilla's love because, through her husband, the small don Angus who taught PPE, she could enter grander university circles.

Drusilla eventually became a writer of novels based on the Greek classics and highly acclaimed in a cultish way. Since she was my godmother, I ended up with the complete oeuvre. I passionately adored them and finished reading the last one on my twelfth birthday, also the day that she died by her own hand. I can still remember the final paragraph:

'The great hero was shot in the heel by the cowardly Paris. And so Achilles closed his weary eyes. But, seeing no more, there came even louder to his ears the songs of the Cyclades which escorted him upwards to the land of the sun.'

DI

Julie became less fiendish after she was elected to parliament. Her seat was a suburb of London so she told Brendan to find a job in the city or else commute to Oxford and she moved the family to Golders Green.

'Do you like it, darlings? How could you not like it? Don't you think the air is fresher here? Do you like your new schools? Have you made new friends?' She could ask a range of questions and never hear the answers. I suppose she felt it was enough to ask.

I loved the house. Its big garden led down to Hampstead Heath where I soon discovered wild animals, eccentric men and a few women who were as wild as the rabbits, badgers and deer. I was Diana, the goddess of the hunt, the moon and nature.

Our mother didn't believe in curtailing her daughters' freedom which was fair enough because she didn't offer alternatives and it saved her a lot of trouble. Both she and Brendan worked very hard making the world a better place, never forget that. Brendan, who had been a general surgeon, turned himself into a knee and hip specialist and worked for the NHS at the Royal Free Hospital. He was no easier to pin down than Julie but he had a different way of asking questions,

'I hear you were out all yesterday evening, my darling Di?"

'Yes, Dada.'

'And what a beautiful evening it was. Did you see the hares running through the yellow gorse?'

Here I would try and work out which answer, yes or no, would more easily lead us out of deep waters. The previous evening I had been camping in the Heath woods with a man called 'Bear' who taught me how to light a fire by rubbing sticks together.

'Hares play in the morning, Dada.'

'True enough. What a nature lover you are. I expect you slept well after all that fresh air?'

I wondered whether the latest au pair noticed I had not returned until dawn. I should point out that Bear was not a dangerous man, merely an ex-soldier who had not found himself able to fit into society. There was never any question of him molesting me.

'Yes, Dada.'

Since it was teatime, I knew he wouldn't have finished work and had merely dropped into the house on some unknowable mission. He would not have time to pursue his questioning or even pose supplementary questions to Millie and Di. Although gathering corroborating evidence was not his style. He believed in freedom too.

Millie's idea of freedom just then was to gather her friends in her bedroom and paint each other's lips red. After they'd achieved womanhood in that simple way, they settled down to read *The Merchant of Venice or As You Like It*. At this point in her life, Millie hadn't decided whether to be a swot or a beauty so she pursued both with equal success. She was top of her class in every subject except maths. She said, disdainfully, 'I'm leaving that for the men.'

So naturally I took up maths.

It could have been Bear who tipped the balance when I started pestering Brendan and Julie to let me go to boarding school.

'Diana does seem a very outdoor sort of girl,' murmured Brendan. I'm sure he hadn't told Julie about Bear. They never talked about important things. But he must have had some qualms about my choice of companion.

'I need space,' I told them, 'or I shall run away.

Merrydown House was in the Sussex countryside which gave it a head start over any other kind of freedom, and the rules, as far as I was concerned, were merely there to be broken. I found a friend there too: Hazel. Hazel and I were the only two Catholics in the school and were taken off to the local church on Sunday by a taxi driver trusted by the school.

I suspected almost immediately that he was an old soldier – just about every man *was* then, even if they did perfectly normal jobs. He was handsome in a taciturn way and listened politely to Bear's war stories as retold by me.

'He was dropped onto an island. Hot as hell, even though it was still May. Crete it was called, and one day the Nazis came floating out of the sky, thousands and thousands of them, driving Bear and the Allies further and further until they were dead or crowded like cattle onto one small beach. Poor Bear expected a German POW camp, or to be drowned as he fled, or blasted into small chunks...'

'Don't say such things!' Hazel was shocked. But she liked being shocked. That's why we became friends.

'I just might climb out of the window onto the roof.'

'It's dangerous, Di. You can't!'

Her mother worked as a secretary to her father who was an MP so we had that in common too.

Our taxi driver was called Tom Pomeroy, which one bright day he told us was an ancient Norman name meaning King of the Apples. He was so hopeless, long and thin. So easily bullied. I bullied him. Forced him to sell me cigarettes and one day I got caught smoking behind the church and he got sacked. Poor old King of the Apples. Not really like big hairy Bear on Hampstead Heath, although they were both outcasts, created by different wars. Their reject status seemed to offer a clue to what the world was all about.

MILLIE

Mummy invited me to lunch at the Houses of Parliament on my sixteenth birthday. 1954. I'd finished my O-Levels (a year earlier than most children) and for once books weren't staving off waves of boredom. Boredom was the principal enemy for all girls of my generation. Almost everything we did was to stave off boredom. Even the word now brings that sense of inaction, of the impossibility of anything interesting or surprising – or just anything at all – happening, and the total incapability of taking action to make anything happen. Now when teenagers lie around helplessly it's called 'depression' or 'stress' but then it was simply boredom.

In the end, and to my rage, Di came too, sulking and hideous in her school uniform. I was wearing a cherry-red dress with a white Peter Pan collar which was my birthday present. I knew I looked beautiful.

Also at the lunch was Mr Mulcahy MP, Julie's friend. As soon as I saw his son Eddie, I felt my life changing, a great churning of the wheels. At first sight, just as the saying goes. I managed to overlook the fact he was also the brother of Hazel, one of Di's friends. He was eighteen, I was sixteen and two days, older than Romeo and Juliet. As we sat in the House of Commons dining room we looked into each other's eyes and found love. My eyes are blue, his a splendid amber circled with black lashes, reeds round a mountain pond.

Up till that moment the visit had been formal, exhortations from Mummy, long lectures from Mr Mulcahy, shorter lectures from me. My exceptionally good memory allowed me to say nonchalantly, 'By the thirteenth century, a parliament, coming from the French *parler* to talk, had become a meeting where the King asked English

barons to raise money for fighting wars mostly against Scotland...'
But all this fell away the moment I looked into Eddie's amber eyes.
He had olive skin, a smallish, straight nose, a well-sculpted, wide
mouth and a tall, spare figure. He was about to go to London
University.

He said, 'You're very unlike your sister.' He could not have
known what a good start he'd made.

'I have another even younger sister called Cleopatra.'

'*You* should be called Cleopatra.'

'We call her Cleo.'

At this point, Di looked up from guzzling a lump of meat. 'I
suppose you'll be sent to Korea?'

Eddie turned from me reluctantly. 'Sorry?'

'There's a *war* in Korea, I believe, North v South. Men of eighteen
and over doing their National Service tend to get sent there.'

'I'm deferring my National Service until after university.' Eddie
frowned and pushed his hair back from his noble forehead.

'Don't you want to carry a gun, stamp out evil in the world!' She
spoke in a low, intense voice.

'Oh, shut up, Di.' She was such an idiot.

'Girls, please!' At the word 'Korea' Mummy and Mr Mulcahy
had stopped their conversation about the Prime Minister's
annoying personal habits.

'But Julie...'

'I am your *mother*, Diana...'

'*Mother*, Korea is being fought at this moment by chaps like
Eddie. I just thought...'

'Thank you, dear. I suspect we don't need your thoughts on far-
off battlefields.' She smiled at Mr Mulcahy.

Looking back, Di's point of view was impressive for a fourteen-
year-old. Although I'm so well educated, I prefer to get it from
books whereas Di was always interested in the world. She was also
fearless whereas I am full of fears.

'We're in the House of Commons, *Mother*, where this afternoon our Foreign Minister, Sir Anthony Eden, will speak about the UN's role in making peace in Korea.'

How did she know that? *I* didn't know that.

DI

The evening when Millie and I returned from the House of Commons, Brendan was making a cup of tea in the kitchen. Julie never made herself a cup of tea.

Millie went upstairs immediately to savour her first male conquest in private so I had my father to myself. I followed him into the living room and sat opposite him, hands firmly on knees. He should see I meant business.

'Brendan.'

He frowned. 'I bet you don't call your mother Julie.'

'I do. And she hates it.'

'I suppose we like to think of ourselves as your parents.'

'*You* may.' I gave him a meaningful look from under my eyebrows and as he stared back at me, blue-grey eyes, brownish hair, thick eyebrows, squarish face, I recognised myself.

'What's wrong, Di?' He sighed and folded away a newspaper.

'I am putting up with Merrydown.'

'*You* chose boarding school.'

'I need to have hope.'

'When I was fourteen – you *are* fourteen?'

'Yes.'

'I tried to join the Merchant Navy. I was tall for my age like you and thought I'd convinced a captain, but he merely rang a priest and the game was up.'

'Were there lots of ships in Liverpool?'

'Lots and lots. Even more priests.'

'Did you run away because of your parents? They always seemed ...' I hesitated '... kind.' Grandad and Nana who we met once a year were small and round. Grandad smoked outside their little house, leaning on the side of the wall, and Nana crossed herself before eating.

'So what do you want to do?'

I floundered.

'Perhaps you would like to go on an outward-bound course this summer?'

'Bound for where?'

Brendan smiled. 'I send my teenage patients to one in Devon. It helps them to get their strength back.'

'I'm strong already.'

'You could use your strength. Climb trees, swim in ice-cold rivers, dangle off cliffs, build tunnels.'

'Like training to be a soldier.' I hoped my voice was nonchalant.

'I'll put you down for it.' Brendan knew me better than I thought.

Hazel was unimpressed by my news. 'It's for charity cases. You know, *duds*, my mother gives it money. I'd never want to *go.*'

'You think everything's very nice so I don't expect you'll ever change.'

'Why ever should I?'

I went by train and bus to outward bound. I felt like an escaping prisoner. Adults had got used to children travelling alone during the war so it wasn't unusual for a fourteen-year-old girl to do such a long journey on her own. I had a suitcase with me which was very light because I packed it myself with tooth things, socks, an extra pair of socks, a packet of sandwiches and a small bottle of Tizer. That was a treat to myself bought with my pocket money. No backpacks for girls then. So I tied my school sweater round my waist and got on with it.

It was a very hot day but I didn't mind that either. By the time we reached the dramatic South Devon coast, my head out of the open window pulled down as far as it would go so that I could smell and feel the movement of the waves, I was ecstatic with the joy of life.

There were several of us on the stubby old bus that bumped its way from station to village. We were all misfits. There was the girl with a misshapen back, a pair of twins who were so blond as to be almost albino, a fat boy, most unusual then, and, just as unusual, an Indian who looked delicate and, judging by his cavalry twills, rather grand. I hoped there were some stronger specimens on the course.

We were met at the village by a thin, harassed-looking woman with hair flying around her head, who herded us into a decrepit van without windows but fitted with two benches.

'Come. Come. Come,' she yapped, like an anxious sheep dog.

Obediently, we climbed into the van. A dark smelly heat overwhelmed us. The Indian, who was next to me, rolled his eyes and I rolled mine back. He turned out to be a son of a VIP who'd been conned into the course by the demented man who ran it, Major Charlie Slipshott.

Slippers, as he liked to be called, met us as we fell out of the van. We gaped up at him.

'All survived, have you!' he shouted, as if disappointed. 'Vi, take them off to their quarters before they start running away.' At any other time he would have been certified, laughing manically as the men in white coats took him away, but it was still less than ten years after the war and army folk with a bit of a pension found solace in all sorts of unmonitored ways.

After my return, I asked Brendan, 'Wherever did you find the Major?'

'Old Slippers? Didn't I say. Came across him in Africa. Later he got nabbed by the Nipps. Never quite the same afterwards. But full of vim.'

Vi, still impersonating an anxious sheep dog, led us across to two corrugated iron Nissen huts which retained the air-force insignia painted on them.

'Mind the barbed wire,' she yapped. If she'd said 'Mind the bombs', I wouldn't have been surprised. 'Girls here. You have a mirror and a basin. Boys over there. There's an outside tap.' It was one of the first times I felt glad to be a girl. While I bagged a bed under a window, a scene developed as the twins fought not to be parted.

'Never mind,' said Vi, capitulating as both Tiggy and Rolo spouted tears. 'I always keep one spare room in the house, you can have that.'

On the first morning Slippers looked us over as if we were new recruits and shouted (he never lowered his decibel level), 'Filthy lot, aren't you! Get your swimming togs and we'll shimmy down the cliff for a nice cool bath.'

We trooped after him, over dry grass and prickly heather till we were on a narrow track and I suddenly noticed the shimmering sea below us. A very very long way below us.

'Down we go!' bellowed Slippers. I later discovered this was his party trick for all the new intakes. He enjoyed unashamedly the pallid terror and shaky protests, better still those who turned and ran.

'Beatle-headed loons!' he called after them. 'Didn't Mummy and Daddy tell you we're outward bound?'

A little girl – Maureen, as I discovered later – sat down in the path and cried. She should have left the course then and there.

Once Slippers had caused what he considered his fair share of terror, he pointed to a path, not easy but navigable as it zig-zagged gradually downward. The old hands took to it confidently and Suraj and I followed. For me, excitement trumped any fear and Suraj, it turned out, when in India during the summer months, lived halfway up the Himalayas.

The sea was bliss. I can still remember it now. Despite the hot sun, the waves were high and rolling towards us with white tops breaking as they fell. Since I had brought no swimming suit or towel I strode in wearing my underclothes, certain that the sun would dry me afterwards.

The following morning, Slippers turned us out early. 'Abject drudges, today we're climbing up instead of down!' he shouted. He was wearing a very odd red hat which I was told had been given him by the Free French in the Second World War, although it was more like the hats worn by the *sans-culottes* who stood by Madame Guillotine and watched the aristos have their heads sliced off. 'Into the van!' He paused as loud groans rose. 'Ha! Perhaps some of you prefer to run.'

In this way six of us found ourselves running beside the van on a day when the temperature reached ninety degrees. Of course we had no water so after a bit we flopped slower and slower.

'Might lose a few here,' gloated Slippers leaning from the window. 'I expect you'll find the van more agreeable now.'

Actually we didn't but we wouldn't and couldn't run any further so we collapsed onto the ground. We were on a wide expanse of scrub grass where a few sheep cropped hopefully so Slippers drove round us in circles, shouting and waving imprecations, 'Vile worms! Creeping toads!' It definitely seemed better to be outside the van.

At that point an antique tractor pulling a ramshackle trailer appeared. Already realising we would survive only by our own efforts, we ran over, screaming, shouting, waving. We must have looked as mad as Slippers who had already driven off at great speed, black smoke hanging in the air behind him as the exhaust pipe barely skimmed tufts and molehills.

'Aye. Aye.' The driver of the tractor stopped beside us with an attitude of resignation. I realised that being accosted by a group of shrieking young persons (teenagers not yet recognised in those parts) was not a new experience.

'We need a lift to a high place!' We all yelled different things but that was the summary.

'Aye. Aye.' He was a man of few words, his face encrusted with weather, his empty pipe protruding like a dragon's tongue.

Meanwhile a line of sheep advanced, pace quickening, bleating loudly until they were gathered round with expectant expressions on their long faces.

'Aye. Aye.' He motioned backward and we saw the trailer was piled high with loosely tied hay which the more enterprising sheep were already tugging out, some standing on their hind legs. It seemed this was a place for innovative energy.

After we had emptied the trailer, without waiting for another 'Aye. Aye,' we bundled into it and set off across the expanse. The bleating sheep were left behind, the sun shone in a deep blue sky and once again I felt the thrill of freedom, a heady ringing in my ears which I still recognise on any challenging assignment.

The high place was a ruined watch tower further up the coast, ruined in the sense it seemed about to fall down but was still at least six storeys tall.

'Get up there you laggards and pea-shoots!' Slippers exhorted unwilling climbers up some very unstable ropes and didn't even turn to look at us. To my surprise, I noticed the little girl, Maureen, already a long way up.

'We don't *have* to climb,' said Suraj, sitting down and gracefully crossing his legs. Although I admired his calm determination, I could never resist a challenge.

I was halfway up, swinging out from a crumbling parapet, when I heard a rumble, a yelp. Stones fell from above, followed by a scream and a falling body. I couldn't actually look because I was clinging to the wall, praying the whole place wouldn't collapse around my ears. I did hear the wallop as the body hit the baked ground.

The drama was so sudden that the world seemed enveloped in a crimson blackness. How did I get down? How did the others on the tower get down?

It was my first experience of death and the shock was great enough to confuse my perception. The falling body belonged to Maureen, a victim for Slipper's obvious rage. But inwardly I did not feel any great desolation, sympathy or horror. Somehow I had always known that tragedy was at life's core. An analyst might point to that first violence as a signpost to my subsequent career, which has included so much death. But I believe I was always like that: poor Maureen losing her nerve and letting go of the rope merely pointed the way more clearly. If I took any message, it was 'Be braver or you will fall.'

I did hear the screaming girls, the silent boys, Slippers bellowing, 'What has that stupid girl done now! Just look, you dolts, and see what happens when you don't hang on!'

I suppose she was laid out in the van. Perhaps I remember sliding down somehow and red blood on the ground. I certainly remember trudging the very long way back to the Nissen huts, none of us talking. I think there was a storm on the way but none of us even mentioned that. I suppose Maureen was eventually taken away in an ambulance. It was too late for dash and sirens.

There were still four more days left of the course and so complete was the silence on the death subject that it might never have happened. If there'd been a telephone we could have called our homes, perhaps some would have asked to be taken home, but we might as well have been on the moon. Possibly Vi's anxiety reached a higher pitch and Slippers became slightly subdued, but on the whole it was as if nothing had happened. If the police became involved, I never saw even one blue-coated Bobby. Death, it seemed, was not the end of the world.

When I got home and Brendan asked me how the week had been, I answered, 'Fine. Great fun, actually.'

MILLIE

My first date with Eddie was at an Italian espresso bar. He picked me up on a scooter outside school under the eyes of a bunch of jealous girls. I felt so sophisticated sitting side-saddle on that scooter, then swinging about on a red plush stool with a jukebox playing 'That's amore'. I can even remember a line, *'When the moon hits your eyes like a big pizza pie'*. Even that seemed romantic at the time, although I had recently fallen in love with Byron and my usual taste in music was for Verdi.

'You seemed older in the House of Commons,' Eddie commented as I sipped my espresso. The espresso machine had only just arrived in London and was as exciting as the arrival of tobacco or potatoes from the New World or opium from China. I had been reading De Quincey's *Confessions of an English Opium-Eater* (1821) and the coffee bar with its pulsing beat and orange lights was as close to an opium den as anything in my experience to date.

'I'm sixteen. How old are you?'

'Eighteen. I'm working in my father's office, then in the autumn I'll start my degree in Oriental Studies.'

He would know about opium dens. 'I'm leaving school this term and going to a tutorial college.'

'In London?'

'In Victoria.'

'London University is further north. In Gower Street.'

When we first met, love made it possible for Eddie and me to carry on conversations like this for ages. Then after a while we moved on to deeper questions. We were serious people who might have seemed dull to some. Looking back at the me then, it's strange that being very clever and very beautiful didn't add up to very interesting. I didn't have any sense of humour for example. Life has always seemed too important to mess about with endless jokes, like Cleo does. Identify the important questions and find the answers, that's how it seemed to me. Love, Marriage, Belief. Big words. Eddie and I felt the same way so, there we go, dull.

Cleo and Di had none of my attributes but scored much higher on the interesting front. They believed that all I wanted was *love* because I loved Mummy so much and even though she loved me more than either of them (she positively disliked Cleo and Di certainly disliked her), she could be beastly to me at times.

Eddie and I never made love before we married. Possibly that is dull too, although perfectly normal for the fifties. All that repetitive *petting* (naturally the female was the pet – cat? dog? bear?) was so *inelegant* and *silly*. Heavens how I longed to pose naked on a bed! Or just anywhere. *Would you like to sin/With Elinor Glyn/On a tiger skin/Or would you prefer/To err/On some other fur...*

I was always an old-fashioned sort of girl.

∞

Mummy only realised I had a boyfriend on my eighteenth birthday. She had been given four tickets for *Tosca*.

'Can Eddie come too, please Mummy? *Please?*' As so often, we stood in the hallway of the Golders Green house while a taxi waited to whisk her away.

'Eddie who? There're only enough tickets for you and the girls.'

She was so pretty, although into her late forties. She wore her red hair in bright curls round her face and pearl studs in her ears making her bright eyes brighter.

'Eddie Mulcahy. You know him Mummy. He's often here. You know his parents.'

'Him. Well, tell Cleo she can't come.'

'Please, Mummy.' There was that pleading again, 'Can't you tell her?'

'Darling Millicent, do you think I have time to talk to a bad-tempered twelve-year-old (Cleo was fourteen) about something as unimportant as *opera*.' She put a wealth of scorn into her voice. 'Perhaps you have heard the word "Suez",' she continued in satirical vein. 'Our young soldiers embarking for Egypt with guns on their shoulders. That's where I'm going this evening.'

'To Egypt, Mummy?'

Mummy, already on her way, swivelled like a dancer at the door. 'Are you sure you really won a scholarship to Oxford? I am going to attend a debate in the house about the Suez Canal. Of course we shouldn't send our boys. We must pull them back.'

Game set and match. I let her go. I never tried to compete. On this occasion I understood that what seemed like cruelty was explained by the fact she never went to university. Many mothers are jealous of their daughters. Oscar Wilde noted, 'As long as a woman can look ten years younger than her daughter, then she's satisfied.' It's known as the Electra Complex. But to be honest, Mummy did look ten years younger than me.

It was the start of the summer holidays and both of my sisters were at home. We sat not speaking at the kitchen table where Helga, the current housekeeper, who was Swiss, fat and spotty, owing to her passion for (Swiss) chocolate, had placed soup made from a (Swiss) Knorr packet, a pile of sliced white bread and (Swiss) triangles of cheese. She was very homesick, poor thing.

If Dada was at home we ate in the dining room and Helga served us stewed meat. Poor overworked Mummy was never at home. I suspect she liked food as little as sex.

Usually, I read a book at mealtimes – I found Swinburne went well with eating – all those florid phrases like a mouthful of creamy soup. That evening I left my book behind.

'I've asked Eddie to come for my opera birthday outing. Would one of you mind standing down?' I felt I was putting it in a grown-up rather than a sisterly way.

'Me! Me!' they both yelled together. This was disconcerting.

'Don't you know we both *hate* opera. All that desperate screeching,' Cleo expanded. 'Don't you know *anything* about your own sisters!'

Di said nothing. It often wasn't worth her speaking when all she was doing was waiting to escape, although I didn't realise it at the time.

'Opera fills me with *ennui*!' Cleo shuddered theatrically.

'But you've never been to one.'

'I can *imagine*!'

She could of course. That was her talent – imagining things. Also, she'd probably heard Eddie and me playing *Otello* and *Madame Butterfly* and *Tosca* on my wind-up gramophone. I liked opera because it was romantic and I didn't take much notice of the fact they all ended tragically. I still believed in happiness then. Dada hated opera.

So Eddie and Mummy and me went to the opera and in the foyer we met a friend of Mummy's called Billie Fiddler. He was not as bad as he sounds, although he had a thick Scottish accent. I was pleased she had a friend because she would be happier. I always wanted Mummy to be happy.

In the second interval after Tosca has pleaded with Scarpia for her lover's life before stabbing him to death, Mummy and Mr Fiddler, who was some sort of union leader, said they weren't enjoying it and went off for a meal. Eddie and I sat on little gold chairs sipping lemonade. I showed off a bit – after all, it was my birthday.

'I'm so looking forward to Cavaradossi singing *O dolci mani*.'

'But it's so sad.' Eddie stared at me. 'Almost unbearable.'

'Virgil wrote *Amor vincit omnia* but I know what you mean. Death is going a bit far.'

Eddie's amber eyes glowed. 'Millicent...' As he paused, I thought how sweet it was that he used my full name, even if I would have preferred to be called Daphne or Penelope or Calypso.

'Will you marry me?'

Had he really said those words? I remember the hot flush that swept through my body and into my face.

'Of course we'd be engaged for quite a long time. Until you've finished your degree and I've finished my post grad and got a job.'

Eddie definitely was dull and he truly loved me and I did him.

CLEO

Weddings bring out the worst in everybody, particularly the bride's mother. Julie wore white of course with a silver trimming and a veil. No, I must have misremembered that, even she wouldn't be so idiotic. She must have worn one of those hideous fifties petal hats that clasped the head like a perverted biker's helmet. Except she would have made it seem charming.

The trouble was that Millie, my famously beautiful sister, had just finished finals and was worn out, overweight from all the comfort-inducing sugar buns and nervous about her beloved, that is, Eddie. She feared she didn't love him as much as Eloise loved Abelard but she really did want to have sex with him. Or someone. She confided that to me. Also, she believed in marriage and they both went to church every Sunday, hand in hand.

Actually I respected them for their belief, even though it was a bit sudden in Millie's case, and now and again I felt jealous enough to go with them. But somehow I ended up making fun of the gurgling priest who never turned to look at us or the ear-numbingly out-of-tune choir or the congregation who mumbled and rumbled like old trains going through a tunnel. That's always been my problem, so blinded by the incidentals that I can't see the point.

The wedding service was in the barn-like modern church nearest our house and Julie had invited as many politicians as she thought would help her career. Since it was early September and the General Election was on October 8th, meaning most MPs were busy harassing their constituents, she didn't get much of a take-up. Worse still, she'd spotted a very pretty, much younger rival standing for Finchley, more or less on our doorstep.

'Margaret Thatcher,' she hissed as we set off for the church (having given up waiting for Di who was supposedly coming from America), 'a grocer's daughter with a millionaire husband and a face like decorated granite.'

'She's Conservative,' I said, mock innocent, 'Why ever would you want her at Millie's wedding!'

'I don't want her, you idiot!'

As I said, weddings make people behave badly. Or maybe that's politics. The Labour Party had been out of office for nearly eight years and swapping beloved Clement Attlee for Hugh Gaitskell (another neighbour) had made little difference. As a would-be journalist, I was going one evening a week to a class on political theory under a bridge in Southwark where all the men wore beards and all the girls wore glasses. 'It's the economy, dear...' our 'facilitator' liked to say. She had a tragic home life and always turned up late with signs of tears. '...forget equality, fraternity, freedom.'

I thought of her when I saw a huge slogan draped over the hall adjoining the wedding church, 'Life is better with the Conservatives, don't let Labour ruin it.'

'I expect Mrs Thatcher put there,' I commented, but not loud enough for my mother to hear.

Of course the car stopped directly in front of it. To do Julie justice, she got out and, perching on her stilettos, gave it a long appraisal, wondering perhaps how to get it down.

'Less memorable than Macmillan's "You've never had it so good."' A guest joined her, staring upwards. It was one of Julie's bachelor admirers, the short, fat one, nicknamed Dopey by me because he looked like the Seven Dwarfs dwarf who had the biggest nose and a habit of shutting one of his eyes. He was actually a brilliant economist – or so Julie, lowering her voice in unconvincing awe, told me now and again. All her men-friends were brilliant and useful, of course.

Leaving them to political despair – the Conservatives were on their way to winning a third term – I went to look for gayer haunts – behind the church for a ciggie, where I found Eddie and his best man nervously hiding, also smoking. Neither was capable of speech and the BM squeezed a wad of papers in his hand which suggested a horribly long speech.

'I wonder if Di will make it,' I said brightly. No response. Di had been in New York for two years and seldom made contact. I did have a deep thought between puffs. I had glanced back as we left our house and seen Brendan and Millie standing hand in hand. Perhaps they were merely practising for the long walk down the aisle but there was something in the sight that held my attention. They had never seemed to have much in common, Millie's obsession with Julie blocking paternal attention, but at that moment, they wore an aura of love. Could love override everything?

Eddie gave a terrified yelp and the show was on.

DI

I was living in New York when the invitation to Millie's wedding arrived. Why ever do people want to complicate their lives? September 1st, 1959. She wouldn't be twenty-one for fourteen days. Funny how I remember the date of my sisters' birthdays.

'Look what my tragic sister's doing!' I shouted to Suraj, who'd handed me the letter where I sat on the floor drinking a whisky sour while reading the *Washington Post*. Suraj (the same chic fellow from the outward-bound course) worked for the *Washington Post* so it was hard to avoid a copy. Anyway it pleased him which was a good idea as the apartment where I was currently resident, a grand duplex on 57th Street, was his – or rather his parents. But they preferred Delhi.

'Why do you always expect me to collect your letters?' He pulled off his exquisitely cut jacket and expensively striped tie and stared bitterly down at me. We had tried being lovers but it hadn't taken – not least because he wasn't sure whether he preferred females or males, more likely the latter – so we had reverted to a bad-tempered sibling relationship. I was good at that.

'When did I last get a letter?' I waved the invitation to him as a distraction. 'Millie's getting married. In September. Do you think I have to go?' None of the rest of Suraj's large extended family left India for more than short visits so he liked to pose as the sophisticated Westerner who'd left behind the narrow old ways. In fact his father was a powerful minister in the government and all of them were far better educated than me and, moreover, Suraj loved them devotedly.

'Of course you have to go!'

I sighed. 'Millie is a sweet girl, hampered by her clever brain and a conventional outlook. But they'll have to pay for my flight.'

'Why not go by ship? I might be able to swing a cabin. But you'll need to allow five days.'

Suraj was my best friend. We met in adult life in Washington where Brendan had found a job for me looking after an American army friend's disabled child. Heather was an angry teenager who could only walk with two sticks and I was concentrating too hard on my own survival to be any use in the carer's role. But I liked my boss who worked in the Pentagon and gave important parties. It was at one of these that Suraj and I recognised each other and shouted as if in homecoming, 'Slippers!'

Escape to New York was entirely through him as was the little money I earned through scraps of information discarded by him but just viable for me to present to the *Daily News*. I had never wanted to be a journalist but in this unlikely way, I found myself treated as one. Americans like to put people in boxes so I needed a tab. *'English woman journalist, freelance, specialising in overseas insider gossip/news/conflicts'* sort of made sense of me. At least they seldom questioned my credentials. Americans are generous that way. *'Specialising in overseas conflicts'* was obviously more of an aspiration than a reality.

'A berth in the *Queen Mary*,' I agreed to Suraj, downing my whisky.

'And I can get the apartment cleaned in your absence,' said Suraj. Sometimes he acted like my mother. Correction: not *my* mother.

Five days on a huge ship. Big waves, hot sun, smooth water, grey skies, too many meals, too many expected changes of clothes, boring, boring, BORING people, that's what I expected. But when I arrived, off the dock, which *was* exciting, I found a man already in my cabin.

I was nineteen but I was feisty and everything new excited me. 'What are you doing in my cabin?'

He was wearing some kind of uniform, thirtyish and very fit

looking, even though he was semi-slumped on the bed. His thigh muscles bulged.

'Good afternoon, ma'am. I guess there's some mistake.' He had a beautiful Southern voice. 'Perhaps they thought you were a man.'

I noticed there were two bunks. It was not a very grand cabin, although it did have a porthole through which I could see the legs of people going up and down a plank. 'I am not a man.' Whatever had Suraj landed me in? Could it be his idea of a practical joke? Up till now, I wouldn't have rated a sense of humour as his strong point.

'Of course, I've no objections,' said the man, standing up with a gallant bow. 'I've always wanted to get to know the mother country better.'

I was beginning to warm to him. 'You'll meet an awful lot of the English where you're going.'

'Is that so?' He seemed genuinely surprised. Perhaps he was mentally challenged.

'In England.'

'Jeez, I'm not stopping. Just thought I'd take a ship for a rest. Too many aeroplanes lately.' He smiled in what I now saw was an exhausted fashion. He took my case from me gently. 'I'll tell you what, why don't we go up on deck and watch the ship leave.' He'd spotted what I'd missed – that the legs had stopped mounting the plank and the engines were revolving louder and more noisily. He held out his hand, 'Brad Wolfe. Pittsburgh Pennsylvania.'

'Diana commonly known as Di Flynn. Oxford England.' I approve of this kind of American formality. Clears the air.

So we shook hands and went up on deck together and stood in the warm rain as the great ship moved away at a majestic pace from the airy wonder of Manhattan's skyline, rising out of the mists like the magic city it is.

I sighed. 'Can't wait to return.'

After five minutes Brad turned his back on the city, 'Let's go find a seat in the dining hall.'

In fact we drank beer in a bar and, after two pints, Brad said slowly, 'I'm on my way to Vietnam.'

The word was heavy with meaning, I could tell (in my head, I spelled it Veetnam as he'd pronounced it), but meant little to me. Remember this was 1959. 'Where *is* that?'

So then, as I sipped beer and puffed Camels, he talked. He'd flown back from there only a month ago with a fever he'd picked up. His boss was still there in Saigon. They were part of an American mission which I now know to be MAAG, the Military Assistance Advisory Group It was all a mess. Diem had no idea how to run a country, except for his own and his family's gain, his army, so-called, was divided into two and to make matters worse, here, in the US, the military didn't agree with the politicians or anyway the politicians' advisers, who really didn't think the North so much of a threat.

'The North?' I repeated. I said very little partly because I didn't have much clue what he was talking about and partly because I was surprised a soldier should bare his soul to a half-witted teenager about whom he knew nothing except that she was English and had claimed rights to his all-male cabin.

'Up there it's a mess too. But at least they know what they want. I guess you can't blame the French for everything but that doesn't get us very far, not while Ho Chi Minh is preparing a route from North to South and who knows what else... You know our great President, hero of World War Two, has had more heart attacks than a nervous girl. Although at least he knows what a mess it is ...'

He just had to talk it out, I suppose, and in a way he'd judged his audience correctly: I didn't understand enough to write a story.

Drinks were followed by dinner. I was nearly thrown out as my trousers broke the Captain's dress code but Brad's uniform prevailed and we ate fish, duck, meat, cakes, ice cream, cheese and grapes, all with attendant wine. At the end of this orgy, neither of us could be bothered with gender specifics bunk-wise and we retired together, glad in my case that the corridor walls were close enough to sway from one to the other.

I pulled off most of my clothes and climbed to the top bunk.

'Ladies first,' said Brad agreeably, as he stripped to his undershorts.

I then climbed down again in search of a lavatory. Next time I tried to climb up, my leg slipped and I found myself in a heap on the floor.

Brad peered down. 'Hey, want my bunk, sailor?'

Seeing his point, I launched myself up and forward. The thing was, Brad hadn't gone anywhere. Having sex when drunk is a wonderfully funny occupation, particularly when you scarcely know each other. It makes me laugh now when I remember how polite we were to each other. Odd phrases stick in my mind:

'I'm married.' From Brad.

'I despise marriage.' From me. We kiss to celebrate agreement.

'With two kids.'

'Kids grow into goats who smell and eat grass.'

Brad pulls off my bra. He touches my breasts so I squirm and wriggle – not much space for that so one large leg dangles over the side.

'You're so young.' From Brad. 'I shouldn't.'

'You should.' From me. He does. We do, although we have to roll onto the floor to really get going.

'Fucking condom.' From him. I watch as he tries to get it out of his jacket and then put it on the appropriate place.

'Need some help?' From me.

I've never understood why so many women make such a big deal about sex. Millie, for example. Cleo is pretty mixed up too. Surely sex is a form of communication like any other. Brad and I were much more comfortable together after we'd shared our bodies.

'You English girls are quite something,' he remarked in the morning. A thin light came from the porthole but it was enough to make my head ache.

43

'I told you already I'm not typical.' I became more interested and sat up in my bunk. 'How are American girls different?'

'They want to get married and have kids.'

'All of them?'

'The ones I meet. Unless they're hookers.'

I lay down again, pleased with my new sisters. 'I've never met a hooker.'

He didn't rise to this one. He was putting on a clean white shirt out of a packet and brushing his jacket. Suddenly the thought of five days together was a bit of a challenge. Maybe I would go looking for another cabin. As he turned his back on me and methodically filled his pocket with lighter, money and clean handkerchief I suspected he was thinking the same.

But then it was alright again. We sat in the grand dining room, although I don't believe our cabin merited the grade, and for the first time I took in that I was on a liner. We were riding on an ocean with nothing to do, freer than the birds who sometimes followed in arrow flight or the fish that we didn't see but whose presence was all around: other worlds surely as important as ours. I was so young and for once I felt good about it.

Brad and I lay together in that not-grand cabin a great deal in the next five days, so much so that Brad ran out of condoms.

It was after dinner on the last night and Brad was still dressed. I had begun to believe that his short-nosed, square-faced look was handsome, in the same way, perhaps, that I thought Brendan was handsome. In my mind, they were both soldiers.

'I'm exhausted,' said Brad. Both their names began with 'B'.

'With me?' That sort of remark always floored him. 'Don't worry. I've should get some sleep so I look perky for my sister's wedding.'

'You're going home for your sister's wedding?' He sounded shocked.

'Unfortunately. Didn't I mention it?'

He became quiet, the small cabin oppressed with his cogitations. 'With your family?'

'That's it. Mum MP Julie Flynn, bride's sister Millie, youngest sister Cleo, Dad Brendan Flynn, doctor, ex-soldier, well Royal Army Medical Corps.'

It is almost unbelievable, but the truth is that he had not thought of me as someone with a family, in fact not as a real person at all. I was a whacky English girl on a boat who had appeared from nowhere and would disappear to nowhere.

'I'm not planning to introduce you,' I said into his lengthening silence. 'Anyway you'll be in Vietnam.'

'You should have told me.'

'What? That I was born of man and woman? That I have siblings?'

'Your sister's getting married.'

'People do. You did.'

He sank down onto the bunk and put his head in his hands. 'Did you say MP?'

'What?' He had been muttering. 'Not Military Police. Member of Parliament.'

He groaned. 'I shall talk to the Bursar.'

'He's dreadfully boring.' My facetiousness was a cover for my sadness that it was ending this way. Nor did it escape me that it was my family, however inadvertently, that had put the boot in. Of course he may just have been exhausted, as he said, and wanting a couple of peaceful nights before he got back into 'the Veetnam mess'. But I think he really was frightened off. A lesson that if I wanted to behave freely, I must be totally independent. Fuck Millie and her wedding!

MILLIE

My wedding to Eddie was utterly beautiful, even Mummy was moved to tears. Or so Cleo said. Di made it back from New York which was wonderful. Cleo had begged me not to make them 'Hideous old maids of honour' (Cleo's description) and, to be honest, it was quite nice to be on my own for once.

The church was decorated with white lilies and Father Ignatius had an excellent singing voice which, I'm ashamed to admit, does make a difference to a Nuptial Mass. I can't understand why anyone without religious faith bothers to get married at all. Eddie and I held hands and dedicated ourselves to God. We were in love and He was our witness.

We'd all been baptised Catholics but Eddie brought me to God and I'll always thank him for that. It gave me a higher purpose which, I have to admit, I took a while turning into action, but in the end I got there. I used to imagine being the abbess of a pre-Reformation monastery. When I mentioned this to Cleo she snorted and said, 'You just think wimples are becoming.'

They are actually. There's a wonderful stone tablet of Abbess Hilda of Whitby, 614–680, wearing beautiful white frills across her noble forehead. Bede, that great historian of ecclesiastic history, wrote about her in 731, 'All who knew her called her mother because of her outstanding devotion and grace.'

DI

Naturally I was late for the wedding. The ship docked at seven in the morning and I had to disembark, catch a train to London from Southampton, get to our house, change and reach the church by midday. I slunk in up the side, no hat, no gloves and one of Cleo's dresses which was much too short for me. I found myself sitting next to my old schoolfriend, Hazel. There we were, sister of the bride and sister of the groom. She hissed at me, 'When did *you* last sleep?'

'I've been on a ship.'

'Who with?'

'A great big GI. Too big for a bunk. Had to share the floor.'

Our relationship hadn't changed at all: I enjoyed shocking Hazel and she enjoyed being shocked. How was I to know that three days later, Hazel would be dead, run over by a milk float, so homely a vehicle for tragedy.

We became quieter and I stood up in the side aisle so I could see dear old Millie plighting her troth. Actually, Eddie looked very handsome: formal gear suited his height and seriousness, and, if Millie looked like a puffball, we all knew she was beautiful really.

It was a full-on Catholic wedding with the singing and prayers in pre-Vatican II Latin. When I look back now, I confuse it with Hazel's funeral which came such a short time afterwards. The happy couple missed it, being in a honeymoon suite on a ship heading for Ceylon when the milk float struck. It was four o'clock in the morning and Hazel had been coming back from a party. She liked parties and I just hope she had a good time. The Grim Reaper doesn't announce his coming, whether you crash off a crumbling tower like poor Maureen, or go under the wheels of an unlikely killer.

Julie couldn't make the funeral either. 'There's a three-line whip', she told me with a self-righteous air.

'Hazel was my best friend,' I said, although I didn't care one bit whether Julie was there or not.

'Funny, isn't it, you chose to put the Atlantic between you.'

'Not funny.' But there was never any point in arguing with Julie.

MILLIE

Eddie's and my honeymoon was a joy but we both suffered for it when we discovered on our return that his sister, Di's friend Hazel, had been buried in our absence. He was terribly cut up, poor Eddie.

Cleo tried to comfort him. Although not religious, she liked to exercise her imagination: 'Now you have a sister in heaven praying for you.'

Which wasn't much consolation. Of course Di was very sad too, until she shot off back to New York, by aeroplane this time.

She said to me the night before she left, 'You know I always wanted to be a soldier.'

And I said, 'No, I don't know because you never told me.'

'It's a kind of complicated story.' Her eyes swivelled away from mine. 'But now I've decided to be a war reporter.'

Then I knew it was important. But, frankly, I could think of nothing to say.

So, after a pause, she added, 'Wars are the most important things in the world.'

So I said, smiling, 'That's because you were born in a war.'

She frowned, and I was silent. Afterwards, I thought of saying to her, *love is the most important thing in life.*

෯

Cleo came round to see our flat. It was in Marylebone, above a furniture restorers, and smelled strongly of vicious toxins used to strip wood etc. She curled up on our new sofa.

'Millie darling, Can I live with you. *Please.*'

I smiled tolerantly. 'But you're still at school.'

'But I *mean* it! I *miss* you!'

''We've only one bedroom and one bed.' I was flattered.

She lay back with her head against the armrest. 'Do you really *love* him, Millie darling?'

What a question from my little sister. She had never been interested in my views on anything before.

'I'm *so* happy!'

'That's nice.'

'I'm *so* lucky! I have a wonderful husband, a clever, handsome, hard-working, loving husband. I have a home of my own and work I adore...' I was doing a postgrad on the minor Elizabethan poets at London University. 'We have enough money. We agree on the purpose of life. We are healthy, happy...'

'You said that before.' Cleo stared up at me, her sharp little face eager to catch me out. Or did she really want to know?

'We share so much, our belief system, our work ambitions...'

'So you don't love him.' She sounded disappointed, cheated somehow, which surprised me coming from her. Even as a small child, she had been the cynical one: why should she place so much emphasis on love?

'I've always been a romantic.' I tried again on a different tack. 'When I put on my silken wedding dress, I felt clothed in a shimmering future. *Nothing in the world is single/All things by law divine/In one spirit meet and mingle/Why not I with thine?* – Percy Bysshe Shelley.'

'I've got it now,' said Cleo, suddenly bounding to her feet. 'Thank you, darling sis.' She kissed me and left the flat in such a hurry that I had to throw her satchel out of the window after her.

'Of course I love him, you idiot!' I shouted, as she collected pens and exercise books that had flown all over the pavement. 'But why would I tell *you!*'

'Because I'm your sister!' she yelled back.

CLEO

With Di in America and Millie married to the boring Eddie, I found myself an only child. I was still at my London day school, studying or rather not studying for my three A-Levels: English, History and French. No one in my school did more. The work was a doddle for someone like me who has always found spewing out a few hundred words easier than buttering bread. Besides, I didn't care whether I did well or failed utterly. What I was actually doing was writing a novel.

Recently, I found a note to myself from this time: *Father disappears. Whereabouts unknown.*

'Your dad's going to work in South America,' Julie told me in one of our hallway crossings.

'How long will he be away?' I called after her receding back. I surprised myself with this question. Why would it matter? All the same I did ask him over breakfast one morning – annoyingly I still had to turn up for school rollcall in the morning.

'Julie says you're heading off to South America.'

'Quite right. Sorry, Cleo, my darling. Should have told you. Getting away from the hospital for a bit and working with a charity. Give me a new perspective.'

I was impressed and forgot to ask for how long.

'Sorry,' he said again. 'Two patients to see before a meeting.' He left. I watched him go, jacket over his shoulder, his hair still thick and only slightly grey, his figure like a younger man.

Within a week he was gone. He hadn't discussed it with Millie either. Her response when I passed on the news was unsurprising: 'Oh, poor darling Mummy!' Honestly...

Di, on a rare transatlantic call, had a different perspective. 'Yes.' Pause. 'He passed through New York.' Pause. 'I'll tell you about it some time.'

Nor did I find out whether Julie had as little information as I did. Her mind was on more important things. Conservative Prime Minister Macmillan had won the 1959 election with 107 more seats than Labour and he was doing all sorts of sensible things like continuing the unravelling of the Empire and forging a stronger relationship with America. Not a great time for the Labour Party.

It seemed, from information eventually and reluctantly divulged by the hospital, that Brendan had taken a six-month sabbatical to work for a small charity called Andes Medical Action which seemed to be based in the mountainous regions of Colombia. His salary was still being paid and he had arranged that it should go straight into Julie's bank account; she did tell me that.

'We are solvent still,' she commented one evening with a grimace – which might have been rage or satisfaction. It was a return to the first four years of my life when I had not seen a father and scarcely believed in his existence. My novel changed its title to *Abandoned Child*.

My prospective publisher (stolen from Julie's address book) roared with horror.

'*Such* a turn-off, dear!' I saw her point at once. Buffy Coldstream was an apparently scatty lady from a grand family, with no money and a love of books, books that made money. 'We'll call it *As you like it but can't have it*; a nod to Shakespeare always pleases the punters. That's what we're aiming for, a highly readable book masquerading as Eng. Lit. You can do it, can't you, dear? With your ma, I bet you're frightfully well educated.' I had so far presented twenty pages and couldn't believe I was in a publisher's office being taken seriously.

'Oh, yes!' I stared with awe at Buffy's scarlet lips which flowed over her mouth and at her lump of grey hair massed on the top of her head.

'And don't forget the sex,' She paused for a moment and narrowed her eyes a little dubiously. 'How old did you say you were?'

'Twenty,' I lied.

'Quite so. Well. It's all in the imagination anyway. A ninety-year-old author of mine's who's been celibate all his life does sex marvellously well. Such detail! He says he gets it from the library. I'm sure you'll manage. It's amazing what we can get past the censor these days.'

My novel was written at top speed during the time we were given for A-Level revision. Probably the first happy time of my life. I didn't realise that I hadn't much to say and little originality, I just went with the flow and for some reason it worked, although even then I had a sharp eye for the peculiarities of people and a vivid way of bringing them to life.

The youthful heroine of my novel finds herself alone when both her parents are killed in a car crash. Tragic Elsie's options range between life with a revolting aunt, hair on her chin which nearly met her nose (very like Julie's friend, late author, late godmother, Drusilla) or a life on the streets. Of course, she chooses the streets. So far, so imaginative. But even I realised I couldn't rely on half-remembered fairy stories of princesses in disguise or princes and beggar maids to reach a 1960 adult audience, however brightly I wrote. I had never been the sort of girl who found fulfilment by spending hours ingesting the genius of the Victorian classics. At heart, I still believed George Eliot was a pompous man.

I decided to experience sleeping rough. Informing Julie (not that she cared) that I was staying with a friend for three days so we could test each other's French vocabulary (so likely), I took a sleeping bag and laid it near St Paul's Cathedral, with a hazy idea of requesting sanctuary if in difficulties.

It was a sunny spring evening, darkness longer coming than I'd expected, when suddenly a man in a pinstriped suit was approaching me, pointing his umbrella. I had been sitting cross-legged but now jumped to my feet.

'Aren't you Julie Flynn's daughter?'

My instinct to deny was dampened by his confident manner.

'I suppose you're coming to the service for Members of Parliament.'

As I was dressed in my oldest clothes and had more or less rubbed dirt in my face to look more authentic, this was an odd supposition.

The man eyed my sleeping bag. 'Or perhaps you're protesting?' He looked pleased with himself as he said this. 'Nuclear bomb protestors like coming to St Paul's. Centre of London, I suppose, which heroically survived the bombing in the war, now faced with a worse threat, that sort of thing.'

I recognised him as a parliamentary aide who had once dropped something in at the house for Julie. I looked round nervously. 'I'd better be going.' I rolled up my sleeping bag. 'Just having a little rest.' If I didn't hurry, with my luck, Julie herself would be upon me.

So I moved to Southwark Cathedral, more downbeat, where I managed a whole night and only a disgusting dog, certainly with rabies, tried to snuggle up. Early in the morning I took the underground to Westminster Cathedral but very soon that was awash with men on their way to Parliament and priests and nuns who wanted to give me soup, so I was just about to pick up my sleeping bag when a voice said, 'Oi there, you girl!'

My spirits lifted immediately, a sensation familiar to any journalist who spots a lead. There was quite a crowd going in for morning Mass so it took me a moment to match voice with man. Was he a policeman who would lock me in a cell? Exciting. An assailant, here in broad daylight in a holy place? Fascinating. Or a rough gangmaster keen to offer me a job? Definitely worth following up.

'You can't lie just anywhere you know!'

He was rough, dirty, unshaven and old, although probably not as old as he looked, given that his coat was tied together with string and his shoes nearly as big as a clown's, as was his red nose. It seemed I had disturbed an angry tramp. He even had a bottle sticking out of his coat pocket.

As I stared, he stood over me mumbling imprecations, drunk before eight in the morning. 'Tens of years I've had my pitch here. Tens of years. And a girl, a snotty girl, mind you, comes along, if you please, and thinks she can move right in. Well, if she thinks that's fair, she's got another think coming.'

At this point he raised his fist in the air but he was so skinny and tattered and tottering that he was far more absurd than threatening. If Millie had been around she'd have quoted *King Lear*. As he held his pose, I sprang to my feet.

'I'm so terribly sorry. I was only here because I wanted to meet you. Look.' I pulled a packet of biscuits out of my bag and, when he seemed disappointed, added a pound note. 'You're famous,' I invented hopefully. 'I just wanted a chat.'

'What about that there?' He pointed at my sleeping bag suspiciously.

Once again, I rolled it up as quick as I could.

'Got a fag, have you?' He took the pound note.

I was in! Tommy was really where my novel started. A nice girl goes into London's underworld of crusty old tramps and lost boys and girls. He gave me underworld street cred. More importantly, through him I met Bernard Briggs AKA Briggs, full stop. Cockney pop stars on the King's Road or in Soho weren't two a penny yet and Briggs was always his own man. Sadly, he ended up in an Indian ashram and expired from too many trips in search of a truer life.

At that time, he was still the poor East End boy who couldn't believe he'd got money in his pocket; since he was also a good Catholic boy and his Auntie Mary had taught him to help others, many an evening he went round with hand-outs for rough sleepers. That's how I met him. He gave me a fiver and told me to get a hot meal inside me. Me the schoolgirl rough sleeper! Quite soon he realised I was a fraud but somehow I insinuated myself into his daily life of shark producers and tacky recording studios.

I discovered his secret early on. I suppose that's why we were friends. It should have shocked me but it didn't. We were mates, never friends. He liked boys. I should have been shocked, maybe told on him, but somehow that never occurred to me. Judging others, with one exception, was never part of my make-up. I just accepted, tried to understand, then wrote about it.

Novelists who use and abuse real people on a regular basis know it's a scorched-earth policy, but I was a child, pretending, and never thought of consequences. I should have known that Briggs would recognise himself in the self-made rich boy with a heart of gold, and a taste for forbidden sex. I'd managed to add those pages, with the help of the Marquis de Sade and Henry Miller. Buffy was thrilled.

When she sent him a proof, Briggs scribbled me a note – first time I ever saw his writing: *'Hey, Cleo, girl. Why did you go and do that? Take me for a fool, did you? Ta ta now.'*

No one did pick up it was him but perhaps it was me who drove him to drugs and that fatal ashram. Or perhaps it was Auntie Mary.

MILLIE

'Raise a glass, Millie. My novel's going to be published.'

That's what she said to me. Cleo said to me. We were standing in the hallway of the Golders Green house. It was a bad moment. I was the clever, beautiful one, four years older and married, a brilliant grown-up with a great future ahead. She was a shrewish schoolgirl who would probably fail her A-Levels and had the good sense not even to try for university. *A bad moment* is an understatement. It was not her place to publish a novel.

'Are you quite sure?' I was only visiting to collect a painting that I wanted to hang in Eddie and my flat. I was not prepared for Cleo. To be fair, the expression on her face showed no triumph, only surprise. I now saw she had a book proof in her hand. She was wearing school uniform for heaven's sake. 'What novel?'

'Oh, you know.' But I didn't know. She was beginning to smile now. A difficult sight for me to behold.

'Let me read.'

She handed me the book. The novel was called *As you like it but can't have it*. My favourite Shakespearian comedy used and abused. Shakespeare. My province. My source of joy. I gulped, read the covering letter and handed it back.

'Congratulations.' I reminded myself that I believed in good behaviour and anyway the novel was almost certainly rubbish. Why would I be jealous of a rubbishy novel? Admitting to jealousy was a step forward. Eddie was seriously Catholic and lately I had become interested in the Seven Deadly Sins. I had been cheered to realise that I was guilty of very few of them but when I pointed this out to Eddie, who was usually on my side, he said, 'What about pride?' Which was quite witty for Eddie.

'When did you write it?' I thought of the splendid wit of Jane Austen; of the psychological understanding of Mary Ann Evans (AKA George Eliot), both needing to turn themselves into men in order to publish; the Brontë sisters, calling up their demons to make art; Elizabeth Gaskell portraying so brilliantly the trauma of woman's lot while eviscerating the man's world of the industrial north. They had broken free from their confines to write great novels.

Was my little sister to join this hallowed team? Of course not. The world had changed. It was 1960. Anything goes. I handed back the proof.

'They're going to pay me £150,' Cleo said in a voice of wonder.

I pulled myself together. 'Lucky you.'

'Escape money.' Were we all trying to escape? She suddenly looked up at me. 'You've done it with your brains and your beauty. A career and a man. I could never do that. I just have to rattle along, using my wits and, as you say, hoping for a bit of luck. You don't have to read the book.'

'Oh Cleo!' I hugged her and felt real tears in my eyes. That was the point about Cleo: whenever you decided she was beyond the pale, she said something that made you realise she quite appreciated her weaknesses and, more extraordinary in our family, she was prepared to admit them. Really, despite the horror of what happened, sometimes I think she's the bravest and most generous of us all.

DI

I met Brendan in P.J. Clarke's on 55th and 3rd Avenue. Suraj suggested it as being unpretentious but extremely fashionable. I said who cared about 'fashionable', but he assured me the beefburgers were first rate and the air-conditioning never flunked out which was important in a sweltering September. Suraj had kicked me out of his parents' flat but we remained good friends. I lived instead in a railroad apartment on 38th street on the East Side, which didn't have air-conditioning but two ancient fans which blew the dust around from the books that lined the walls. 'Railroad' described the layout of the apartment: three narrow rooms, like old-fashioned train compartments, leading one from the other. It was very Manhattan – not the high-rises, obviously.

One morning I woke up to find Wystan Auden, the poet, in the next cubicle to me. He was very nice and merely murmured, as I walked naked past his bed, 'Angela didn't mention she had other guests.' His English accent gave me a surprise.

'She didn't tell me you were coming either,' I said, looking round nervously for something to cover myself with. But as the only obvious candidate was the sheet over the poet, I decided to carry on as if it didn't matter. He stayed a few days and we exchanged polite words over a first cup of coffee or a last glass of wine. Once I did share my views on Vietnam and his wrinkled face wrinkled even more in what I assumed to be agreement, but otherwise we were ships passing in the night.

New York was filled with interesting and sometimes famous people who didn't feel the need to interact with me. Journalists were different. I was learning from them, that was the point, and if the men – there were always far more men than women – attracted me, I slept with them. I was nearly twenty-one, no longer very young, and looked back on my growing up with a faint sense of disbelief. But my father, that was something else. He had always seemed more than mere 'family'.

'Hello Di.' Brendan was there ahead of me, standing bulkily in the cool, red-lit darkness.

I went over for a hug. He smelled of aeroplanes. He smelled English too, although I didn't know why. 'I've booked us a table.'

'I've come straight from the airport.' As we walked to the table, I saw he was carrying a bag.

'You're travelling light.' We sat down.

'Where I'm going, I won't need baggage. I'm picking up medical equipment at the airport. What would you like to drink?' I had forgotten the echo of Ireland in his voice.

I ordered a lager and he ordered a Jack Daniels. We both went for burgers and fries. I had never eaten a meal with him on my own outside of the house. It felt good. I gulped at the iced water and sipped the lager. I'd been drinking very little recently.

'So tell me what you're planning?' I asked, assuming an interviewing manner before he could question me. 'All I know is you've taken a sabbatical and heading up some mountain in Colombia or is it Peru.'

'I'm working for a small charity.' He cupped his glass in his big hands. 'You're quite grown-up, aren't you?'

I sat back in my chair. I felt pleased he'd bothered to stop off in New York and arrange a meeting.

'You were very young when I came back after the war.'

'I can remember it.' I didn't say how important it was to me.

He spoke in a sudden rush, not looking at me at first, then his eyes stared appealingly. 'I didn't want to come back. I found someone I loved in Italy. She thought I was important. She loved me. Only me. I was the centre of her life. Your mother loves her career. She's

admirable, your mother. An extraordinary woman... extraordinary.'
He paused. His face was flushed red. Sweat at his hairline.

I turned my head. I wanted to go away and leave him to his life.

'Di. Please!' His eyes strained for recognition. I remembered he
had been my hero.

I gave myself a long space, hoping he would fill it. But he didn't. I
tried to speak without bitterness. 'You had three daughters. So you
came back. And now we're all grown-up, you can go.' Perhaps he
was behaving in a perfectly reasonably way. Julie was impossible, we
all knew that. She didn't value love, just admiration and success. 'Do
you mean it's not a sabbatical? You're off for good?'

'I don't know.' He looked down, I thought shame-facedly, then
he summoned the waiter and ordered a second whisky.

'Where is your...' I hesitated, 'girlfriend?' I had become the
parent drawing out secrets from a reluctant child.

'Elena lives in New York.' So that's why he was in New York. I
was an optional extra. 'She's a doctor too. She works in the Bethesda
Medical Centre. She was married and has a fourteen-year-old son
who lives with his father in Chicago.' His eyes turned to me again.
'She's coming with me.'

Now we both were silent. I'd found my father and lost him again
in the same conversation. 'So that's why you came here.'

'I wanted to see you. Someone from the family needed to know.
We're going to a dangerous place.'

'We?'

'I'm sorry.'

'I like being on my own. You don't have to worry about me.' He
wasn't worrying about me.

'I've always felt you were the strong one. If I told Cleo, she'd just
make stories about it. And Millie would take it too seriously.'

'And also tell Julie,' I supplied, which wasn't very nice of me. I
drank iced water while he ordered another whisky. 'You're going to
be drunk,' I said, sounding more and more like an anxious parent.

'I don't expect you want to meet her?' He had perked up, confession done and dusted.

'No actually. One mother's enough for me.'

'She's not very motherly.'

'One non-motherly mother's enough for me.'

He got the point and ate his chips which had grown soft and cold as we talked. I began to think the whole thing was pointless and looked through the window to the bright lights of the city. Out there I had a life. He hadn't asked one thing about what I was up to. Then he began to talk about when he'd met Elena.

'We were both working in a military hospital in Naples near the end of the war. She was worn out by everything she'd been through. She said to me, "I nurse Germans first, then I nurse Yanks and British." I said, "But you must nurse your own people, the Italians." And I watched as her black eyes filled with tears, "Where was I when my brother died? When my father and mother were taken and shot?"

'Mussolini had come in on the wrong side; she was born in the wrong country. She went back to study after I left, became a doctor and emigrated to America. She said, "I have no family in Italy. I don't recognise those despicable," – she used the Italian word *spregevoli,* her beautiful mouth curling in revulsion – "those *persone spregevoli* who accepted Hitler, and I mourn the others who died as partisans." She used to say, "My head is *sfollati*. It should be somewhere else."

'My war had been so different to hers. I'd felt in the right place, looking after the right people, even if they were sometimes our enemies. I was strong and proud of myself. I saved people's lives. Once I was in the desert and I found an exploded tank with fragments of three men in it and one more still just alive. I kept him going by sheer will-power all the way to Cairo. I just wouldn't let him die. No one could believe how far he'd come.'

As he talked on, his words merged with memories of the stories that I'd heard as a six-year-old girl. I didn't want to stop him but I only partly listened. After a while he got back to Elena again.

'Of course I fell in love with Elena. Falling in love made winning the war perfect, complete. I was a hero to myself and to her. I made her life possible again. We lived together in a little flat overlooking the bay. The sun shone. Fishing boats appeared on the blue waves. We planned a future together. I hadn't seen Julie for four years and she had diminished to almost nothing. There was half a war between us. When I thought of her, I told myself she'd be fine, well able to take care of herself.' He stopped talking.

'When did you remember us?'

He looked at me vaguely. 'I said I had a wife who was obsessed by politics and had three daughters, although I'd only seen two of them. Elena said, *"Allora, è finita."*'

'You mean you wouldn't have come back to us? You said you decided to come back. But you didn't. *She* sent you back.'

'What?' He was slumped in his chair. 'I'm exhausted. Whatever time is it in England? I've got to get to bed.'

He managed to call the waiter and pay our bill. I watched without saying anything. But I didn't want our meeting to end like this. 'When are you leaving?'

'Tomorrow evening.' He seemed to come back to himself and looked at me again. 'I didn't mean to talk like that. Going on about the past. Sorry. Jet lag. The drink in me. Don't think too much of it.'

I thought of asking him if what he'd said was true but I knew it was.

We stood together on the warm street and I said, 'Which way are you going?'

He said, 'East 2nd Street'

So I walked with him. I still loved him and didn't want him to be hit over the head by some drunk from the Bowery. We hugged when we said goodbye, then I set off for a cross-town bus. I looked back and he was still standing there watching me. I felt as if I'd been orphaned.

63

CLEO

'*Minister's Schoolgirl Daughter Writes Sex Romp.*' Not a headline that you easily forget. I can't say I was very pleased by the tone of the red tops when *As you like it but can't have it* (Is that the worst title ever invented?) was published. In fact I was no longer a schoolgirl. I tried to believe the book had sensitive nuances and even deep truths if you looked hard enough. Dig in a novelist's soul and you'll find a conviction of the book's genius lurking behind the knowledge of its fatuity.

The novel was launched with a party in The Pheasantry on the King's Road, and Julie arrived ten minutes early, incandescently angry, red hair roaring off her head like flames.

'How dare you! Are you a complete airhead! Do you never think of other more serious people! Why am I the last to know!'

Various answers to what were not really questions came to me. 1/. With you as my mother I had to swim or sink. 2/. If I'm an airhead your genes must take 50 per cent blame. 3/. My publisher's serious about me. 4/. I'd have told you if you'd ever asked me what I was up to.

Instead I stood at the doorway with a glass in my hand, black kohl round my eyes and my skirt short enough to show off my slim young legs and said sweetly, 'I thought you never read the *Express*.'

'Fool! My PA reads every paper. She tells me everything that refers to me. Have you never noticed I am a politician?'

I put on a considering face. 'Not really. Tell me, what do you think about nuclear disarmament? Or then again, should we support home-grown British or go off to Big Daddy US of A?'

At that moment Buffy appeared between us, twice the size

of Julie, a cigarette dangling from her scarlet lips, booming with bonhomie. 'How kind of you, Minister! We're so honoured. So frightfully honoured. We hardly dared hope... We know just how busy you are. You must be so proud of your daughter...' As the younger daughter of an earl who ran away to Soho to make some money, Buffy flattered and cajoled with all the sycophancy of generations of royal courtiers.

I could see Julie faltering, the flames dying down round her head. She took a step back.

'I have to be at the House...'

Buffy took a step forward, waved over a waiter. 'Of course. Of course. One drink, perhaps. A toast to a great new future... a brave new world for a brave new spirit!' She pulled me towards her and raised my arm in a victory salute.

I'm afraid I smiled gleefully.

Julie stared at me. It felt like it was the first time she'd ever looked at me or certainly the first time she'd seen me. I wonder what she saw? A girl not unlike herself at that age, neat, pretty, although not as pretty as her, determined, although still with little idea where she was going. A writer? If she had thought that, it wouldn't have meant much to her. The only books in our house were Brendan's medical treatises, Millie's set books, and the occasional political biography presented by the author to Julie, *Aneurin Bevan: the Man who raised the flag*, humbly presented with admiration and kind regards to his successor... etc, etc.

Julie stared at me and I stared back. This was *my* evening. I had started a diary recently.

...Party a riot! Julie come to pour cold water. Seen off by Buffy, looking like a drag queen. (Is one?) We drank champagne and an ancient journalist from the Standard begged me to join his team. Ugh. On the other hand, depends what he pays. I didn't know anyone except Tommy the Tramp, Millie and Eddie. Tommy

drank his own bottle in a corner and was found asleep there the following morning. Millie was all dressed up in orange frills like a fruit sherbet and Eddie in a black suit like an undertaker. Briggs didn't show but there was The Times Lit Ed called James? and the Financial Times chap called Tony? and the Express chappess called Mo? and the Mail called Herbie? and some radio people keen to get a bit of me, so I wasn't alone, quite apart from Buffy and her posh girls shrieking 'Jolly Good!' She pays them a pittance so they make it up with noise. I wonder if I'll be a bestseller...

The truth is, when I got home, on my own, alone, lonely, fairly drunk, very drunk, I felt low, not bubbly. I sat at the kitchen table and sniffed. Even produced some tears. Di would have been made of sterner stuff but she was in New York. Even Brendan would have showed interest but he was who knows where. Had been there for three months. My head was slumped on the table when Julie appeared at the door. Her appearances in the kitchen were rare. I squinted up.

'Ah.' She looked vaguely my way as if trying to recognise something alien. 'Here you are.'

I didn't look up. She had to do better than that. I wrote an alternative scenario in my head: *What a triumph, darling! I am so proud of you!*

'Time for bed, I think,' said Julie. Did she move forward a fraction? Possibly but not enough to make any difference. 'It's been a long day.'

Did she actually want me to question her about the trials of political life? It seemed so. On *my* publication day! 'Night.' There was no point adding, 'See you in the morning' because I wouldn't...

All Julie left behind was the smell of her scent which I never did identify.

MILLIE

Mummy came to tea on Sunday. I felt sorry for her. She seemed so tired. We had been to Mass and I thought how much some quiet time would help her. She looked beautiful of course. But I could see beyond that and recognise the toll that public life was taking on her. No husband to support her. I looked lovingly at Eddie who was pouring us a glass of wine.

I'd put lilies in a vase to please her but I think they were really for me. Mummy was too busy to care for flowers.

CLEO

I am a novelist. I tell stories. I look for stories. I make up stories and life is never boring. But, amazingly, against all the odds, *viz.* family history yet to be revealed, I am capable of love. Only *I* know this, and one other. Plus Millie, I suppose, who believes everyone is born loving. She must do if she thinks our mother loved her.

I discovered love in 1962 at the age of twenty when I went on the second CND march. Anyone who was anyone and under twenty-five went on at least one of these marches from Aldermaston to London, organised by the Campaign for Nuclear Disarmament. I went along in my habitual spirit of critical involvement. I didn't join movements, I *inserted* myself, as a spy might, expectant and wary.

First of all I met Neil Hooper-Bowles. Despite his silly name, he came from a left-wing family. He was tall and broad and yellow-haired and most unlike the usual ratty Marxist–socialists. We walked together in the rain and I soon realised that he liked to believe he was an anarchist. It was odd to hear him extolling the virtues of violent action as we wore out our gym shoes on protesting against the bomb.

'I expect you read the *Black Fox*,' Neil said. We were having a comfort break at a garage and, while he was employed in fashioning a recalcitrant roll-up to give him worker credentials, a 'brother' handed me a copy of the inky mag. I decided not to mention that I earned a paltry living by writing gossip for the *Standard*. After my first novel was published, I'd refused to go to university, assuming a second, even more brilliant than the first, would pop out of my head. I was still waiting

'Thank you,' I said to the 'brother'.

'I could give you more? A dozen or so?' The question marks were not very hopeful.

I looked at him more closely. I saw he had a satchel filled with copies. He had a large dark head coated with the wild frizzy hair that would eventually come into fashion, above a small, neat body, not much above my height.

I indicated the satchel. 'That bag must be heavy.'

'I was hoping you would fling the mags, to rhyme with rags, far and wide, let them fly like sycamore seeds, strike the earth and grow into great trees.'

'You just want to get rid of them.' A man with a loud hailer was exhorting us onward and the rain was turning my personal copy of *Black Fox* into a sodden lump. 'This won't fly anywhere.'

I looked for Neil. 'We've lost Neil.'

'He'll have found a bird. He always does.'

I could see him now striding ahead with a long-legged girl whose bouffant blonde hair made her look like a dandelion. 'What sort of girls?'

'Stupid. Pretty. He likes them to think him a genius.'

'*Is* he?'

'What do *you* think?' He stopped. By now we were walking along side by side. 'I tell you, I'm fucked if I'll lug these rags anymore.'

As it happened we were passing through a small town which seemed defined by waste paper bins. I watched as he emptied copies of the *Black Fox* into three bins.

'That's better.'

'Won't Neil be angry?'

'I'll say I gave them all away, that people were fighting over them. He's so conceited, he'll believe me.'

'You didn't say he was conceited before.'

Can we please stop talking about Neil!'

Love is so peculiar. Why should Lennie Levy, as he turned out to be, strike love into my youthfully cynical heart? Was it because the story I'd been spinning about Neil and me had been derailed by a dandelion? Was there a vacancy where Cupid could strike his dart? Not just for then, *nota bene,* but for ever.

We laid out our sleeping bags, mine inherited from Di when she left for America, on the same schoolroom floor. Someone had drawn the CND peace sign on the blackboard. I can't see the sign now without remembering how our fingers reached out and curled together as if made for each other. His were delicate and pointed, made for touching, although on that occasion we lay fully clothed in our sleeping bags for a long uncomfortable night.

When the next morning, in sudden summer sunshine, Neil returned to claim me, he seemed a large, embarrassing stranger. I was walking beside Lennie.

'So that's where you got to!' He could have been referring to either of us. 'Hey,' continued Neil, 'Is that an empty satchel I see!'

'Yeah, sure thing,' agreed Lennie enthusiastically. 'All gone.' He gave me a broad smile. Did I say his mouth was wide and full? 'Cleo was a huge help.'

'Jolly good!' This was more public school than anarchist-speak.

Sex or rather sexual attraction is just as odd as love. Lennie had none of the obvious attributes that at the age of twenty I thought I wanted. Even his penis, when we got round to that, was on the small side. 'Got round to that' encompasses the whole complicated business of being a girl in 1962. The convention was that no well-brought-up girl had full sex before marriage which didn't mean they didn't, but they didn't go on about it like now. It also meant that, *sans* pill, they tended to get pregnant, which meant they did get married and that made the convention true, if only after the event.

Despite '*Minister's schoolgirl daughter writes sex romp,*' I hadn't had full sex or 'gone all the way' when I met Lennie. Lecherous older men were my speciality. Until I met Lennie, anyone under the age of forty seemed both callow and threatening. After all they might take me *seriously* when I didn't even take myself seriously. There was never any risk where the lecherous old men, each with a wife bringing up the children in Surbiton, were concerned. But it was all play-acting and really rather disgusting.

Bob Hood springs to mind under that heading, a drunken journalist on the *Standard* who preyed on muddled young women.

I should have known better when after one of the usual post-work pub evenings he offered me a lift home. Actually, it was what I wanted, a rite of passage, but I needed to be drunk enough to let it happen. Well, partly happen.

'You're ready for it,' he mumbled lasciviously, as his bony fingers fumbled inside me. Twitched and poked. Fingers, you note. Perhaps he never went further with any of his conquests; maybe he was loyal in his own way to his wife in Surbiton. More likely, he had no wish for more little Hoods.

We wriggled about on the sofa in my flat where I lived in fashionable squalor with four other girls – or women, but really we were girls. I had fled from home, and more importantly from Julie, the moment I earned enough money to pay rent. None of my flatmates were around that evening, pursuing their own encounters elsewhere. Whenever I read about housing problems for the young, I can't help wondering if it's the rise in standards of hygiene that's caused the present shortage. Our kitchen, bathroom and lavatory all inhabited the space of a modern bathroom. Even drunken Bob Hood exclaimed in some horror when he felt the need for a piss.

'Phew! Girls together, eh!'

'Eyes on higher things.' I hoiked up my pants.

'Time to catch my train.' Did he say that? Not very romantic. But it was important for both of us to deny what had/had not taken place before we met in the office the next morning. Denial has had a bad press in the last decades, blamed for depression, anger, lack of anger, stress and more or less every mental and some physical ills.

But I needed denial.

'Morning, Bob.'

'Morning Cleo. Another hot one. Yul Brynner's in town. Any chance you can get to him?'

But then along came Lennie. Why did I love him? Our second meeting was at a CND event a week after the Aldermaston march. I knew so quickly that I wanted him in my life forever. He knew it too but he had so many other goals. All I had was writing or rather not writing. It was the Easter holidays and he was living in his parents' house in North London.

'Do you want to come to my house?'

'If that's okay.' We hardly knew each other and he invited me to his parents' home! I would have stabbed my heart with my winklepicker rather than take him to Golders Green where Julie resided. Of Brendan there was no news but only a shadowy sense of absence, a mac in the hall closet, marmite in the kitchen which only he liked, the radio in the living room which only he listened to. It was eighteen months since he'd left. Millie, a married woman, went in and out, hoping to find a receptive Mummy but usually talking to the housekeeper who was Hungarian and made large goulashes which nobody ate. I should have been nicer to her but the house had never brought out the best in me. At least I didn't live there.

Lennie's home was in leafy, red-brick Hampstead, not far from Julie's domain, although I disguised that from myself. Sam and Judith Levy, Lennie's parents, were both academics and it was only when I met them and heard their accents that I realised they were Jewish; in other words Lennie was Jewish. If this makes me seem a moron, I can only point out that in the English middle classes, we didn't talk about such things. Despite the war, the camps, the horrors of the newsreels – that was over there in Europe. In England it was deemed polite not to notice if someone seemed a little bit different. Now it might be called anti-Semitic behaviour, since the implication of being 'different' was inferior, but then it was considered politeness.

Sam and Judy talked differently, behaved differently and I fell in love with them nearly as quickly as I had Lennie. To them I suppose I was different, even 'the other', but they were clever enough and kind enough to welcome me.

'Lennie is such a schmuck. Where has he hid this beauty? Please come in so we can admire you.'

'I haven't known him long.' An understatement for a second meeting.

They drew me into their house which was dark with bookcases, tables, high-backed chairs, two pianos and standing lamps with brown shades.

'Papa, let the girl breathe.' It was true that Papa had my arm in a grip, but it seemed to me friendly and caring. I smiled at him.

Judy made tea that first day, despite Lennie refusing her offer and taking me upstairs to his room. She carried up the tray, rattling the teacups all the way up two flights, until Lennie came out and took it from her.

'Mama, you are so nosey. You would break all our teacups, brought unbroken all the way from Germany, to satisfy your nosiness.' They laughed at each other. I heard that laugh with astonishment, a laugh full of love.

Yes, they had taught Lennie how to love but they had also taught him about freedom. Lennie needed no one.

I was in awe of the whole family. There was also a much older daughter, a doctor who had married a doctor and produced three boys.

'That lets me off the hook,' commented Lennie after we met her one evening. 'I don't have to be a doctor and I don't have to have kids.'

'Surely your parents don't care about such things?'

He kissed me without answering. We were lying together on his bed. It seemed that his room was private space once he had shut the door. We kissed when his parents were in the house but only made love when they were out.

The first time he started undressing me as if this was a foreseen event, I let him out of sheer surprise. He turned me round and round in front of him, commending and sometimes touching the parts that particularly pleased. 'Your nipples are surprisingly dark for a fair girl like you but I like it.' Touch. 'I like them very much indeed.' He gives me a turn and runs his hands over my buttocks. 'Small and neat, charmingly compact for a girl.' By the time he'd finished with me and started undressing himself, I was in no state to say no to anything. If he hadn't produced a condom, I would never have thought of the need. I was in love and we made love. Apart from the time when I wrote my first novel, there'd been nothing like it.

Luckily, Sam and Judy were out often, to music at the Wigmore Hall, lectures at the Cadogan Hall, meetings at King's College where they both worked. Occasionally there were concerts in their house. For me, it was all magic and they were part of it.

But Lennie was in his last year at Oxford. He went back to Oxford to take his finals. I knew almost nothing about him, although I believed that once I knew his family, I knew everything. During the time when we were meeting, he was working every night, sleeping for a few hours in the morning and working again until we met. He never told me that and I never guessed it. I was in the fog of love.

But then he never asked me about my writing. So I kept my published novel secret, only hinting that I was working on something. I imagined his parents reading 'the sex romp' and I was ashamed of it. On their tables there were books by Proust and Wittgenstein and most of all by Schopenhauer. I read the titles of his works with a sense of gathering inferiority. *The World as Will and Representation, Studies in Pessimism.* If I had actually dared open them, I might have found a clue to Lennie's nature: '*A man can be himself only so long as he is alone, and if he does not love solitude, he will not love freedom, for it is only when he is alone that he is really free.*'

More obvious than this was a poster above his bed which I discounted in the same way as I discounted posters against the bomb, which means I suspected they were right but couldn't bring myself to sign up.

'To live alone is the fate of all great souls.'

No one could say I wasn't warned. All but the strongest women at that time had the importance of men marked into their DNA. I prided myself on my scornfully ironic take on the world but when I discovered Lennie was off to America the moment he'd taken his finals (I heard from his mother), I reacted like abandoned women the world over: I suffered in silence. Or what amounted to silence,

'I hear you're off to America in a few weeks.' I didn't even add a question mark.

We were in Oxford – a picture-dawn, a May Ball – walking through those beautiful parks where weeping willows mirrored my emotions, if more gracefully and honestly.

'Yeah.'

'That's exciting.' A long pause while I summoned up courage, me, the sharp brave one, unmanned (I was about to write) by love. 'What are you going to do?'

'Travel, I guess.'

Only Americans said 'I guess.' He had already crossed the Atlantic and left me.

'I don't expect you'll write.'

'I never want to write another word.' He sounded angry but I didn't know him enough to understand why.

Lennie was escorted to the airport by his parents. I wasn't invited. We fucked the night before and that was it. It was 'fucking' now and not making love. I tried to hate him but only remembered how we'd agreed about so much: no God, Peace not War, you only live once, never ever believe anything anyone says. Make your own road. He had read economics because Sam and Judy had asked him to.

He loved Sam and Judy but on that last evening he made fun of them: 'Of course they want me to be a Captain of Industry.'

I said, 'But they're academics, they're so, so...' I struggled for the word, '... cultured, interested in the arts. Your parents are wonderful. You're so lucky.'

He stared at me without seeming very interested. 'Yeah, yeah. We all have to make our own road.' It was his farewell.

I should have slapped his face. Or killed him. But I didn't.

DI

I flew to Vietnam a few months after the Buddhist's protest – death by public burning. May 1963. I financed myself with money Julie had suddenly wired over, announcing she'd sold our London house. Good riddance, I thought to myself, although sparing a nostalgic memory or two for the Heath. Where was poor old Bear now? There were many Bears in Saigon. But I still didn't have a press card.

Then I discovered that Brad Wolfe was in Saigon. Well, he was about to be reminded of a few days on a ship crossing the Atlantic. It might be nearly four years ago but I flattered myself he wouldn't have forgotten the English girl who behaved like a hooker.

So I did a bit of deft stalking and went to his office. I dressed as I imagined his wife might, even applying lipstick. I spoke in authoritative Merrydown House English to the young soldiers manning the doors and desks. It was so easy. This was still early days in Vietnam.

Brad came out to me and I smiled apologetically. 'Needs must,' I said or something equally crass. In such situations, it's best to say nothing.

'We'll go out.' He led me by the elbow to a bar in a hotel, not my own one luckily. I was disconcerted by the erotic sensations that his touch set up in my body. Not in my brain, I told myself. I couldn't help wondering if he felt the same. I'd forgotten his height, his strength, his over-powering maleness.

We sat in a dark bar and I felt the same sort of edgy vibes coming off him as on that ship. That surprised me. By the stripes on his uniform and the layers to reach him in his office, he was an important man now. I needed him to be an important man on my side. He ordered drinks, raising his eyes when I asked for a soda. We settled at a small table. He concentrated on his beer before looking at me.

'I thought we'd said goodbye.'

'Sorry.'

'What are you doing here?'

'I'm interested in mess.' I assumed he wouldn't recognise his description of the situation in Vietnam given during our shipboard romance, but I said it anyway.

'You've seen nothing yet.' I picked up a faint glimmer of humour. I didn't remember that he had a sense of humour. 'I've been here from the beginning and I don't get it. How could *you*? How can anyone from our end of the world work out why a man would sit cross-legged and set himself alight.'

'That's Buddhism,' I said.

'Here, it's politics. Vice President Tho is a Buddhist. And the President's brother and political advisor announced, "If the Buddhists want to have another barbecue, I will be glad to supply the gasoline." You must know that.'

I did know that. Hard to miss it in Saigon. As he talked, I was reminded again of the man I met on the transatlantic ship. He had talked to me as if he needed to get it out of his system. As if I, the inexplicable English girl, flicked a switch in his brain. I hadn't understood a word of it at the time. Now things were different. I said nothing and listened.

'Kennedy kind of knows what he's up to. He's an internationalist. Likes to twist and turn, doesn't think like a soldier, but round here, that's not such a bad thing. He's always pushing for increased ops up North; "covert" is still his favourite word and who's to say he's wrong. In either case. I could tell you things about the VC attacks that would make your hair stand on end...'

He stopped abruptly and I assumed for a moment he'd noticed that he was letting go but he was only reflecting.

'What I think is, we're getting ourselves into a real war – only have to see what happened to the French – without anyone putting up the flag. Now we live in a democracy, wouldn't you say?'

I made no answer.

'Our President's the leader of the free world. Leaving aside the world, don't you think someone should tell the American people what's going on?'

There was another, longer pause, so that I wondered if he was actually talking to me as press. Perhaps he wanted me to report his piece. But somehow I didn't think so. He still gave the impression of a man speaking to himself.

'Say, they have a nice room at the back here. How about we visit it?' He pushed aside his drink and leant forward. I saw that he had forgotten that I was a Labour minister's daughter and I was still the same Brit 'hooker' who'd rolled around with him on the floor of his cabin. The abruptness of this suggestion heightened his attraction for me. I thought of Julie telling me once that men only want one thing. Her only bit of advice – with the implication that I wouldn't want it. Yet I hesitated. I hadn't come here for that.

'Wrong call.' He moved back. But I could see he was still hopeful.

'Are you still married?'

'Yeah. For better for worse.' He was beginning to lose interest. I needed to ask him about a press card but selling my body for that was too crude and maybe he couldn't even help. On the other hand, I had never turned down a man who attracted me. If I held off any longer, he'd be out of there.

'Okay.'

We walked down a passageway.

'Sorry it's so small.'

'It's three times bigger than the room I'm living in.' This brought no reaction except that he started taking off my dress, the one chosen to look like his wife's.

Sex repeated falls into patterns. If it was good once, it will be

79

good again. We stayed in that cool little room (rich men must have used it) all day, ordering in sandwiches round three o'clock. Daylight-light went from the one small window, the city madness ebbed and flowed, streetlights flared, sirens passed, re-passed. A helicopter came down low. I never wanted to leave that room.

'They're sending me home. They don't think me reliable.'

'Are you?' We lay on the bed, sculptural limbs entwined.

'I understand too much.'

I couldn't think what to say. 'Where will you go?' *Home to your children*, I wanted to say.

'They'll give me leave, then put me in an office in Washington DC, the sort of place where they can keep an eye on me.'

'You make it sound like a lunatic asylum.' I thought to myself that I'd always known he was there, somewhere in Saigon, and now he wouldn't be anymore.

We stayed all night long. Now I thought I knew why he didn't care about going back to his office or being with me. I was incidental to him. You're on your own, I told myself, and don't forget it.

Dawn came, pink and muffled, a momentary lull in the life outside. We were both loners; I suppose that's why we clicked, he because of marrying the wrong wife, me, because – but we can never understand ourselves. Or perhaps I'm just not interested enough. Not important enough.

We took turns in the cubby-hole that called itself a washroom. We dressed slowly and I still hadn't asked him about the press card.

We sat side by side on the bed.

'Are you going to stay here?' That was the nearest he got to showing concern for me.

'I don't know.' He kissed me kindly. It was a kiss for a wife and, if I was supposed to be pleased, I wasn't. 'It depends what happens.'

'There'll be plenty of things happening.'

So, we parted.

CLEO

My anger with Lennie had one good effect. It made me work seriously on a second novel. Now I had a missing lover as well as a missing father. I went to the Royal Free Hospital where Brendan had worked. And forced a harassed woman behind a desk to give me Dr Flynn's last known address – with the air of someone not just washing but scrubbing her hands.

Since my mother was theoretically not missing, I decided to beard her in her den. The House of Commons, away from its chambers, has always surprised me by its scruffiness. Of course there was no Portcullis House, so people swapped desks and grabbed their chances. Julie did a bit better than that, sharing an office with two MPs who had the lowest rating for appearances in the chamber. I found her alone, apart from her slave, Miss Gilley, who was bowed over her typewriter. Julie dictated as she ran her fingers through her curls.

She looked up with surprise. I very seldom came to see her. She never invited me. I settled myself in the rather grand chair opposite hers while Gilley's fingers remained poised in mid air.

'However did you get past security?' Hardly a friendly welcome for a youngest daughter.

'Journalists have these tricks.' Frankly, we'd given up being polite to each other. 'I was thinking of going off to find Brendan. It would make an interesting trip. I might write it up.'

'Your father...' A surprisingly human look crossed her face, weary and uncertain. She said nothing for a moment, before rallying. As I knew she would. 'I suppose you don't read the papers?' Her voice was strong and hard.

I thought about this. 'Of course I write for the *Standard*. They pay me. But I'm not fool enough to read it.'

'At your age I read them line by line, The *Daily Herald,* The *Daily Worker,* the *Express* for political gossip, *The Times,* the *Manchester Guardian.* I wanted to know what was happening in the world around me. I wanted to be part of it so I needed to know.' She paused.

'I learn about life from people.' I tried to sound defiant rather than defensive. I was twenty-one years old, a published author.

'So you don't know that our Prime Minister, Macmillan, has just sacked seven members of his cabinet, a third of the total. They're calling it the Night of the Long Knives which likens him to Hitler, if you've heard of the dictator who started the Second World War.'

'Exciting for *you*. Not much to do with *me*.' I wish I'd had the nerve to say, *Until you show some interest in my life, I'll show none in yours.*

She didn't give up. 'What it means to *you* is that Macmillan's made himself so unpopular, he might have to resign which might lead to an election and the Labour Party could be back in power and your mother in the cabinet. Or at least the government. I'd ask for Housing...'

At this point she began to talk to herself and my bellowing, 'Might!' in ironic tones had no effect all. As it happened I was right. The Conservative government didn't fall until the following year and that was because of sexual scandals. Think Profumo.

But I supposed most people would find her derision at my ignorance understandable. Except that she had created it. She never understood that. Also, I was a lot more aware of the world than I admitted to her. Sad.

When she stopped lecturing me about Labour politics, I started in immediately. I was not ready for the scene to end.

'I've got an address for Brendan from the hospital. Somewhere to start. I'll go to South America via New York. See Di.'

Again she wore that disconcertingly human face. I waited.

'How will you pay?'

Naturally, I hadn't a clue. My advance of £150 for my novel had long gone and my so-called salary from the *Standard* wouldn't keep a poodle in curls. Most of the girls working on the gossip columns relied on their boyfriends – or their mothers. Julie eyed me pityingly before turning to Gilley. 'I wonder if you'd leave us for a moment, dear.'

I sat up in anticipation. Secrets about my father?

As the slave scurried away, she spoke briskly. 'I've put the house on the market. In fact I've sold it.'

'My home!' I lied with a tragic face.

'You don't even live there.' True. 'I shall give you all some money. I've already sent some to Di.' Guilt money.

'Wow! An heiress!'

I could have been a bit more charming, particularly as the next morning, I had a surprising telephone call. The ringing woke me from a befuddled sleep and I located the communal telephone with half-closed eyes.

'Yes?'

'Darling, such thrilling news!' It was Buffy. She hadn't called me for ages, despairing, I suppose, of my ever producing a second novel. 'Some idiot wants to make a film of your book. And, on top of that, I've got a New York publisher lined up. The Gadarene Swine look like they're heading your way!' I'd forgotten how she gushed while remaining as cool as steel.

'How much?'

'You know how money bores me...' Oh, yes? '... How about I introduce you to Bertie Bull. A dear old homo friend of mine. Toughest agent in town. Come to the office tomorrow and I'll dig him out for you.'

It was only when I put down the phone that I remembered that I was ashamed of the novel. Everybody knew a film took a book further downmarket. I poured myself a large glass of Hirondelle. I pictured Lennie seeing the movie in New York and disowning me thrice. *She was just an easy lay, never a girlfriend. Would I ever have cared about someone who could write a vulgar monstrosity? She's so behind me, man.* From Lennie I moved on to imagining the horrified wonderment from his intellectual parents, Sam and Judy. 'Is that dear Cleo's name on the screen?' By now the disgusting wine was flowing, which is not a good sign at eleven in the morning.

I rang the *Standard* and said I was ill. Then I went back to bed.

In the evening as I finished the bottle, I picked up the phone and booked a flight to New York. Where was South America anyway?

DI

I was drinking beer in a Saigon bar when I heard that Cleo had arrived in New York. Our group of Western reporters and advisers was increasing, even though there were another two years before the US declared there was a war on. A newly arrived reporter said, 'Have you met this Cleopatra? From London, I'm not kidding you. So wired you'd need danger money to touch her.'

I said nothing. Life was far too interesting where I was. Diem had handled the Buddhist suicides badly and things looked rough for his government, actually more dictatorship. I still hadn't achieved a press card but there wasn't a great crowd of us like later, and I could usually find someone to feed me information, true or false.

'So do you know this Cleopatra? You're a limey.' That was Doug having a go. I liked Doug. He was shrewd, knowledgeable and had a real grip on Vietnam's history. Trouble was he was fat, wore glasses – which is why he was press not military – and had BO. Worse still, from his point of view, I was sleeping with his mate, Chuck – who was not so shrewd, not so knowledgeable but as handsome as you got in Saigon. 'I don't know all the girls in England.'

'There can't be that many called Cleopatra.' Doug had a point.

'Hundreds of thousands now that Elizabeth Taylor's played the role.'

'That movie only came out a month ago.' Doug again.

'Fuck off,' advised Chuck who was a man of few words. I gave him an approving glance. Men are so much less self-conscious and have no real understanding of other human beings. It makes them far more restful. I imagined Cleo, stirring. Why was she in New York?

Perhaps she'd spot my name in a NY magazine that sometimes published my pieces.

The bar we sat in was not popular with most foreigners. It had no real air-con, and threatening figures of unknowable nationality – not easy to tell a 'good South Vietnamese from a bad North Vietnamese' – wandered in out of the darkness. We pressed dollars on them, and joints, and waited expectantly for titbits. 'The monks, they run the show. They join with Ho. Diem boom boom...'

'Let's beat it.' That night there were five or six Americans sitting round and no one came to entertain us. I was the only one who refused the ritual passing of the joint and didn't get up and down to refresh my glass. I'd given up alcohol and all kinds of smoking. Why would I want to be out of control in these surroundings? In some moods, Chuck shrugged and told me I was an uptight Brit. Tonight he'd drunk and smoked too much and wanted a beautiful Vietnamese girl who said he was her king and would smoke puff for puff. Tonight I was too much for him and he didn't like the way I looked like a boy. Recently, I'd cut my hair as short as his. I could see all that in his cloudy blue eyes.

We drove back to the hotel. I'd been living in Chuck's room for the last two months and it was time I got out. I moved when he was in the restaurant, eating the ritual hamburger. Luckily Ping was behind reception. Ping (real name Nguyen Thanh Dung) was a weaselly Vietnamese with a touch of French around his nose, half my height, but we understood each other. Unlike most of the people in the hotel, we had chosen to live in Saigon. He wanted money and power; I wanted a cause.

'I need a room of my own, Dung.'

'Ah ha.' Not a man to waste words, he checked the books. 'All full.' I waited. 'You want maid's room?'

'I especially want maid's room.'

'Maid's room hot.'

'On my own?'

'Maid bunked off to mummy.'

I passed him money. 'No disturb. Chuck no find,' I commanded, then frowned. I didn't approve of pigeon talk and sometimes gave Dung (Ping) English lessons.

'I show.' So down we went to the bowels of the hotel and it *was* hot and very small but I felt great. I sneaked back upstairs but Chuck had already disappeared, so I was able to gather my few things, stuff them in a bag and set up residence. Now I had my own little hole. I knew Ping would guard my privacy.

Months passed slowly. I learnt to speak Vietnamese from a very old man with a white beard and brushed up my French with Ping. I hung out a little with Doug, enough to cadge a few stories. No sex. Somehow, I wasn't up for it. I managed to blot Brad out of my thoughts but he entered my dreams. I hoped he was troubled by dreams. Ping said to me one day, 'You a feminist lady. *Oui?*'

I laughed. 'Where do you hear about feminists, Ping?'

'American smart lady say she feminist.'

'Do you think I'm smart, *alors?*'

'You learn how to be smart.'

'*Merci bien*, Ping.' I thought Ping was my best friend and smiled to myself. Sometimes I helped him behind reception. If I stayed a whole day, he handed me a packet of dollars with Eastern ceremony. I told him he was my boss and started calling him 'Boss' instead of Dung or Ping. I liked watching people coming in out of the rain – it was raining all the time then – shake themselves and head for the bar, if they were foreign.

I knew my life was stagnating but I couldn't see any better way forward. Now and again I got a piece accepted by the *Saigon Post*, an English-language newspaper that had recently started. Mostly, they wanted me to review Western books or write about fashion. That's journalism for you. I detested books and fashion equally. But I did get whiffs of an America that was beginning to wonder what was going on in this far-off country. Doug commented, 'You've sold your soul to the idiots who think politics don't matter.'

The weather turned dryer and cooler and suddenly it was November. That's the month when everything happened. It reminded me all those months ago when Brad had said, 'There'll be plenty happening'. Then we'd parted.

On November 1st, All Souls' Day, Diem and his brother were arrested and shot, hands bound, in the back of an ARV armoured carrier. They'd just come out from Mass in Cholon but not many Europeans wondered about the state of their souls. Perhaps President Kennedy did; at least he was Catholic and said to be distraught, feeling the Americans had botched the whole business; not that he was against the coup.

Twenty days later, on November 22nd, Kennedy himself was shot and the Western world held its head in shock. I heard the news sitting beside a pool in the American Embassy, not my usual beat. Some under-secretary or other had looked me up – I wondered if Brad had made the link and then berated myself for being such an idiot – so I got out Brad's wife's dress and walked along.

There were cocktails and nibbles. No Brad, of course. The American Ambassador, surprisingly a woman, was gracious to me. We were both surprised at the other, I guess. There was a moment of confusion when she asked if I was related to Minister Flynn and I denied it. I honestly had forgotten about my mother. Then Doug spotted me and I got included in dinner and somehow I was still there after midnight, dangling my feet in the blue water, and listening to Doug and a few other only slightly drunk soldiers, diplomats and CIA, although most of them didn't advertise the fact, not telling each other what they knew while making it clear that they knew more than anyone.

Most of the lights had gone out in the embassy but there was still a big presence guarding the place; after all it was only twenty days after Diem's assassination and the next government was scarcely in place. Suddenly – I don't remember quite the order of things, how we were told the news of Kennedy's assassination – but one minute it was an ordinary evening at the embassy, and the next there was screaming and weeping and people seemed to be all around, as if the partying had started all over again. Except now it was horror and disbelief.

Everyone stayed up all night, and for that night at least, they forgot I was a Brit. In my dress, I became a woman and an American, the sort of person people wanted to cry with.

When I finally got back to the hotel, I crawled into my bed like a ghost. Who was I? Whose war was I fighting?

At nine o'clock, Ping came to my room. He sat on my bed. 'You know what?'

'What, Boss?'

'You go home. Room for maid now.'

Why did he choose that day to throw me out? To protect me? 'What home?' I asked.

He shrugged. Ping was never sentimental and I didn't blame him. Both his parents and his two elder brothers had been killed in the war with the French.

'Give me a couple of days.'

He nodded.

The couple of days stretched but I was gone before Christmas. Doug and Ping waved me goodbye. They were both on the way up. I put on a brave face. '*Au revoir.*'

CLEO

JFK, President Kennedy, was assassinated soon after I arrived in America and the country wallowed in misery and stories of conspiracy. But I didn't move in political circles so it didn't affect me much. New York was my sort of place. People believed me when I said I was a published author – well, I was, but I never saw myself as 'author' even as I proclaimed it in a humbly boastful way. In fact my novel had not yet been published in the US, despite Buffy's excitement and all contracts signed. But a movie was being made. Well, not quite yet, but the script was well underway. Meanwhile I was open to offers.

Between all the networking with old, hopefully powerful men (few powerful women around) and making superficial friends among the young, I forgot about looking for my father and, although I didn't forget about Lennie, my energies were diverted.

I shared a one-room apartment in a grimy corner downtown with a girl called Hash, after hash browns. 'It's my colour and I'm proud of it.' She looked white to me but she came from the South where she counted as a 'nigger', as she declaimed. I was only slightly shocked when she pronounced the 'n' word because Di had once ridden a horse called 'Nigger' on Hampstead Heath. I recognised that, even if the New York I played around in seemed open to all colours, that was just my ignorance. 'Haven't you heard of Harlem, girl?'

Hash and my paths didn't cross often but she liked to open my eyes a little when she got the opportunity. She was determined to be an actress and once told me she'd slept with 125 men, five for her own pleasure, twenty when compelled to by circumstances and

100 in the line of business. 'But you're so small, Hash,' I commented idiotically. I still wasn't jumping into bed with people. I liked to think it was out of love for Lennie and suggested as much to Hash who said, 'Lord, Cleo, no man's worth that.' Maybe she was a feminist.

One freezing evening in early November, she gave me a ticket for a play she was acting in round the corner. The ticket was handwritten in red crayon so I guessed there wasn't a run on them. In fact there were six us just about filling three benches in an unheated basement room. Very off-off-Broadway.

'If darkness comes at noon, then midday brings the dawn.' This was Hash's first line, standing in the middle of the bare stage, and I can still remember it because when Di arrived in New York, it became a mantra between us, a suitable commentary to the nonsense of life. I can't remember anything more about the production, except there were two naked men (both darkly handsome) who stood like sentinels on either side of Hash as she pronounced.

Later I saw other productions just as inexplicable. Some of them were hailed by the *Village Voice* critic as *'breakthrough drama'* and some disappeared without trace. Once Vietnam protests got going, of course, they tended to have more meaning. There's nothing like a cause to concentrate the creative juices. I can say that because for years I skated on the surface. Feather-brained, as work-horse Julie would say.

That first evening I met Holden. He was sitting next to me, smoking pot throughout. After a while I asked if I could have a puff and he obliged, although not very generously, snatching the cigarette back after one drag. Holden was an ugly man, round face with a small nose, always slightly sweaty, and a big stubby chin which was not the fashion then. Afterwards we all went to a crummy West Side bar where the beer cost half anywhere else and it was only fractionally warmer than the basement. Once more Holden and I found ourselves sitting next to each other.

'I'm a novelist,' I informed him before he could even ask.

'Yeah? Guess what. I wrote a screenplay for a Brit novel. Pile of shit with a fucking dreadful title but I've injected a splinter of backbone. Never know. They might even make it.'

That's the thing about New York – well, Manhattan in those days – you could go to a nothing, nowhere place and meet genuine talent, even success. And people with whom you had links, of course. Somehow I wasn't surprised when it turned out Holden was referring to *As you like it but can't have it*. Should I disown it?

'The author was very young. Still at school,' I murmured warily.

'She couldn't even do the sex bits. Any dumb fool can do the sex bits.' Suddenly suspicious, he peered through the frosty dimness. 'You don't happen to be acquainted with the unfortunate author?'

Against the odds, this exchange formed the basis of a new friendship. Holden, it turned out, was the lover of one of the darkly handsome men but he liked women as friends. 'I loved my mother, you see, and I could never fuck anyone made in her exquisite image.'

Holden was a very rich and successful screenwriter who just happened to prefer New York to Hollywood, probably because of the Gay thing. Men were just becoming 'gay' then.

Although apparently waspish, Holden was very kind. So was Sean, his lover. They lived in a palatial flat in the Dakota (the same building where John Lennon lived and died seventeen years later). I spent a good part of my time in their spare room.

One afternoon, Holden walked me down to the *Village Voice* and introduced me to Norman Mailer: 'She's a Brit novelist.' Holden nodded at me as if he was showing off a horse.

I knew I'd read a Mailer novel but couldn't remember the title. Mailer was heavy and hairy and eyed me lasciviously which was quite a feat, considering I was wound about in coats and scarves. I accepted the largest glass of wine I'd ever seen. I had recently realised that it wasn't just America that was bigger than the UK but everything in it – cars, apples, frankfurters, men, women, high rises, newspapers, food portions and, most enjoyably, glasses of wine.

'I'm such a fan,' I ventured after a second glass, a dangerous statement since I still hadn't remembered the name of any of his books. I unwound a scarf or two.

'Any relation to Di Flynn?' By this time he was surrounded by glasses as if he was preparing that Mozart piece for glasses and orchestra, but he still *could* remember my surname. That's a real American memory in action. I stared without answering. 'She wrote a little piece about Saigon's French legacy for us. Not bad,' he snorted.

The snort put me on Di's side. 'My sister.'

'Is that so.' He seemed more interested.

Later, Holden told me I'd passed the Mailer test.

'What's that?' I asked.

'Being English. Having connections.'

So I was *right* about the city. Making connections. Perfect for a novelist. Although it seemed weird that a sister counted as a connection, particularly when we were so unconnected. I now knew Di was in Saigon but nothing more. The *Voice* did publish a piece of mine: 'Literary London: the demise of the Victorians'. I mugged it up from a copy of *The Times Literary Supplement* found in Holden's flat.

Holden, of course, wanted to write a novel. He said, 'You know J. D. Salinger – Sonny to his family – burgled my name for his fucking book. Our mothers prayed at the same synagogue. I was eighteen when the fucking *Catcher* first came out in serial form so maybe he burgled my life too.'

Sean made violin motions and wiped his eyes. Sean was my new best friend. He told me he had Irish and German roots with the Irish winning, but since he'd fallen for Holden, he was trying to encourage the German. 'You can't imagine the rubbish that man spouts. Self-pity on the outside and icy confidence inside. How do you think we come to live in a place like this?'

'What about his novel? He sounds despairing about that.'

'Despair comes to those who choose. Have you seen his filing cabinet of words and phrases? Writing his novel, or, let's be honest, not writing it, is a mode that gives him huge self-respect.'

I felt so relaxed with Sean that one late night when Holden had gone to LA for a meeting and we'd stayed up smoking pot, I told him about Lennie. Three days later, he informed me, with a meaningful look, that an old friend of mine would be waiting for me in Washington Square at 1400 hours.

'But it's the coldest day of the year.'

'Yup. Dress warm.'

Snow was falling in great dollops as I hurried downtown. I'd borrowed Holden's deer-hunter hat (it later appeared in the film of that name) which only just cleared my eyes and nose. Below it I wore his wolf-fur coat and boots I'd bought in army surplus. Dead man's boots, I presumed. Vietnam still seemed very far away.

I really didn't expect Lennie to be waiting so it wasn't a surprise to find the square only inhabited by a few brave dog walkers and three or four tables of intrepid chess players, so unmoving that they were gradually turning into snowmen. I walked round twice, clapping my hands and stamping my feet and eventually one of the players looked up and barked, 'Can't you shut the fuck up.'

I watched white flakes falling on his black beard and thought, *Stay? Or go?* He turned away before I'd made up my mind. I went to a bench and, pushing off the snow, sat down. Seeing Lennie like that made me feel weak and breathless. I put my head in my hands. A dog snuffled along my boots. A small dog covered in curly reddish hair. We stared at each other with understanding.

The dog went and a pair of legs covered in washed-out jeans stood in front of me.

'I thought it was you.' Lennie took off his hat and shook the snow off it. 'I guess I look like Father Christmas. How are you, Cleo?'

'You've got snow on your beard. How long did it take to grow?'

'I wasn't watching. How about we catch a coffee.'

'You've grown an American accent too.'

'I'd forgotten how sharp you are.'

We both looked at each other in a friendly way, if not loving. I certainly didn't want to look as if I was chasing him. We went to the usual dark bar and agreed a whisky suited the occasion better than a coffee. I'd forgotten to steal Holden's gloves and my hands were so cold the ice in the glass seemed warmer. There was a bit of a chicken-game moment as neither of us asked the other what we were up to. Instead I told him about Holden and Sean and he told me about his room in a converted warehouse near the Brooklyn Bridge. 'It still smells of gunpowder,' he said which I decided not to question.

Then a girl came in. She reminded me of myself when I wasn't dressed like Holden, small and compact with a contained watchfulness. She sat by Lennie.

'Hey. Al said you were here.'

Lennie nodded at me: 'An old friend from London.'

'And who are you?' I assumed the air of an interviewer.

'Tara. Did I break up something?' Without waiting to be reassured, she addressed Lennie. 'Are you on for tonight?'

'Sure. 6pm at the Greeks.'

How annoying was that! I was about to get up and go when Tara got there first. I watched her through the door. Her breath made pretty twirls as she hit the street.

'Who's she?' I said.

'Tara,' said Lennie.

I allowed a pause to develop.

'She's not my girlfriend. Well, only occasionally. She works at ABC News. We're part of a "Watch Vietnam" group.'

It was clear that I was a failure in everything: love, work, politics, the world. 'I'll have another whisky.'

Lennie brought back just one for me. Now I was an alcoholic too.

'What are you up to?' He leaned forward. He'd become the interviewer.

'I write. I can't do anything else. I don't want to do anything else.' The second whisky had an instant beneficial effect. Surely he knew I wrote. But then I had never told him about my first novel. I sat back on the bench and surveyed him kindly. 'And how are you keeping the wolf from the door?'

He smiled. 'You sound like my mother.'

'How *are* your parents?'

'Now you sound like my sister.'

We smiled at each other. This was better.

'Did your dad come back?' He looked reasonably interested in an answer.

'No.' Pause. 'I am supposed to be looking for him but I got diverted.'

'And is your high-powered mother as infuriating as ever?'

So I'd told him that. We'd known each other such a short time. Did I love him or was he my protection against loving anyone? 'My eldest sister married at the first possible moment. My next sister dashed off to Vietnam and I'm here. I suppose that answers your question.'

'My parents just visited. As paid-up Labour Party members, they told me all about Gaitskell's death and George Brown trying to take over but Harold Wilson sweeping all before him, talking about a new scientific age at a triumphant conference and your mother made shadow something or other which boded well for her future. I guess they were trying to lure me back. Strange method. I could feel their love hurtling towards me like grappling irons.'

I said, 'What *are* you doing here?'

'I'm learning to play the piano.' The words were defiant, very serious, and I responded in the worst possible way.

'But your Sam and Judy would be thrilled.'

He stood up at once. 'I knew you wouldn't understand.'

'To rephrase, you mean you had to get away from doting parents to do what they want you to do.'

He didn't answer but put some dollars on the table and I had time to feel sad it was ending like this, Mum and Dad spoiling the party. Then he pulled me out from my bench. 'How about a fuck for old time's sake?'

However casually made, I couldn't risk turning down the invitation. I shivered all the way to where he took me. Not his room but some crazy Village hotel painted a dirty grey, or maybe it was just dirt. On the way we kissed and I thought our lips would be frozen together. I wouldn't have minded, I loved him so much.

The room we made love in (I made love anyway) was very hot with that special New York sensation of great underground pipes blasting up burning breaths. We tore off our clothes and didn't bother to remove the coverlet. We rolled off the bed and lay on Holden's wolf-fur coat, both of us with shut eyes, wanting only to feel.

We hadn't put on a light and the snowy whiteness came through the grimy window until the evening dark wiped out even that.

'I'd forgotten.' That was Lennie.

We crawled back into the bed and lay together but I could feel his mind beginning to race away.

'Where do you learn the piano?' I whispered. I needed to have him a little longer.

He told me all about it then, about his teacher who'd been a concert pianist, played at the Carnegie Hall, but one night got such terrible stage fright that he had to be hospitalised and never played publicly again; but he was the most charismatic teacher in the world. I listened carefully, suspecting that he would leave me again and I would have only what I could remember.

He told me that he waited tables at night in a club from 8pm to 3am and then they let him use the piano for the rest of the night. I pictured all the concerts in his parents' house and felt certain that one day he'd go home. I would be there, I promised myself.

'And what about you?' he inquired eventually. Seriously. That was a surprise. It wasn't just the beard that was different.

'I told you, I'm being a writer. At the moment scraps of journalism but soon I'll start a... (I edited out 'another') a novel.'

'How do you pay the bills?'

'Writers are natural scavengers. Succubi. Spongers. I live off other people.' The thought depressed me. 'I expect I'll go back to London soon. I can get my old job on the *Standard*.'

The temperature in the room seemed to drop. We had no future together.

Lennie murmured, 'As Oscar Wilde said, "Be yourself, everyone else is already taken."' He sat up and went over to a small basin in the corner of the room. I watched him wash. He dried himself on his T-shirt. I watched as the black hair under his arms stopped dripping in little peaks and cohered into a soft mass. He'd paid when we came in. There was no need to leave together. I wondered if he'd kiss me goodbye. Then I thought, we're both in Manhattan which is a small island so our paths will cross again.

When I got back to Holden's place, Sean was only dressed in underpants and looked particularly beautiful and athletic. He asked eagerly, 'Hey, did you see him? How did it go?'

'You Americans are so upfront,' I said. 'But thank you for getting us together. It was good.'

'Good,' Sean repeated with a bemused expression on his face. He was such a romantic.

MILLIE

When I found out I was pregnant I went to church and prayed. In other words, I told the Blessed Mary before anyone. Although I suppose She would have known anyway. I found Holy Mary, Mother of God, much more approachable than my own mother. Darling brilliant Mummy was now edging closer to real power with Harold Wilson leader of the Labour Party and an election certain next year, 1964. Naturally I couldn't blame her for wanting to get on, particularly now Daddy had gone. Both my sisters had gone, of course; to America or Asia or somewhere.

I told Eddie eventually before he rushed off to give a lecture on the historic links between Christians and Muslims. Nobody was much interested, he said, but he was not downhearted. That was one of Eddie's strengths, a sturdy belief in himself, without accompanying arrogance.

'I'm going to have a baby, Eddie.' Saying the words out loud gave me a most peculiar feeling.

'Oh darling, darling, darling.' Eddie clasped me in his arms and I realised that what I was feeling was happiness. It struck me suddenly how skewed my beloved poetry and literature was because it was almost entirely written by men or, very occasionally, by women who hadn't given birth. Love to them was love between a man and a woman or two adults anyway; romantic, sexual love, or occasionally reverent love for a mother. But they had no chance of expressing the wild glory of another creature growing inside your body. Even the genius Shakespeare couldn't go there.

'Shall I stay? Shall I cut the lecture? There'll only be three students.' He was so eager, so excited. My happiness grew.

'Don't do that, darling. We'll celebrate when you get back.'

Men do feel love for their children, I wouldn't deny that. Eddie loved Calypso deeply. But no man can ever know that act of creation. Holy Mary Mother of God knew, knows. It wasn't just because of Mummy being so otherwise engaged that I told Jesus's mother first. I knew who I could trust.

Oh Mummy, why couldn't you understand all these things? Why did you give birth to us all when you wanted us so little? There, now I've admitted it. Didn't you realise how dangerous it was?

DI

Cleo kept telling me how alike we were and I was too tired and depressed to tell her to shut up and stop talking gibberish. Eventually she said that as it was Christmas Eve and we had both been baptised Catholics, shouldn't we go to Mass. I expect she said it to get a rise.

'Come on, Di. Have a drink.'

'I don't drink.'

'At least dress.'

I'd only been back in New York a week when Cleo tracked me down. Apparently she knew the grubby hotel where I had landed up. I didn't ask how. We were so unalike. I wanted to do something with my life and she just wanted to write stuff down. I suppose she would say I wrote stuff down too but that's just a means to an end. Did anyone care about what was going on in Vietnam? Look at LBJ! A man thrown into office by another man's death, with a quite different agenda, different advisors, a different approach. If he *had* cared, he would have commanded the US to flee the battlefield, bringing back all the generals and soldiers and advisers and reporters. That would have been heroic. But he cared about problems at home.

Cleo and I walked to St Patrick's Cathedral. Don't ask me why we went to such a posh place. We were staying in the posh apartment owned by her gay friends who were in Key West avoiding Christmas. I thought of how I'd stayed with Suraj and felt ashamed that the two of us were such spongers. Cleo said she was housekeeping, but I never saw her do anything except raid the drinks cabinet. She said they wouldn't be back till New Year's Eve and they'd love it if I was there, so I chose the maid's room, another maid's room, and moved in. At least there was a television.

The church was crammed. I'd forgotten about believers, that clubby confidence and energy. Most of them looked well-off in their furs and cashmere. I still hadn't got used to seeing money on people's backs.

It was a surprise to find the old liturgy grabbing me. Not grabbing, that's unfair, holding me. *Domine non sum dignus.* Who says that anymore? Lord I am not worthy... Everyone thinks they're worthy. They're taught about self-belief as if it was a virtue.

I made a stab at praying in St Patrick's. Conventional stuff: *make me a better person, make me do good in the world.* I didn't ask for protection. I never wanted that.

We went back to the apartment and Cleo telephoned Millie who burst into tears. While she recovered enough to speak, Cleo raised her eyebrows at me in a what-an-idiot way which I refused to recognise. Millie was so remote from me that I felt nothing but goodwill for her.

I said, 'Hey, Millie. Don't cry. We haven't spoken for ages. How are you?'

'It's just so nice you rang,' she managed to snuffle out. Her voice lowered to a small whisper. 'I'm spending Christmas with Eddie's parents and they're missing Hazel so much. Your *friend* Hazel.' That came out as a bit of a hiss.

'We've just been to Mass,' I said, ignoring the Hazel line and trying to shock her into a better mood. It sort of worked, except that, after a burst of pleasure – 'That's so lovely!' – she returned to sobs.

'Ask her whether she's pregnant?' Cleo shouted in my ear so that Millie and the whole world from New York to London could hear.

'But how did you know?' Millie stopped crying abruptly and Cleo smiled her cat's smile. 'I was about to tell you. Cleo, you're such a witch.'

Cleo took the phone and they started bandying insults mixed with compliments. I wandered away to the window.

I stood watching the snow drifting over Central Park, thin stuff with no hope of piling up on the sidewalks. 'I'm going for a walk.'

When I got back, Cleo had drunk half a bottle of gin and said belligerently, 'I was waiting for you to call Julie.'

'Why?'

'Why am I waiting or why am I calling our mother on Christmas Day?'

Julie didn't answer her number anyway so Cleo drank some more gin and we went out for the Christmas dinner she'd booked at the Plaza. When I asked how she was going to pay, she looked astonished and said, 'Holden has an account here. He loves me using it because he's on a diet and he's afraid they'll close it.'

The point about Cleo is that she has no real hold on reality, which makes her good fun. Better still, and much more surprising, Suraj was sitting at the next table with his wife and family.

'Slippers!' We shouted our password happily. I made a mental note to thank Cleo for insisting I borrowed a respectable jacket from Sean's wardrobe (he had skirts too if I'd wanted them).

So we sat with Suraj and his family and I wondered at the beauty of his young Indian wife while Cleo – amazingly given her alcoholic intake – carried on a witty conversation with Suraj's father about the problems of having a novel turned into a film: 'It's turning a panther into a lion.' Suraj's father, who was a man of the world, nodded politely.

Over coffee I confided in Suraj about my humiliation in Saigon, a total failure. 'Without a press card, I couldn't get into the press briefings and just made do with scraps from the table and a few friends I'd made. I never got into the inner circle at all.'

'So what are you going to do now?' Suraj had a clear vision about work, but less so in his personal life – he looked with so much love at his wife that I almost forgot he was gay.

'This morning I prayed.'

He said nothing.

'In St Patrick's. With Cleo. Then we rang my sister who's pregnant.'

'So you're going back to help her with the nappies.'

I said nothing. He was making me feel worse. 'So what *should* I do?' I said in an ironic tone, but he answered seriously.

'Go to every newspaper or magazine that sends a correspondent to Vietnam, or, better still, a paper that hasn't yet but might like to, big up your six months there, your knowledge of the language, not many can boast of that, get a job and get your press pass.' He said it with such conviction that I had to believe it was possible.

CLEO

I tracked Lennie down to his room. It was another freezing cold day; the snow had melted for a day or two into rain, then froze so that grit decorated the sidewalks and roads like dirty rice. I took the subway to City Hall, walked, and got lost in the tall warehouses somewhere behind the Brooklyn Bridge.

In the end it was chance I found him, a poster stiff with frost hanging out of a window: *The secret to happiness is freedom and the secret to freedom is courage.* It had to be Lennie.

I spotted an open door, climbed wooden stairs and found myself in a room filled with Singer sewing machines, dusty black and grimy gold, row after row. Although no expert, I could see that they hadn't been used for a while. It was as if there'd been a plague, alien attack, an earthquake: Pompeii must look like that. Ghosts, a roomful of ghosts, bent over their tables. If I stayed much longer, the machines would start whirring. I went through a small door at the far end and found Lennie asleep on a camp bed. It was two o'clock in the afternoon so I felt justified in waking him up. I was still surprised by his beard as he opened his eyes.

'What time is it?'

'Afternoon.'

'I know it's afternoon. I don't get to bed till eleven.'

I remembered that he worked in a club, then played the piano till morning. 'There'd be room for a piano in that room next door.'

'If I had a piano.'

He was not unfriendly, I told myself, and sat on the bed. The room was quite male-body smelly but that too was not unfriendly. I wondered whether he would want to make love but the friendliness didn't seem to be in that direction and I hadn't come for that either. I thought. I think. 'I like your poster.'

'What? Oh. Let's go and get a coffee.' Already half-dressed, he pulled on clothes quickly and I followed him out.

'Where are all the workers?' I swept my hand at the empty benches.

'Politics. Unions. Corruption.' He showed little interest in explaining and walked quickly, running down the stairs and slapping his hands together as we hit the cold air.

The small café/bar steamed and hissed and sizzled with kettles and coffee machines and frying pans. When Lennie put his fingers round a mug, I noticed each one wore a plaster at the tip. 'Why the plasters?'

'You can wear out your fingertips beating the ivories.' He gulped for a few minutes. 'You're still here then. I thought you were going to Hollywood to watch your trashy novel being made into a film.'

Had I told him that?

'I'm going off soon. In fact I came to say goodbye.' A lie. I came because I loved him. But it actually was true that Holden had told me that *As you like it and can't have it* was nearer being made. 'The producers are talking about James Stewart as the tramp and Elizabeth Taylor as the girl.'

'How many producers?'

'Three. Four. But the Studio has control.' Which might be true.

'So much money is wasted on movies.'

There seemed little to say to this. 'How *are* the ivories?'

'Do you really want to know?'

Could it be he didn't know I loved him? But of course he didn't believe in love. He believed in freedom and courage. 'Do you believe in happiness?'

'Weird question?'

'Your poster says courage leads to freedom and freedom leads to happiness so that suggests you want it.'

He put down his cup. It was heavy, made of thick china. 'Another guy put up that poster. Before I moved in. I believe in music.'

I gave up then and allowed myself to be washed by a great wave of self-pity. I stood up so he wouldn't see my tears. Of course he snatched my hand. 'Don't go.'

'I'll look you up when I get back.'

Later that afternoon I booked my flight to LA.

✇

I was right about the studio having the power. It wasn't for much longer, but this was 1964. I was led through great buildings containing sets to the office of one of my producers. I was disappointed immediately by his appearance. Instead of being a magnificent presence smoking a cigar while a glamorous starlet pleasured him under the desk, Norman Shoubunkin was small and nervous, wearing a short-sleeved striped shirt and a bow tie.

As I was shown in, he looked at his watch, 'I can give you ten minutes, Miss...' He gave up on the name.

'Cleopatra Flynn.' I deduced that his rudeness was due to lack of power and assumed him to be the third or probably fourth producer in line. I smiled charmingly. Often my name combined with my English accent came to my rescue on such occasions. When I had checked in at my ten-room hotel, squeezed between two white palaces ('boutique' hadn't been invented then), the reception had been all over me: 'Hey, I can tell you're not from London, Ohio.' I deduced from this that Californians were less sophisticated than New Yorkers.

I saw I needed to explain myself to Mr Shoubunkin. 'I'm the author of *As you like it and can't have it,* renamed *Dark Secrets* when I last heard. I was just passing through and thought I'd drop in.' It struck me that if you passed through California you were liable to end up in the Atlantic, so I repressed a giggle and offered another winning smile to compensate for geographical failings.

'That so.' He was a man of few words.

'I wondered if James Stewart and Elizabeth Taylor had been cast? It's so appropriate she was born in England and Jimmy Stewart is such a hero.'

He pressed a buzzer on his desk. Action! Then looked at his watch again. I calmed myself by thinking that I had only come here to impress Lennie and could leave whenever I liked.

The young man who had led me in reappeared. Now I saw him from the front, I realised he was startlingly good looking with brilliant blue eyes, black hair and gracefully tailored features.

'Coffee. And don't forget the sweetener.' Later Reuben (would-be acting name Ben Anton), who was the young man, explained there were only two modes in Hollywood: rude and charming.

I never found anything out about my book/film from Mr Shoubunkin but Reuben filled me in: nothing was happening. As a consolation, he invited me to supper at a hotel where, he informed me, people went to be seen.

We had a small table, cramped by a flatulent, orange-coloured plant, but we could peer out between its leaves, or so Reuben assured me, and hail or accost when appropriate, if anyone famous appeared whom he'd met. No one did.

My lack of cinema savvy shocked Reuben. 'You'll never manage things on your own,' he advised, blue eyes electric with intensity. 'Without an agent at your side, you're dead in the water. Think Lucy in *The Searchers*, abducted, raped and scalped, and that's before the movie had even started.' Reuben lived and breathed films. He had grown up on this very lot, his mother a Puerto Rican bit player and his father a producer whose name had never been divulged by his mother, leaving him free to claim by turns Joseph L. Mankiewicz, Howard Hawks, Preston Sturges and Fred Zinnemann.

'You're so handsome,' I told him. 'You're sure to be spotted.'

'You don't think the nose too feminine?'

I studied the straight, medium-sized protuberance he was now fingering. 'It's perfect.'

'Think Natalie Wood, *Splendor in the Grass*. I told that to the medics. They're used to doing Jewish girls who want little turned-up pointy things. I can't tell you how often I drew this nose. I went under the knife with only a teensy anaesthetic to make sure I could scream if they tried to reproduce the flirty little beauty they created for Ann-Marie or Annette or Annalisa.'

Reuben made me laugh. He made a pass at the end of the meal but sighed with obvious relief when I said I needed sleep more than sex.

'It's such a currency here that you have to ask. Like who pays the bill.'

'The best-looking men are all gay in New York,' I told him.

'I thank you, Ma'am. I did give men a try-out but they're so much more violent than women. *Actually* – do I sound like a Brit? – I *adore* a woman's body, soft and round and smooth, without all that bristly hair. *Actually,* you're just my type. Think cat-like Vivien Leigh in *Gone with the Wind*.' He smiled to himself.

I felt happy standing on that pavement with Reuben. The warmth, so relaxing after the East Coast freeze, the palm trees along the sidewalks, the cars, gas-guzzling spaceships, all seemed a suitable up-yours to Lennie. I smiled contentedly and at that moment Reuben grabbed my arm and hissed maniacally.

'Oh my God! Who is that *dancing* towards us? This *is* your lucky day!'

I gazed where he pointed and among the suddenly parted pedestrians, I saw a tiny gnome-like man who was indeed dancing, skipping and hopping towards us.

'In public! No escort! A few yards distance!' Reuben was no longer lowering his voice.

Of course I couldn't enquire who the famous person was. As we and the rest of us outside the hotel stared with avid respect, the great man passed into the hotel, doormen bent double, *maître d'* rushing out, two huge hosts in tuxedos greeting, whispers spreading.

'Fred Astaire...' Reuben breathed out the name and joined the crowd closing behind the idol. I was in the home of stardom, I thought, and even felt sorry for poor old Norman Shoubunkin, sitting in his empty office with no power but rudeness to an unimportant English novelist. Stardom was the thing. Perhaps Reuben of the beautiful Natalie Wood nose would make it. I wandered away.

In the middle of the night but already daytime in London, I rang Julie. I only ever had the urge to contact my mother when I was very far away from her. 5,437 miles was pretty good. Slightly to my surprise, she picked up.

'Guess what, Mum, I'm in LA.' I pictured her in her parliamentary office, neat and pretty, giving her secretary a hard time. Thoughts definitely not on her daughters. Or maybe she'd let mother-to-be Millicent in a little closer. I doubted it.

'Is that Cleo?'

'That's me. Daughter number three. Born 1942. A war baby.' I was already regretting the impulse to call her.

'Where did you say you were?'

'Hollywood. I just saw Fred Astaire in the flesh.'

'So your novel *is* being filmed. Well done, darling.'

I caught the surprise. But I was her 'darling' so how could I be a spoilsport with the truth? 'Yes. It's all incredibly exciting. Almost unreal.' Certainly *that* was true. 'I saw the producer today, Norman Goldberg,' – (more impressive-sounding than Shoubunkin) – 'and I met the director too, Reuben Anton, quite young and very good looking.' At least the description wasn't a lie.

In all honesty, I've never felt truth quite the ultimate target that most people seem to. More like a golden bullet. Find me someone who bangs on about the truth and I'll find you a liar. I gave a lecture once about the truth of fiction, and halfway through I remembered it was supposed to be about the truth of historical fiction so I repeated the same things but threw in *War and Peace* and

Le Rouge et le Noir and *Gone with the Wind*. My real point was that everything is made up once it comes from us ridiculous humans: history, historical fiction, fiction and everyday life. All based on lies.

'So glad,' she said. True? False? 'And thanks for ringing. I've got to go into the chamber now. See you back soon, I expect.'

'Sure. I'll let you know.'

I'd say that was our most genial conversation ever.

'

MILLIE

I always looked at Calypso with wonder. I'm not a natural mother, being unconfident, self-conscious and over-protective, all of which makes the wonder even stronger. I peered out of my study window and watched our au pair taking her to nursery, a determined little sprite with black curls and bright blue eyes. She'd been walking for a while now and insisted on pushing the pushchair, despite the au pair's protests. Even from behind I could see the effort she was putting in, from her stumpy little legs to her arms strained upwards. When they'd turned the corner, I sat down at my desk where I was preparing a lecture about English medieval mystics. But sometimes, after a few minutes, I pushed the books and papers aside and wept. I liked to believe the tears were of happiness.

Eddie used to say I was too emotional and cried far too much. He said he never knew whether I was rejoicing or suffering. I have a feeling Mummy said the same, although my tears then were mostly of suffering – *as she refused to return or even acknowledge my love.* That's what six sessions with an NHS therapist taught me how to say. But it didn't stop me crying. Even the Mother of God hadn't been able to stop that. I was beginning to learn that my feelings were not as biddable as my mind.

When Caly was about to be three, Eddie persuaded me to visit the Weeping Madonna of Syracuse because he liked the idea of introducing her to a miracle on her birthday.

He said, 'I want her to believe in something outside everyday life, and a plaster cast of a woman's face that sheds real tears as certified by the bishops of Sicily fits the bill perfectly.'

We spent a week in Sicily but, to my relief, we never did find the

Madonna. After all she was weeping for the sins of the world, which didn't seem very appropriate for my innocent little daughter. But our sex life was reinvigorated by the warm sun and the beautiful Roman mosaics. When we got back to London, life seemed boring and I blamed it on Eddie. It was very wrong of me and I talked to my friend, Father Ignatius, about it.

He said, 'Married couples often come to me with difficulties and I listen and try to help them.' His nice red Irish face became sad. 'But I don't seem able to change things. Perhaps you could encourage him to become more outward-looking. Book tickets for a concert. Go on a walking holiday.'

He should have told me that life was a vale of tears and I'd just better get on with it or I'd never make anyone happy and certainly not myself and absolutely wouldn't reach the heavenly kingdom. But back in the sixties, priests were already undermined by modern thinking and didn't dare give the tough side of Catholic teaching, not if they were gentle and kind like Father Ignatius.

Actually Eddie was undermined too. He liked things to be simple and the new look to the Catholic teaching made things much more complicated. Ever since our marriage, I'd seen his little red catechism book by his bed – *Who made me? God made me. Why did God make you? God made me to know him, love him and serve him in this world, and to be happy with him for ever in the next.* Then one night it was gone, and Eddie said, 'I'm trying to work out the new teaching.'

Sometimes I compared my life to my sisters, so free, creating new worlds for themselves, and I felt a little bit jealous. But then I looked at Caly. Cleo came to the tea party I gave for her second birthday. She stared at the children with amazement. I asked her why she was so surprised.

'Most women of my age have children,' I pointed out. We were sitting at the same table as Caly and her nursery friends, all little girls. 'It's what women do.'

She laughed, 'I suppose that's why Julie had us, to show the world she was a real woman. Did you ask her to this merry event? Calypso is her only grandchild after all.'

'She's on a trade mission to China.'

'You do keep in touch. China, that's something. On Nixon's trail.'

'I read it in the papers.' I didn't want this conversation. It was a repetition of too many others. I wanted to be happy watching Caly and her friends being happy in our new, sunlit dining room – we were both earning after all and had just bought a house in Islington. I wanted to listen out for the doorbell when Eddie came home and share his joy in the scene. I was saving the cake till then.

'My friends are on the pill,' said Cleo. 'You do know about the pill, do you? Although I suppose it's against Catholic teaching. Come to think of it, a priest might find it a bit suspicious you've only got one child.'

'I don't know why you came.' I moved to the other side of the table and helped a little girl called Mary eat her jelly. I could feel Cleo watching me. I was determined to love her and not make a break between us. It was important to me that we were sisters but sometimes she amused herself seeing how far she could push me. She never understood until much later that there were no limits.

The doorbell rang and I hurried to let Eddie in. He thought Cleo was jealous of me but I never believed that. She was just interested in what made me tick, as she was in everything to do with people. It was food for her novels and her novels were a way of protecting herself from the difficulties and emotions of real life. I always understood Cleo better than she realised and knew that her chippy cool was just a disguise for her sensitive, loving nature. She'd have screeched with laughter if I'd told her, but it made me less surprised when what happened, happened.

When the birthday party was over and Eddie was reading a story to Caly in bed, Cleo and I relaxed over a glass of Blue Nun. As she lay back on our new Habitat sofa – this was my life and I was proud of it – I noticed how physically like Mummy she had become. This was ironic considering how much Cleo hated her. Cleo's hair seemed to have gained a reddish glow and more curls and her face was more defined and purposeful.

'Are you writing another novel?'

'Scared you'll be in it?'

'Again,' I commented which made her smile. She *could* admit to things. 'I don't mind being your token old-fashioned married woman.' When she got back from America, she wrote a witty tale on being an English girl in New York. I wasn't in that one. It sold pretty well, apparently.

The next one was much fiercer, cruel really, about a girl who is beaten up by her husband and has to go to hospital and into a hostel for abused women. It shocked a lot of readers because the man was, apart from the beating bit, so very nice and kind and ordinary and they had two nice ordinary children. And, even odder, they were not from the rough, dangerous working class, but the well-behaved middle class. It was also explicitly violent. So it got a lot of attention, including from critics accusing her of 'meretricious violence'. I suppose that sold a few extra copies.

My role in the novel was ignominious: the best friend who refused to believe that the husband, called Lionel, could be beating up his wife, Lucy, even when she had the evidence of a black eye and eventually a broken nose. I forgave Cleo but kept the novel well away from Eddie as Lionel bore a distinct resemblance to him. Eddie never hit me, of course.

'You know I don't talk about work in progress.' Cleo held out her glass for a fill-up. She really knocked back the drink.

She was very secretive, not just about work but about everything. For example, I knew she had a secret love but never who it was nor, indeed, how serious. I tried another subject.

'I'm thinking of giving up work. '

'That's classic. So you can be the perfect wife and mummy, I suppose. Or have you got bored of snotty students skipping classes?'

I'd known she would disapprove so I ignored her mean comments. 'Eddie's inherited some money from a godmother who he didn't know existed.'

'That's handy.' She held out her glass for more wine. 'I guess I'm doomed to write for ever. It's a life choice, not a job. I'm trapped. Even if one of my books was finally turned into a film and made me a million dollars, I'd still be stuck to my typewriter. It's my boulder I'm forever rolling uphill like poor old Sisyphus. It's up the top in the evening but by morning it's at the bottom again.'

I noted that, although not clever, Cleo could use her education when she wanted. But she was only building up to a rant.

'Writing's a disease. Like scabies or rabies or psoriasis or polio or brucellosis, anthrax, botulism, cholera, necrotising fasciitis or...'

I interrupted her, 'I always thought you *loved* writing.'

She gave me one of her round-eyed looks, 'Wives *love* abusive husbands.' Then she started again, 'Like leprosy, yaws, Lassa fever or zoonosis, chikungunya...'

'Please, Cleo.' As she shut her mouth I made the mistake of saying,' I bet you haven't any idea about chikungunya.'

'Chikungunya if you don't mind.' She sat up, put her glass down, and began to recite, 'Chikungunya is an infection caused by the chikungunya virus. It causes muscle pain that can last for weeks, months or even years. About one in every thousand people who get chikungunya dies. There is no known cure.'

She looked at me and smiled triumphantly. 'My next novel will feature a handsome doctor working in the Hospital for Tropical Diseases.' She sank back with her drink. 'On reflection, I think my analogy of Sisyphus rolling his boulder is more accurate for my addiction and servitude to writing than a disease. Many diseases can be cured after all, whereas Sisyphus and me are doomed for ever. Can you remember, Millie, how long he lived for?'

Cleo had always liked to dominate the conversation but, now

that I was grown-up, I no longer minded. Eddie came in just then and I smiled calmly as if we had been chatting about the best age for Caly to start playing the piano. I don't think he understood about sisters. The poor man had lost his own sister of course in the milk float accident.

Eddie picked up the mostly empty wine bottle, tipped it and raised his eyebrows at me. My policy towards adult heavy drinkers was to let them have as much as they want. Smoking I felt different about, and the moment I was pregnant with Caly, I banned cigarettes from the house. Cleo was extreme, that was the thing, and she needed alcohol to keep her steady. At least that's what she told me and at that time I believed her. Everybody drank so much then. On the cigarette front, she usually stood on my doorstep and had two quick ones before she rang my doorbell. If I spotted her from a window, she'd cry, 'Just having my fix.' She's my sister and, as I've mentioned, I loved her.

'Do we need another bottle?' I said to Eddie.

DI

I'd decided not to go back to Vietnam without a press card but it became more and more obvious that a Brit was not very likely to be employed by a US paper when it came to writing about their sensitive war. Then in 1965 I met Ollie in the Oak Bar of the Plaza Hotel. Not my usual stamping ground since I didn't drink and I didn't dress up. But there I was, dragged there by Suraj.

Ollie was born English and worked for an English paper and they wanted him to report on this war that Prime Minister Wilson was trying so hard to avoid. But Ollie loathed the idea of upping sticks to Saigon with a thoroughly unpredictable war as daily fare. He was old enough to have done his UK National Service and be sent to Korea – except that peace was agreed just before his ship left Southampton. He, along with several thousand young national servicemen, were already aboard.

'I puked with joy,' he told me. 'It was the most joyful puke over the rails, seaboard-style puke, than anyone has ever enjoyed.'

Ollie was not the right man for Vietnam, that was obvious. I remembered Suraj's wise advice. I said cheerfully as if my heart wasn't doing flips, 'Hey, Ollie, why don't I go to Vietnam instead of you? I've been in America nearly as long as you and I've already spent six months in Vietnam. I know everybody, even some of the top brass in the military. I've been invited to a White House gala next week.'

This was true. I had the invitation propped up on the grimy window ledge of my newly acquired flat, a squalid place inherited from Cleo's beloved. Sean told me about Lennie when I stayed in their apartment that Christmas after my return from Vietnam. He knew far more about Cleo than I did. He told me that she obsessed over a guy called Lennie, Jewish and a peacenik in a-march-down-the-streets-carrying-a-placard kind of way. I even seemed to know he was learning to play the piano. My God! The world is going mad and he's playing the piano.

Fast forward two years to 1965, Cleo long-gone, and I find myself at a Vietnam protest evening organised by the Committee for Non-Violent Action and there is Lennie playing the piano: 'The Stars and Stripes' backwards, that sort of thing. I guessed who he was instantly. I went over and leant right across the piano so he had to stop playing, kind of threatening – it always made people believe I was drunk when I behaved like that and they found it even more scary when they discovered that I never touched alcohol.

'I'm Cleopatra's sister.' He could have doubted me. I've never looked the least bit like Cleo, but, to do him justice, he put out a small white hand (not my type at all) and muttered 'Hi' – before adding, with more conviction, 'How is she?' I liked that. He was still British after all. He put his arms across the keys either to protect them from further marauders or from exhaustion. Most young types like him in Manhattan were exhausted.

'I live in New York,' I replied. 'She seemed okay last time I heard from her. She's published two novels in two years.'

'Yeah.' Now he really did look exhausted. He drank deeply from a glass of beer on top of the piano. 'I'm going back to London.' He drank again. 'My mother died.'

'Sorry.' Death happened.

'Yeah. My father wants the support. You know. I'm his only son.'

'Tough.'

'The real world,' he murmured or *perhaps* he murmured. After this meeting, Lennie handed over his unpleasant flat to me. So there was the stiff white, gold-embossed invitation, where Cleo's beloved had lived, complete with tattered flag out of the window, *The secret to happiness is freedom. And the secret to freedom is courage,* except that the word 'courage' had been defaced to read 'rage'.

Ollie didn't say yes immediately. 'I'll think about it. See who you can talk to at The White House.'

Washington was too much a company town for me. I'd got used to grubby downtown Manhattan, and the famed open spaces and classical buildings of central Washington left me cold.

It was strange to put on a borrowed dress and high heels and totter (why do women want to perch up high like idiots?) towards the grand White House portico. On the way – apart from the gardeners, I was the only person not in a car – I gave myself a little lecture about cooling it. No need to insult anyone. Listening, that was what I was there for.

So in I went, prepared for anything and anyone except one. The first person I saw, leaving aside the President who was very tall, was Julie, mother Julie, the UK's Minister for whatever she was at the time. So that was why I'd been invited. Goddam! To use the local parlance

But there she was, toes pointed daintily, frock wasp-waisted, bright eyes lighting on me as a bird on a tasty morsel,

'Diana, I am so glad you could make it,' she trilled.

'Hi Julie.' I bent and kissed her cheek, petal-soft and turned toward me. I was at least a foot taller.

'Is this your *daughter*?' A bulky, yet handsomely older American, a Senator perhaps, perhaps a warmonger, stared at me with surprise.

'I live in the States,' I said with a slightly accusing air, as if America had made me big.

'She's a journalist,' said Julie, the first time I'd ever heard her try to promote me. This man must matter.

'Not the sort who wants to catch a fellow out, I trust?' he drawled, raising eyebrows across a tanned face. A fat cat face.

'Depends on the subject.' I realised I found the man attractive and was annoyed with myself and even more with him.

'Diana spent six months in Vietnam,' said my mother. 'She has a lot to contribute on the subject.'

I turned to her, happy to oblige her proud mother act. 'I'll be going back shortly, as the correspondent for an English newspaper.'

'That's wonderful, dear.' It seemed unreal, the glamorous setting, with the President of the USA in view, my charming mother, my own wishful thinking and this handsome man who moved his gaze from Julie to me with calm goodwill. Whoever *was* he?

Then I saw Brad. He was looking directly at me. He had a woman with him. A wife-type just as I had imagined. She even had crimson lips and a busby hairdo.

Fainting has never been my style but I know when to beat a retreat. As I found a gilded ladies' lavatory, I caught myself thinking, *this is Cleo territory, she'd enjoy it for the story she'd make of it.* The idea soothed me.

When I came out again into a thickly carpeted corridor with panelled walls, Brad was standing there. He was on his own. 'I scarcely recognised you,' he said.

'It's been a long time.' I'd never felt so ugly in my life. Normally, I don't rate ugly. Ugly/beautiful – who cares? I suspected Julie was to blame.

'How are you doing?' Brad was the persevering type.

'Was that your wife with you?'

'Sure. That was Judy. I'll introduce you. Was that your mother I saw with William Holden? I noticed her name was on the guest list. Where are you living now?'

No wonder I'd found Julie's companion attractive, like millions before me. I tried to accept Brad's casual manner. After all, he'd come to find me and it was not as if he was a beautiful physical object either. 'I've been living in New York ever since I got back from Vietnam. I see you on the television now and again. Behind McNamara.'

'I'm an old stager now. Part of the original military adviser brigade.' He looked round and indicated two chairs. 'Let's sit down.'

I remembered how he'd always liked to talk to me, which made me something more than an available fuck. I regretted the last thought. He pulled the chairs closer to each other and we sat down. I took off my shoes and felt better.

Brad started in at once. 'You see what's happening? We're in a war. A real epic war, not some little thing over there we can end any time we throw enough men and money at it. Do you know how many of our men are heading out there now?' I thought I might, but said nothing. 'So many and mostly poor or black... drafted.' He put his hand up to his head and I thought he was feeling for his cap and was disappointed that he found only hair – which was thinning a bit. He swung round and faced the door to the grand salon where the party was still rocking. 'How many men in there are going to Vietnam?'

I liked him in this angry mood. He must be approaching forty, old for a soldier. 'I'm sorry Brad.' I put my hand on his arm.

He frowned. I noticed he had a glass in one hand; his fist was so big I hadn't seen it before.

'Do you wish you could fight?' I asked. I thought the war was a disaster but I admired men who fought. How ridiculous is that! I wanted the good guys to win. And I wanted the good guys to go away from Vietnam so that the bad guys could sort things out for themselves. Kill each other, if that's what they wanted. Oh, hell, this was 1965. There was still hope. Brad had been quiet so long I'd forgotten what I'd asked him.

'Up till now it's been more about bombing than fighting. Talk "Rolling Thunder", bombs coming out of the sky and going right through the ground, except that's there's always more ground and more men to dig holes, fox-holes. Talk to the foxes about that. I don't fight but I fly in there in a big fucking plane and there's a man with medals at my side and he says, "All this bombing ain't getting us nowhere, what we needs more feet on the ground," and I say, "Yessir," because he is right but I can't help thinking too that all those foxy yellow men in their holes and on their trails are going to keep on coming, so I say, "Yessir," and then I add, "It'll take a whole lot more to be done with those Commie bastards." And the General or whatever says, "You're so right, Wolfe, we need more soldiers, many more, a whole fucking army of young American soldiers. Honest, bright-eyed, God-fearing men. Solid American boots on the ground. No slimy, slitty, shitty, yellow folk you can't trust as far as you can throw them. The so-called Army of South Vietnam. I ask you. How fucking right you are our fucking Colonel Wolfe. We need the draft to spread a real good net, that's what we need, married men as well. Where did I get such a good advisor as you, Wolfe?" And I say, "Thank you, sir."

'And, believe me, by December, two weeks' time, there'll be 200,000 laughing GIs thanking me for giving them the opportunity to get on the tail of Ho Chi Minh. And nearly as many generals saying, "Thank you, Wolfe. Gee, Wolfe you've really got this sewn up. Where did we find you?"'

I don't believe he said all this quite like this, but he did say a lot and he saw he was beating himself up in front of me because I was still the little English girl to him who fucked around like a whore. I thought of saying *You didn't make the war, you're just another victim* but it sounded stupid even inside my head. What did I know? Maybe it was the Brads of this world that screw things up. After a long while when his ranting was sort of winding down, I grabbed his arm so that he stopped altogether and looked at me.

'Won't your wife be waiting for you?' I said.

He drew his thoughts back to me. His blue eyes were red-rimmed. His fingers were red too where he'd crushed the glass with his fingers. Not dripping with blood but definitely red.

'Maybe.' That was all he said.

So I squeezed my feet into my shoes and we parted.

MILLIE

I made a friend when Calypso went to school. Our daughters were in the same class and neither of us worked. We were both clever and didn't have enough to do. Eventually Helen had three more children and I saw less of her but at that time we were close. I told her things that I usually reserved for the confessional.

I suppose I went on about Mummy. Anyway, one day over lunch in John Lewis (our girls attended a convent in Cavendish Square), Helen said in a challenging sort of way, 'It must be amazing having a brilliant, famous mother. No wonder you adore her. I'd really love to meet her.'

It took months but eventually I arranged a tea. Helen and I waited in the drawing room, helping our two little girls, one fair, one dark, make a Fairy Queen puzzle. I was reminded of Spenser's *Fairie Queen* poem, published in 1590 and taken as homage to Queen Elizabeth I, '... *cloudily enwrapped in allegorical devises...*' That too seemed a link with Mummy.

She arrived smiling, although her ministerial car waited outside in a threatening sort of way. An assistant who had come with her waited in Eddie's little study.

Helen was awestruck, which made me happy. Mummy said to her when she revealed she hadn't been to university, 'The Labour Party is determined that university will be open to all and, by that, I mean women too. In fact, particularly women.'

When she went after half an hour, not time for even a cup of tea, she added, 'I always say to the women in my constituency, "Children are a gift of God but then we must do the rest."'

Helen said, 'She's just so impressive.'

I said, 'I wonder who is the *we* who must do the rest.' But it felt disloyal to say even that and since Helen only looked bemused without speaking, I let the subject drop.

Later she told me that Mummy's visit had been an absolute highlight of her life.

DI

That Christmas, after the White House gala, and before I went back to Vietnam, I went home. Where was 'home'? Well, it turned out *not* to be in Julie's well-appointed mansion flat opposite Westminster Cathedral and usefully close to the Houses of Parliament, but in Millie's Habitat-furnished house in leafy Kensington. Eddie had abandoned academia for the city and clearly was making money.

Millie looked plump and pretty, and Cleo and I admired the exquisite Calypso who recited 'Goosy Goosy Gander' with great charm while Julie did political speak with Eddie and in the basement a nameless girl cooked a huge goose which explained Caly's choice of nursery rhyme.

While we waited to eat, Cleo got as drunk as possible as quickly as possible on sherry, then turned on the television, saying loudly, 'I'm warming it up for the Queen, although I guess you socialists won't be watching.' She gave Julie, who adored the Queen – as Cleo had just informed me – a malignant glare.

'Give us a break, Cleo!' It was obviously foolish of me to try for a family Christmas. It was only a gesture, not based on any true need – and only a certain amount of love. And when had I believed in the traditional? I allowed myself a moment to wonder whether Brendan's presence would have made a difference – with no resentment, because I liked to imagine him happy with Elena in some Inca hideaway.

Cleo left us halfway through lunch and went who knows where, but I soldiered on, enjoying the calm of Eddie and Millie, tolerating Julie's assumption that her news was all that mattered.

'The Labour Party under Harold Wilson is carrying through

an expansion in the social services, health welfare, and housing, unparalleled in our history. And that is not even to mention our ambitions to completely overhaul the education needs of this country. Have you heard of the plans for the Open University? To reach all kinds of people?'

'How wonderful, Mummy,' Millie and Eddie nodded agreeably. 'It's a magnificent idea.'

I imagined her red rosette fluttering. The word Vietnam had not passed her lips. Perhaps it was with some lingering sense that I might be able to make her behave like a mother that I accepted her lift in a taxi to Cleo's flat where I was staying. To my surprise she asked me to come on with her to her flat in Westminster. Out of sheer curiosity, I accepted. We were shown in by a porter and went up in a panelled lift and into a panelled flat with plain dark sofas, lamps with pleated covers and cream walls.

'I only rent it,' she said.

An unwelcome thought struck me: that she was lonely and I should feel sorry for her. I pushed it aside. 'I'll only stay for a minute. I'm still a bit jet-lagged.'

She gave me her vague, I'm-thinking-of more-important things look. Perhaps I was jet-lagged, otherwise why did I form my next sentence. 'You know Brendan came to see me on his way to South America. All that time ago...' I paused but when she said nothing, I still didn't think better of it. 'He told me about Elena. What she meant to him during the war. It seemed like a real love story.' I behaved as if this would be no news to her and not very important anyway, but I saw her blue eyes half shut before fixing on me. I suppose I wanted a reaction, a bit of honesty between us. Jet-lag? My imminent journey to a war zone? How foolish can you be! I continued: 'You knew she'd gone with him, didn't you, that they disappeared together. You had no use for him anyway.' I stared at her and again that feeling that she might be pitiable threatened. I suppose I didn't care enough to torment her. Brendan had got away from her to happiness, however his adventure ended. She wouldn't like that.

'He was going on a charitable mission,' she said coldly. 'He was on his own.'

I goggled, then let it pass. 'I suppose it's strange he never wrote.' It was strange, I guess, I'd never thought of it before.

I can only describe Julie's face as haughty as she answered me. 'Perhaps he came to a tragic ending.'

I laughed. It was simply impossible not to laugh – was actually funny that she could imagine I would swallow that line. But I guess she thought I was jeering.

So that was the end of our conversation. I was shown the door without even a peck on the cheek, me, the intrepid reporter who might never come back from the wars. Thank you, Julie.

I walked back to Cleo's flat, Westminster to Notting Hill Gate, checking whether I felt nostalgic about the city where I'd grown up. The thing was that I'd spent most of my childhood trying to escape, to Hampstead Heath, to boarding school and eventually – Whizzo! Gazooks! – to the US of A, so in the end I gave up trying for any emotion other than relief. The evening was cool and dim, lit up where there were Christmas decorations. I was surprised how few people there were on the streets, except when I passed a pub and the pavements were crowded with noisy men in Santa hats and girls with tinsel in their hair. I went via Victoria, Sloane Square, Knightsbridge, Kensington and up Church Street where I passed the new Biba store whose fame had even spread to New York and a non-fashion-spotter like me. I spent a moment assessing the school-girlish models, flat-chested and skinny-legged in short tunics coloured purple and plum and gold. No stupid bras or corsets for that lot; some things had improved in London.

Cleo lived in a modern-build flat in Pembridge Crescent, not far from the Underground station. Portobello Market was a few minutes away but the flat was utterly without character as if she was avoiding letting slip any clues to her character. The night before she'd said, 'I only exist in my novels,' which was odd, considering that she also said, 'My novels are crap, rubbish. I wouldn't recommend them to my greatest enemy.'

I was due to meet my new English editor, Frank Hogan, the next day, Boxing Day. He gave a famous party every year and Cleo had assured me it was an honour to be invited. She had been invited the previous year and spent a fortune on a blue leather dress with tassels which only came half way down her thighs, so she told me. She explained that the less material a dress took, the more it cost and then suggested I wore army fatigues. As I took the emergency stairs upwards – I prefer stairs where possible – I wondered warily and a bit wearily what state I'd find her in.

Gloomy premonition fulfilled: Cleo was out cold on the living-room sofa but when I sat down on its end and stared at her crossly, she woke instantly. Sisters have this effect on each other.

'Hi, Di! Di, hi! It must be nice to have a name that rhymes with "Hi!" – so friendly, or would you say more "breezy"?'

I thought that half asleep and totally drunk, she still enjoyed playing with words and was rather impressed.

'Now Cleo rhymes with Leo or Theo, two male names. I wonder what's the significance of that?'

'Easy.'

'What?' She appeared genuinely interested.

'You're paralytic.'

She sat up, looking I must say very pretty with her sharp pale face and long hair and neat figure. 'Cleo does rhyme with quite a lot of distinguished Italian words, '*Dio, mio...*'

'Do you always drink so much?'

Her blue cat's eyes opened wider; apart from the long hair, she really was getting to look more and more like Julie.

'If I'm having Christmas lunch with Julie, I consider paralytic drunkenness the only sensible course of action but, to be honest, and as you're shortly off to a war zone, the true answer is yes. I find large quantities of alcohol suit me very well. I feel much better, make more friends of the sort I admire, mostly other drunks, and work longer hours. Buffy once told me that a lot of her authors write best on a hangover so I'm only following professional advice.'

'I see.' I really couldn't think of anything to say. She seemed to be talking complete drivel but, as a non-drinker, how could I know. Instead I found myself holding out my hand and clasping hers.

We both stared down with surprise at our joined hands. Having gone so far, I found myself going further. 'I'll always be there for you.'

Cleo smiled, a grateful, sweet smile. Then she took her hand away. 'Yeah, I'll summon you from a paddy field with a host of Vietcong rising from the jungle ahead.' But her voice was wistful as if she took my offer seriously.

CLEO

I drank heavily, huge amounts, mostly of wine, but I was not choosey. Under certain circumstances, I could knock back Pernod, absinthe (or is that the same thing?), Vermouth, Campari, and the drunkard's staples: vodka, gin, rum and whisky – the final two definitely a last resort. I was not alone. All the most successful people in what is kindly called the 'creative industries': writers, agents, publishers, journalists, painters, advertising chaps (they mostly were chaps), TV, radio, film producers – film directors less so because they were so exhausted from first trying to get a film and then making it. Some politicians drank too, think Winston Churchill, a straight alcoholic if there ever was one, or George Brown on the other side. Julie didn't drink at all and that was certainly more typical of the Labour Party. A glass of beer versus a crate of wine. Nurture winning over nature. Perhaps I should write a treatise about drinking habits in the sixties before drugs kicked in.

Alcohol suited me wonderfully well. I woke up at 8am with a hangover so that, since other people, books, the world outside, were unbearable, there was nothing else to do but write. After groaning, more groaning, and eating whatever there was in the fridge, at 9am I sat down at my desk, an ancient card table that felt unthreatening. There I stayed, hoping and usually achieving some sort of outcome, until 1pm when I met with another creative person at some nice trattoria and broached a soothing draft of Chianti or Corvo or Frascati. At 3pm I walked, wandered, dithered, perhaps pretended to research, although novels were almost never researched in those days.

At 5pm I sat at my card table again and pretended to improve what I had written in the morning. I had read this was the habit of poor old Virginia Woolf and liked the concept, if not the practice. At 6pm I had my first drink (discounting lunch), usually on my own. My flat was bright and new and after that magical first drink, I felt able to congratulate myself on my success as a novelist, as an independent woman while still in my middle twenties. Moreover, drinking a bottle or two a day could even lead to surprising, and positive outcomes.

One early evening in the summer of 1966, I decided to go and ring the doorbell of Lennie's house. Just because I was a high-achieving alcoholic didn't mean I'd forgotten Lennie. He was and remained the love of my life but I hadn't seen him since we both came back from New York: so I would never have decided to ring his doorbell and certainly not have carried the venture through, without that First Drink – Pouilly-Fuissé.

So, emboldened by a delicious cold glass of French burgundy, I took a taxi to Hampstead. Taxis weren't expensive then, but it was still a luxury which gave that evening – a dulcet one with pigeons cooing and people strolling (or vice versa) – a special feel.

'Here we are, miss. Have a nice evening.' In those days the cab drivers were all Londoners and assumed you were too, so you bonded in stories of narrowed roads and increasing traffic lights. This was better than politics, on which subject, despite their working-class backgrounds, cabbies held uniformly fascist views. One evening, after a bottle or two, I mentioned my mother's name, then at the Department of Health, and received a diatribe against her and those like her who thought the country was made of money. This taught me a cheering lesson: the working man dislikes politicians, even when apparently on their side, nearly as much as I disliked my mother.

The doorbell of Lennie's parents' house was a round brass button, and the sight made my heart beat so fast that I had to lean against the wall, resulting in the bell ringing. I jumped back. The door was painted black, the tall house built of red brick with a dark creeper crawling up the side. It spoke of good sense, intelligence, sobriety, success that has been earned by hard work. The door opened very slowly and an old man wearing a yarmulke peered out, small eyes beneath bushy eyebrows. He was bent and thin and it was hard to recognise Lennie's father. Then I remembered his wife had died.

'You are looking for someone?' How true that was! All my life, actually.

'I'm looking for Lennie, Mr Levy.' Such was my respect that I nearly said 'sir'. My legs were trembling. Such is love for a courageous modern woman.

'A friend of my son. Come in. Come in.' I had forgotten his accent. Obviously, he hadn't recognised me but he showed me politely into the living room. While he shut and tidied away a small book and took off his yarmulke, I noticed the changes in the room. Sadly, the piano lid was closed. It was his wife that had played. Judy. I pictured her at the piano stool.

'You have arranged to meet him here? He no longer lives here now, but you know that.' His eyes were keener than I'd first recognised. 'You are perhaps a business acquaintance?'

'No. Just an old friend.'

He smiled a little. 'Not an estate agent then. Lennie is trying to persuade me to sell this house. My daughter too. You know my daughter?'

'I met her once. I am very sorry about your wife.'

'Thank you. Yes, it is a great loss. A very great sorrow to me.'

'I remember your musical evenings. You created your own world.' Did I remember that? Surely I only cared about Lennie? And yet it did seem true in my memory.

He smiled again. 'Ah, yes, that was Judy. I was just a follower. And now all I have is a good girl they have found to look after me. She likes to speak in German to me and I say, "No, Elsie, we are here in England where I want to be."'

Although there was no self-pity in his voice, I felt his loss and his loneliness rising around him like a heavy mist. I understood that he'd let me in because he wanted someone to talk to. I thought what to say but his cleverness – I remembered he had taught philosophy or ethics or maybe a bit of both at King's College – was a barrier to my usual witty prattle. While I searched for a suitably impressive subject, he stared at me seriously.

Eventually he broke the silence. 'You are in London, perhaps, for Lennie's wedding. Although of course we must now call him Leonard. He is marrying a good girl, Rebekah, very successful in the money world, most unusual for a woman and of course we approve. Judy and I have never been the sort of people who feel that high office should be only given to the male of the species. But Judy cannot meet her. You know Rebekah, I'm sure?' There was a question mark here but it was impossible for me to speak. In my wildest dreams I had not imagined Lennie marrying. I felt more desperate than any time in my life for the wonders of a second drink. The alternative was to run from the house, screaming and tearing my hair.

Since I said nothing, although probably gulping strangely, Sam, Mr Levy continued, 'My daughter is very pleased with Rebekah. They were friends already. She sees her as a thoroughly modern girl.' He paused and eyed my mini-skirt and black fish-net tights, before adding, 'Not up to your style, it is true, but a modern working-girl and, since Lennie, or Leonard as we must learn to call him, has taken on work at my brother's firm, they will be very well suited. So my daughter has taught me. Have you been to a Jewish marriage before?'

'No.' My voice came out in a squeak.

'It lasts for a long time but, assuming the cantor is good, it can be most impressive.'

I stood up, possibly with tears in my eyes: they were certainly at my heart. 'I am sorry, Mr Levy, I am no longer a friend of your son...'

He held up a hand to stop me. 'Please. Please, sit down. I have remembered who you are a moment or two ago and I am enjoying our conversation. Since I have given up my academic work – I had a little stroke – or so they said but I think it my mourning for my wife, although that is a very big stroke – I do not see many young people. Stay, please. Wait, I'll find you a glass of wine.'

That's what I mean about alcohol sometimes rewarding you with a positive outcome. I had arrived as the result of the First Glass and by the end of several tiny, engraved glasses of sweet white wine, we had become friends. My desperation to flee Lennie's Jewish wedding ejected us into my Catholic background which I exaggerated for effect, and soon we were discussing the nature of goodness and I suggested, with Sam's apparent agreement, that he was surrounded by Good Jewish Ladies – his carer, his daughter, his loathsome-to-me but obviously good soon-to-be daughter-in-law (I refused to say her name) – and what he needed, I repeated it more than once, was a Bad Catholic Friend, in which category I came top.

Heavens knows what else I said as the potent jewelled glasses filled and refilled, but I could feel his old man's kindness and his enjoyment in my whirling mind (What is creation but unleashed energy?).

Lennie would always be the love of my life but Sam became a dear friend and confidant. In a dark hour, he accepted me fearlessly.

DI

'Crossover', that's what they talk about most. Not the grunts, of course; they talk about going home or the beautiful girl who might or might not be waiting for them back home or the hot girl they picked up last time they were in Saigon or the weed that spins you away or the AK47 that jammed again when lined up like a duck on a range.

'Crossover' comes from the generals and the advisers and the politicians visiting, and some of the press who like reporting what the generals say as if it were true, so that they will get their questions answered at press briefings, except neither the questions nor answers about the progress of the war make any sense because it all comes back to 'Crossover' which is meaningless and even if it had any meaning no one is willing to put down the truth, mostly because they don't know, but also because the war has been going for years now and has its own rules, uncontrolled by anybody. It's like a party whose hosts lost control a day or two earlier and have quite forgotten why they're giving it but still try to pretend there's a reason.

The generals have convinced the politicians (well, semi-convinced – think of party-goers wandering round in a daze but hoping for something to hang on to) that 'Crossover' is the answer to everything. Hallelujah! And what they think it means is the moment that so many of the Forces of Evil (Vietcong, North Vietnamese Army) have been wiped out by the Forces of Good (South Vietnamese Army, US and allies (not many)) that THEY (the Evil Ones) CAN NO LONGER MAKE UP THE NUMBERS, the wondrous end is nigh! Once that happens, the thinking (if you can call it that) goes, then the Forces of Good will sweep all before them and the war will be won. 'Crossover' has triumphed.

The odd thing is that there has never been any sign of this happening, even when battles are fought with an officially reported forty to one, Gook to GI death rate. Allowing for a gross falsification of the numbers, there were still more dying from the North than the South and US of A, but somehow the North kept coming. The trouble about basing your war on a game of numbers is that it ignores history, politics, cultural factors and geography. Some of the American officers I interviewed thought it fucking unfair, wrong too, of course (proving they weren't normal human beings), that the Ho Chi Minh trail was run and supplied by women as well as men. After all this time, no one had a clue about the enemy and mostly didn't want to.

I am writing this in September 1967. Some of it may end up as a letter or two for Cleo, unreal though she seems. So I got my war. This is my life. Vietnam correspondent for an English newspaper, when they bother to print my reports. Obviously the English are only as interested as observers are likely to be. I wonder sometimes whether my mother, the politician, Prime Minister Wilson's mate, can take some credit for that. She certainly hated war because it took Brendan away. For the first time anyway. Just how often is the political personal!

Some of my pieces make their way into other papers, usually remnants of the Empire where there are English language publications, The *South China News*, for example, in Hong Kong. I like the thought that my words are getting into odd corners of the globe. The *Village Voice* takes something now and again which gives me a bit of US cred. But even if I'm not big-deal famous – the new television reporters are taking that slot – I reckon my Brit outsider (woman too) POV has something to offer.

I'm just back from Da Nang, the big American airbase on the coast. Once you've got your accreditation card with its little red and yellow stripes you can hitch a helicopter ride to anywhere in this country. After two years here I'm almost one of the boys. They know

I don't panic and only ask questions at the right moment. More often than not, they tell me the truth – even the marines. 'I just want to go home and go to school' or 'I'm fucking scared. You know what I mean, ma'am.' Actually I didn't, but I tried to look suitably sympathetic. I would have been scared to kill someone though and now and again a new boy with head shaved like a criminal would even admit to feeling the same.

My friends in the 1st Cavalry Division (Airmobile) called me 'Britgirl'. 'We've got Britgirl along,' they'd report over the thunder of the helicopter, and I'd feel proud. I had a name. These last few days have been tough. I went out from the base with a company of marines who were ordered to clear out (i.e. kill) some Vietcong who'd been coming in too close for comfort. Problems, none of them new, included no certainty how many VC were in the area, inability to separate good South Vietnamese from bad North Vietnamese until the green tracer bullets are heading your way (US tracers were red), no knowledge of terrain, hostile terrain e.g. swamps, cliffs, jungle etc.

We never set out further than a couple of hours out of the camp, like duck-hunting on a rainy morning. The men were from Virginia, Minnesota, Alabama (black), Idaho. In the American army everyone comes from somewhere and likes telling you about it and I like hearing. Mountains, grassland, cities, there they were, and duck-shooting made a bit of sense to them all. Being as tall as many of them and dressed the same in combat camouflage, with helmet and flak jacket, my presence on an op like this didn't cause any stir, even though I carried a notebook instead of a gun. I stayed back, of course, but I saw what I saw.

First we crossed the inevitable miles of paddy fields which sensitive GIs found so beautiful when they first arrived. Now they were just wet and a bore. Jungle came next, disappearing into rising ground. On the edge lay the villages, thatched huts and pens for the pigs or chickens. This was where things could go wrong if your leader was nervous, stupid or an instinctive killer. An instinctive killer often was stupid and nervous too but happily I didn't see too many.

Yesterday morning we were led by Rogue. This wasn't as bad as it sounds because Rogue actually was his name. D.G. Rogue from Wisconsin. He was distinguished by his height: six foot five at least and broad. A VC would have to be a very bad shot to miss him. I liked Rogue but I drew a breath of relief when he went down on his stomach, crawling along like a vast snake. He was a nice man, married with a pregnant wife called Gloria and a dog called Mut who he loved nearly as much. I watched him bend double and go into one of the huts. After a few minutes his head came out again and he waved me forward, 'Hey, come and see, Britgirl.'

Since the rain was drenching me through to my tee, I obeyed with alacrity. There were two young children in the hut and an old crone stirring a pot of rice.

'Just look at that,' enthused Rogue. 'Granny's promised me a portion. Did I ever tell you Gloria's mum is Chinese. Given me a real hankering for home-cooked rice.'

I smiled and stared. Something was wrong. Then I got it. The pot was far too big for a family or even the whole village, which was a few huts and not many more people.

'She could feed all of us with that lot and have some left over.' A drip had started above my head and I moved a step back.

Rogue already had a bowl, procured by his Vietnamese interpreter but he put it aside at the tone of my voice. I'd been out here longer than him. Yet I hated what I was doing. I wasn't a soldier. Why had I spoken? But it was too late.

Rogue handed the bowl to the old woman, went outside and gave the order to search the village and land nearby. Tunnels were one of the ways the VC evaded capture and killed the invaders. That's what the Americans were to them. Same as the French but with more firepower. The whole place was riddled with tunnels.

They found the entrances easily enough, threw in grenades and pulled out eight or more dead soldiers, two of them women. I didn't count after a bit. It was the first time I'd killed anyone. Quite a haul for a first time. I could hear the old lady wailing as we left and the high-pitched crying of the children.

Rogue was quietly pleased. He had the good sense not to give me any credit. Perhaps he knew I would have hit him.

We should have gone back to the base then, mission more than accomplished, but it had all been so quick and easy that Rogue, after reporting over the radio, decided to carry on. Maybe he wanted an honour to take back to Gloria.

The rain was still heavy, casting a silvery sheen over the trees and undergrowth ahead. I thought it was like putting Vaseline on a camera lens, making everything soft, mysterious and unknowable. My complicity in those deaths had made me jittery in a way I'd never felt before.

We must have walked for half an hour when the point man ahead gave a cry, followed by a scream. We all dropped to the ground. Then the man behind me – I never liked to be right at the back – gave the same kind of scream. It was obvious we'd walked into a trap. The usual procedure when this happens is to call in the helicopter and hope they blast the enemy to hell. But they were too close around us for that and the trees effectively screened us from above. The only chance was to call in back-up and hope those same trees gave us a bit of cover, plus the undergrowth.

As I crawled under some dense and prickly bush and edged as near as I could to Rogue who was on his knees and firing rounds in all directions like a dervish, I asked myself whether this was my punishment, meted out by those ghosts of the underground dead and commanded by the old lady, a wild Valkyrie, grey locks flying.

It was over quickly. With the amount of firepower on both sides, small battles like this are over quickly. I lay under my bush, under Rogue who had fallen on top of me and the bush. In the eerie silence, groaning gave your position away. I felt rather than saw ghostly figures closing in. Then came the bangs as they finished off any American wounded. Footsteps walked right up to Rogue, then moved away again. He must be very dead. I had no idea whether anyone had escaped but I knew the back-up was on the way so I lay where I was, comforting myself with a prayer or two, 'Holy Mary Mother of God pray for us sinners, now and at the hour of our death.'

The most hardened soldiers often told me how they found themselves praying in dangerous situations when they would never own up to any religious belief in normal life. Soon it was silent again and I moved Rogue a little and peered through the bush. A thorn pricked at my forehead and I though how odd it was that it should still hurt as thorns do. I pictured the crown of thorns on Christ's head and thought that must have hurt him too.

The marines came in quickly, with the medics. They took Rogue from over me so I was able to push the bush aside and sit up. I don't think they'd noticed me. The rain had stopped and a sharp light was shining through the trees, lighting up the marines' tense faces under their helmets, striking sparks off their AK47s. They were looking outward, guarding this little space. Someone nearby was radioing a report. 'Eight down,' I heard him say. So some had escaped. Not Rogue. Still nobody noticed me. Perhaps *I* had become a ghost.

'Hey,' I whispered. I was lucky not to get shot. Two men lifted me onto my feet. I don't often feel like a woman but I did then. They looked at me, amazed. Perhaps they thought I was a spy. I wanted to explain but my voice wouldn't work so I took out my notebook and my accreditation.

'She's a reporter!' yelled someone.

'Some lucky broad!' yelled another. Probably they weren't yelling but it felt like that to me.

We went back so fast that we might have been flying. A tank appeared and I was put in it. Then I was back at the base and I was fine, nothing wrong with me at all. Covered in Rogue's blood, that's all.

Near-death experiences are common in Vietnam; I'd interviewed men whose eyes were still opened wide and far-seeing from their recent proximity to the Grim Reaper – as Brendan used to call Death. His description came back to me as I lay awake that night – and now I'd had one myself.

Rogue. Me underneath him. You could say his death saved my life. That was a kind of crossover. You couldn't say that he saved my life because he had no choice in it, but it was his death which perhaps he owns. Do we own our deaths? Choices we make? Life choices? Enough. I was a soldier, kind of, and soldiers aren't introspective. Or shouldn't be.

CLEO

I got married in October 1967. To a silly little twerp called Hayden Bristow, a journalist of course who liked being close to successful people, and my novels continued to be successful, even if I wasn't. I was a mess. I need hardly add, a drunken mess. Think hours of 'witty' chat with other drunks in the bars and restaurants of Soho. I was pretty, let's not forget, and much younger than Twerp Hayden who had been married twice before which proves that a/. he wasn't averse to marriage and b/. he took it lightly. So that's why he married me. Postscript: he might have been impressed that my mother was a minister in the Labour Cabinet.

So why did I marry him? Not sex, more's the pity. The fact he protested undying love and his desperate desire to marry might have had something to do with it. I'd never expected to hear that from anyone. I suppose I was flattered by also becoming part of the circles he moved in. Marriage seemed the next stage, perhaps, or perhaps it was just an experiment, like sleeping rough outside Southwark Cathedral. The truth is I have no idea why I married him.

The venue of my wedding was the Chelsea Registry Office in the Old Town Hall on the King's Road which, through the waves of aforementioned drunkenness – the event was after lunch – I could see was agreeably grand.

When I invited Millie – the only person I asked apart from Buffy – she carolled, 'Oh how *absolutely* lovely! I didn't know you'd found The One!'

'Of course I haven't,' I answered cheerfully,

'Oh but Cleo...' Her voice trailed away so dismally that I decided I could stretch the truth.

'He's very engaging. Writes brilliant pieces for the *Spectator* and various other rags.'

'You mean he's *Conservative*!' This time her voice expressed Shock, Horror.

'He's not political,' I said briskly. 'More interested in capitalism.'

'I think Mummy will feel that makes him Conservative.'

I was beginning to be irritated. 'I wouldn't *dream* of inviting Julie. She'd probably talk through the service, or whatever it's called, about how for the first time in British history the government is giving more money to education than defence. Hooray! But...'

Buffy, when I popped into her office on my way to lunch with Hayden at the Gay Hussar, was more straightforward. 'Atta girl! Get the first one out of the way, that's what I always advise.' She returned to her mountain of manuscripts which always remained the same unattainable height, before shouting as I walked out of the door, 'Don't let married sex interfere with your writing, dear. The pen is mightier than the orgasm!' This last a shrill bellow so that a young secretary passing in the corridor shimmied away, giggling nervously.

In point of fact, sex was never a rival for my writing. Frankly, I could still take it or leave it, and mostly I left it. I did perform perfectly well for novelistic purposes, crossing the bounds of good taste with the best of them. I found sex most fun when I was drunk, and for that, one man was much the same as another, assuming they didn't enjoy beating or other painful practices. Writing about such things was one thing, performing them or having them performed on me was quite another.

As I said, I didn't marry Hayden for the sex. Come to think about it, I probably married him to spite Lennie – which was pretty silly, considering Lennie didn't know I knew he was married and certainly didn't know (or care) that I was getting married. But I knew and it made me feel better about myself. At the last minute, knowing he wouldn't make it, I telephoned Sam Levy and invited him to come along.

My wedding took place on a cool October afternoon in the middle of swinging London. This is relevant because Hayden, who was old and sharp enough to know better, swallowed all that hyped-up freedom as if having hair to your shoulders and smoking spliffs was the same as lifting the working class out of poverty or saving every trapped wife from male abusers. Mother Julie could have taught him a thing or two about that.

But Hayden was a capitalist who allowed himself all kinds of liberties in its name and believed his own ugly eccentricities – like swearing at strangers who annoyed him or peeing in the street (similar activities in his view) – showed he was part of the new avant-garde. He was a muddled man with a brilliant turn of words that made him what he was, and a fearless self-promoter who, when looked at without a glass in hand (my hand), was a nasty piece of work, a shameless shit or a... Words fail me. He would have done better.

So we married, he forty something and marrying for the third time, me twenty-five and marrying for the first and worst reasons. The wedding itself began demurely with my few guests effectively in character. Buffy, arriving with the accustomed cigarette drooping dangerously from her lips, lost a fight with the attendants who told her to put it out or they'd put her out. Sam did come and took a seat near the back. He looked worried and coughed at intervals. Perhaps he was hoping for an opportunity to object, which never came. I waved and turned away. Millie wore a hat with flowers on the brim and a dress with beads and tassels. Although conventional by nature, she was aware the hippy movement gave her the chance to show off her beauty. I smiled at her approvingly and she asked doubtfully, 'Who are you marrying?'

Hayden was very late arriving, having a deadline to complete, on the Beatles as the Impersonation of the Anti-Nuclear Movement (that old thing). Or so he'd informed me. There being no iPhones in those merry days, one never had a clue whether anyone was lying about their activity or whereabouts. Fifteen minutes after starter's orders, he dashed in with a gang of friends who'd obviously been having a good lunch. Subsequently I discovered it had been the play-off of a pub darts match in which Hayden had participated, expecting to be disqualified early. Drink was taken.

'Oh my dearest bride!' He whirled me round, utterly drunk. Have I mentioned how handsome he was with a perma-tan and chestnut hair that whirled above his broad shoulders and legs that were not as long as he believed? Banging her desk, the registrar demanded order like a schoolteacher with naughty children, and the latest guests lounged unrepentantly to the back of the room.

So I was married. All omens bad. Hayden and I were not unalike, both talented with the gift of the pen but in an ultimately superficial way that made us ashamed of ourselves. We were not long enough together for me to get a real grip on his back story, but it seemed to consist of an East European country where he spent his childhood, probably a disappearing mother (if only that had been mine) and a loving grandmother who brought him to England and spoilt him rotten. It is not a good plan to marry your grandmother but that's what he attempted before and after me – plain girls with bad skin and thick legs and, presumably, kind hearts. Eventually, he notched up a score of six, with myself the naughty soldier out of step.

The wedding party took place at The Pheasantry on the King's Road. It was set back and screened by an arch with over-large Greek-style figures, not quite welcoming, not quite threatening. A late nineteenth-century city folly. Up to a year ago it had been my club of choice where the drunken literati and would-be literati had gathered. Now there was only a night club in the basement and apartments above. Hayden owned one of the apartments and that's where we all squashed in.

Through the bright flow of champagne, I was surprised to see Sam still with us, sitting quietly on a sofa, wondering perhaps at Hayden's purple corduroy trousers with orange velvet patch pocket (I *loved* those trousers – perhaps they are why I married him).

I took my drink and sat beside Sam who, finding no water, drank nothing.

'Thank you for coming,' I smiled inanely. 'I didn't expect it. Not your scene.' Which was an understatement. It is a painful fact that I had caught sight of Lennie a week earlier, with a clean-shaven face above a dark suit. He looked calm and confident. Actually, I waylaid him for a minute and told myself I liked his stare of terror and something else – excitement? Admiration? Certainly not regret. His good wife, Rebekah, was expecting their baby as Sam, the proud grandfather, had told me. I would never make a stalker because I had fled then without either of us saying a word.

'I'm fond of you.' Sam answered my question.

'What?'

'I believed it was an important day.'

I suspected by then that my obsession with Lennie was all a fantasy but it suited me to keep it going. It gave me the sensation of loving someone and, practically speaking, it had brought me Sam who really did love me. Perhaps I was Sam's fantasy or perhaps he was trying to help a lost soul or perhaps I merely amused him. As a novelist I have a duty to look from all sides and only pick what suits the occasion. Sam loved me.

'I'm afraid it is more impulsive than important,' I admitted.

He smiled, and was about to push himself up, up and away, when Buffy loped lopsidedly towards us. She subsided heavily beside Sam, making his part of the sofa rise a foot.

'Such a pleasure to meet you. Cleopatra has told me so much.' This was a lie.

I saw she was drunker than me and decided to say nothing. Buffy was my editor and, as a matter of fact, gave me very good editorial advice, along the lines of, 'Darling, you didn't really mean to bang on about Vietnam, did you, when bally old England's not even in the war. Thanks to that pipe-smoking chap.' I always did what she said. What was Vietnam to me? That was Di's story.

Of course I had wanted my extraordinary sister at my wedding, however ridiculous and impulsive it might have been. I had taken a note round to the paper who published most of her reports but I doubt she ever got it.

At the wedding party, Millie, sentimental after only one glass of wine, pronounced, 'Even if you don't want Mummy here, there should have been three sisters at your wedding.'

In order not to cry, I ground my teeth at her, 'You'll call us the Three Musketeers next!'

I didn't love Hayden at all. It is a shocking fact. If I'd loved him even a little, things might have turned out better. After most people had gone, we went into his bedroom and tried to have sex together. Neither of us tried very hard. He kept reaching for a glass on the bedside table and at one point complained in a childish whine, 'Were you always so heavy?' His biggest involvement came with his own cock which was a fine size and stood up proudly whether I was anywhere near it or not. After a while I went into the bathroom but was too drunk to think any of the deep thoughts I'd hoped for.

So I went back to the living room, found another bottle of champagne and brought it back. That excited Hayden at least.

I suppose that if serious drugs had been used by the group we moved in, we'd have fallen apart quicker, but drink was our primary drug of choice and Coke the sugary freshener in the nice glass bottle. Young bodies can take a lot. I was still only twenty-five.

My only sensible decision was to put off moving in with Hayden, not that he tried very hard to persuade me. Nor were my reasons important; I simply preferred my flat which was lighter and more airy, the idea of moving all my things made me reach for a drink and I didn't want his cock proudly flashing at me when I was trying to work. Actually, now I write them down they seem like pretty sensible reasons. Maybe they even made me a feminist.

DI

I left my hotel to go to the press briefing, known as the 'Five pm Follies' because they were held in an old cinema, a theatre of the absurd where briefing officers purvey a mixture of truth, evasion and falsehood. Amazingly, some reporters – the majority, to be honest – still believed them. It might have been a Summer of Love in New York but in Saigon there were war-time rules.

I lived in the same hotel as before. But I had a proper bedroom and my neighbours were mostly other reporters. Saigon was where I came to eat, wash and change my clothes – and go to the odd press briefing. The authorities need to know you exist, a woman with a Brit accent, not threatening, maybe.

On the way I met Ping (once Dung), my friend Ping who used to be manager of the hotel and had let me sleep in the maid's cupboard. While I was away in New York, he moved from the leisure industry to politics – the killing industry – and was now called by his proper name, Nguyen Van Dung. He was still little and skinny but wore smart suits with the jacket slung over his shoulder and talked English fast with a strong American accent. I disapproved of Ping but he was still my friend – and useful informant, of course.

We stood on the street, not far from the cinema; it was hot, noisy, smelly, crowded and raining. Dirty water carrying cigarette stubs surged round my boots. I always wore boots now.

'You good, Di? Going in there for a laugh!' He indicated the building behind us and laughed himself.

'You look well Ping. Very prosperous.' When I used words he didn't understand, he frowned and clicked his teeth. 'Hale and hearty, I'd hazard a guess.' It was only a game really to remind him of the days when he wasn't important.

'Ah, Di. Times bad. US choose bad people.'

'Not you. Is that it?'

'Not listen to correct news. Believe government. Some time even believe Buddhist.'

'I've got to go in. Let's have a coffee. 8pm? Usual place?'

'Sure. Sure.'

I left him. Sure he might be there. Sure he might not be. He might have something interesting to say. He might not have. And he might not say it if he had.

I joined the other reporters, past the Korean guards, and into the gallery. Said hi to the ones I knew and respected, Bob from US TV, Don from ABC and Julian from the BBC. I had time to consider the effect their pictures were having on American viewers and whether words were on the way out. Even thought of Cleo who can only see words, if you can see words. Sat down, got out my notepad and checked on the stage for the usual suspects. They were there alright, prepared to reel out the figures to prove America, sorry, South Vietnam, was winning the war. Uniforms. There were a lot of uniforms up there. And then I saw Brad.

His presence there set off a roaring roll of drums in my head, a fleet of helicopters coming in to land. After all, I hadn't seen him since Washington, nearly two years ago. Why was he here? There were no particular top brass in town and that's what he did, shadowing bigwigs and failing to impress on them the truth of things. He looked square cut as ever but paler, a little grey even.

The press briefing took its usual droning, adenoidal progress, thirty statistics for every word, and I didn't take in anything. At question time, I managed to pay a bit more attention as Julian quizzed the figures in his rather grand English voice. It was obvious to everybody he was right but it wouldn't change anything.

I walked slowly out of the building and Brad was there waiting for me. It was still raining but it suddenly seemed beneficial, refreshing.

'Hi Brad.'

'Hello Di. How are you?'

'What are you doing here?'

'Shall we grab a beer?'

'I don't drink.'

'A coffee, then.' He took my arm and we walked along the pavement together and all the strident theatre of Saigon became background.

We sat opposite each other in a dark bar and he ordered a beer to my Coke.

'I came to find you,' he said. 'That's why I was at the briefing. I've been thinking of you. I've been worrying.'

I smiled. 'I don't take risks.' I thought about lying under Rogue, his blood seeping into me. 'I do my job, that's all.' I noticed that he was staring at me with great intensity. 'Why are you like this now? I've been here for ages.'

He sat back against the bench, passed his hand over his head. 'I'm divorced. I came to ask whether you'd marry me?'

I didn't understand. Was he being funny? 'You mean so I get out of Vietnam? Get out of danger?'

'That would be good.' He seemed unable to explain himself. We stared at each other.

In all the times I'd thought of Brad I'd never thought of marrying him. Marriage was not on my life-time agenda. Besides, I had met him when he was already married; the fact that he was divorced didn't change my image of him: he was a married man. 'I don't see what marriage has to do with us,' I tried. I wondered whether he planned to say he loved me. But love wasn't on my agenda either. I thought of Brendan with his beloved Elena far away somewhere, maybe in the farthest place anyone could go, the place I'd caught a glimpse of yesterday. For the first time in years I felt like a drink.

'Can I come to your hotel?' Brad leant forward to me.

'Of course.' This was easier. I could deal with this.

We made love better than ever. This was no snatch and grab, this was slow. We needed to make a space together. I knew he'd come all this way to find me and I discovered he wasn't grey at all. He was golden. Strong. I crawled over him, checking muscles, checking heart beat, estimating the thickness of his skin over his veins, where the blood ran hot and happy.

The rain fell close to the window, my hotel window high in the sky, and I thought of the silver curtain falling over the jungle as we approached it yesterday and how it stopped so that when I crawled from the bush the body bags shone in the sun. Shapeless sculptures of the dead.

I crawled over him, stroking him, licking him, cajoling, avoiding his arms pulling at me. I was in control.

I put my head on his chest and felt him grunt and pant and it was a love song of desire. I allowed him to hold me so that we were face to face and his eyes were anxious and red-veined and they too were a love song of desire.

I kissed his lips and he kissed mine and the length of our bodies touched, right down to our toes.

It was the middle of the night when we separated, when our bodies separated, and even then a while before we spoke.

I came back from the bathroom and lay beside him. I rolled over towards him.

'Why don't you smell of sweat like real men?'

'I'm an American? Don't you have deodorants in little England?'

I thought *is this married couple's banter?* and frowned.

'You weren't serious about marriage, were you?'

'Not now. Now is perfect.'

'Without the wedding bands?' I thought, bonds.

'Yes.' He put a hand across me proprietorially, perhaps the way a husband might relax with his wife, but I let it lie.

He didn't stay all night. Probably he was avoiding words. Fine by me. We had a date for eleven the next morning. But I overslept. I never oversleep. In my dreams the dead came out of their bags and all of them had faces like Brad.

We sat in a bar and drank American coffee, tasteless and too much of it. We sat side by side on a padded bench left over from the French and he held my hand.

'I heard you were on a bad op not long ago.' He was part of my world. Also part of the system. He made me look at him. 'I want you to marry me and come to America.'

I stared down at the croissant he'd brought me – a good French croissant. Do oppressors only leave their food behind? 'You want me to come and live in Washington, surrounded by politicians. I left England to get away from all that crap.' That was a reference to my mother. Thinking he might not have understood, I added fiercely, 'My mother.' But it felt like a lie. Julie didn't matter.

'I guess you're a bit like your mother.'

'You don't know Julie. You've never met her.'

He stared at me. 'I met her in the White House. You were there too. The next day she was at a meeting.'

'You *can't* mean we're alike?' I heard my voice rise.

He smiled. 'Not if you don't want to be.'

Now I was curious. 'Give me one word.'

He didn't have to think. 'Driven.'

We were both silent. Could I really be like Julie, of the pretty ways and ice-cold determination?

There was a pause while I banished Julie and he thought of his next move. He said, 'Maybe you want me to come back here as one of the 10,000 military advisers? I could hang around waiting for you to get wounded or killed.'

We both gulped at our coffee. Brad put down his cup first. 'I'm going to take early retirement. I want to marry you and make a home with you in California, not too far from the sea.'

I laughed. I don't know why. The surprise? The shock? I saw he was offering me happiness. I could see it shining in his eyes. He didn't even mind me laughing. He smiled too.

'I love you. Don't you understand that? You don't have to stay here. You can come away with me. We'll retrain. We'll become businessmen, artists, entertainers. We don't need this.' He waved his arm to the window.

As if on cue there was an explosion, a small explosion, probably a motorbike back-firing. Vietnamese motorbikes ran on the sort of fuel that exploded regularly. I laughed again. 'You want me to give up my whole life.'

'No. No. I want you to start a new life!' He was impassioned. If we'd been alone, we could have kissed and made love.

For some reason I pictured Bear on Hampstead Heath. My broken warrior. A man I admired. 'You want me to run away?'

'You don't have to be part of this war. It's not even your war.'

'Bad things happen; best if they happen elsewhere?'

'What do you mean?' He wanted to understand me but I hardly understood myself.

'That's how people operate. Since I was very young, I've known bad things happen and I can't turn my back on them. Now I have a role. I'm a tiny fish in the pond but if I only change the minds of a few people, that makes sense of my life.' At the same time as I was speaking with absolute conviction, I thought *I don't want to drive him away*. I said, 'Something big's coming up. The Vietnamese I talk to know it. Probably your generals do too but don't want to admit it. Early next year. Maybe even during the Tet holiday in January. Your 10,000 military advisers probably have an idea too but they're blanking it. Or being blanked. You see, I need more time here.'

Brad sat back against the bench. What did he himself know? Why should I think he knew less than me? Rumours always flew round Saigon.

'I won't be able to get out of the army for a few months, possibly not before spring.'

'So I'll stay through Tet. I'll watch the firecrackers and eat the cake.'

Had I promised to marry Brad next year? To live with him and be his love. It seemed absurd. I leant against him. My body seemed to feel I had. 'When can you come back to my room?'

'This evening. Get in some beers.'

'I don't drink.' I smiled at him. Maybe we'd have a beer together. Suddenly he seemed like a mirage. How could he be smiling at me like that? Perhaps I had died under Rogue's corpse. I grabbed at Brad and ran my hand over the thick warm skin of his face. 'See you later.'

MILLIE

Mummy invited me to lunch at the House of Commons as she did periodically. It must have been January 1968. For most of the time she talked about the 'I'm backing Britain' campaign which encouraged workers to put in an extra half hour without more pay and which was endorsed by Harold Wilson.

I don't expect she meant to make me feel uncomfortable, she wasn't thinking about me of course, but her excitable talk of duty and all hands to the wheel and serving your country with hard grit, 'How many hours do you think I put in?' as she glanced at me for a moment, were not the right words for the mother who had given up work because her husband earned plenty, liked her fresh for him in the evening and they both hoped for another child.

'I know you work hard, Mummy,' I agreed feebly. 'But you look very well.' As I said this I suddenly noticed that since I'd last seen her – only Christmas after all – she had changed. Her aura of lightness which came partly from her quick mind and partly from her pretty figure topped with the halo of red hair, had morphed into something more solid, more querulous, less confident; in short – older.

I watched her with this in mind and somehow was not altogether surprised when she said at the end of the meal as we sipped our coffees, 'Do you ever think of your father?'

The real answer was 'No' or perhaps, 'Almost never.' If I did think of Dada it was in relation to Di who had hero-worshipped him and modelled herself on him. It was always Mummy for me. What could she be thinking? (This guessing at her thoughts was, incidentally, an exercise of the imagination I had practised since childhood.)

'He went away so suddenly. So long ago. It must be ten years ago,' I prevaricated.

This made her impatient, as almost anything I said did. 'Don't you ever wonder where he went? What happened to him?'

'I know you tried everything to find him.' I didn't really know that. But I had always taken it for granted. 'I think you said the charity he worked for lost touch with him.'

'Well, I expect they did.' She was still impatient.

'It was a very dangerous area,' I began again. 'That guerrilla group – what was it called? – was very active. So tragic.'

She gave me a pitying look. 'You have a tender nature.'

Even I could see this was an insult and began to weary of her game. 'Have you heard some news of him?'

She blushed, the redhead's blush which painted her cheeks with scarlet and then reappeared in blotches on her neck. 'Of course not,' she snapped. 'Why ever would I? What a ridiculous idea! I suppose you've been talking to Di.'

Now I was really taken aback. Why or indeed how would I ever talk to Di about our vanished father? 'I can't talk to Di. She's been in Vietnam for years,' I muttered. 'As far as I know, still is.'

'She writes to Cleo.'

'They became closer in New York.' I tried to make my voice non-committal but I could see some inner rage was keeping Mummy's face scarlet. I did my best not to look because it made her seem ugly. *To me, fair friend, you never can be old/For as you were when first your eye I ey'd/Such seems your beauty still...*

'I expect Cleo tells you everything – at least when she's not pissed out of her mind.'

'I love Cleo.' I tried to sound dignified and wondered if Mummy knew Cleo had got married and not invited her.

'So has she told you things about your father?'

'No,' I said because it was true and I couldn't say anything else. That was more or less the end of our conversation and certainly the end of any mention of Dada. Gradually, the red turned to pink and she began looking at her watch. As throughout our lives together, I braced myself for our parting. And, as throughout our lives, she remembered at the last minute to ask a question about my world,

'How is Calypso, darling?' Ridiculously, I was pleased she'd remembered her name.

'Very well, Mummy. She has started to learn how to read already.'

'That's good. Give her a kiss from her grandmother.'

DI

When Brad left Vietnam, between Christmas 1967 and New Year 1968, I was surprised to find myself bereft. It was a weird sensation, physical in its intensity, so that I felt cold even in Saigon's stifling heat. I looked around me on the most crowded streets, aware of being alone for the first time in my life.

'I'll be back on St Valentine's Day,' he said, 'and by then I may even have bought a home for us.' Home again, not house.

I told myself I only partly believed him but when he was gone I discovered I did. To test things out, towards the end of January, I slept with a French cameraman who usually hooked the prettiest Vietnamese girls, some of them procured by my old friend Ping who had slid even further upwards in President Thieu's bureaucracy but wasn't above any profitable business.

'Why you with that French?' he asked me. 'He shit.'

'I'm testing my love for another,' I told him. 'It's a regular thing we do in England.' We stood in the foyer of the Majestic, as usual teaming with multi-national press.

'He shit. You crazy.' He put a skinny finger to his head. 'That American big boss. Good man.'

'Your English is going downhill. Want some more lessons?'

'Wanna Coke?'

We went together to the bar and got our Cokes and found a quiet corner. I could see he had some news for me. While Brad was around, I had taken my finger off the pulse of the city. I had the slightly unnerving sensation that Ping had sought me out. Usually, it was the other way round.

'I think you go home with that boss.'

'How do you manage to know everything, Ping?'

'I your friend.'

'And you want me to go home. Come to that, why aren't you celebrating Tet with your family?'

Now that I knew the reason Ping had stayed in Saigon, I saw mine was a silly question, from a woman in love for the first time in her life. Besides, hadn't I told Brad that something was cooking up, even if Tet was supposed to be recognised on all sides as a truce? When had the VCs or NVA ever kept agreements?

I suppose we'd all got used to Saigon being a place for rest and relaxation. You took a helicopter ride to join the war. Only twenty minutes but it was a ride outside the city. So it was a shock when heavy firing began right in the centre of town. It was New Year's Eve and most of us reporters were booked in for parties. But it was obvious immediately that this was a huge story, and in a matter of minutes we were jostling for places outside the Presidential Palace (no President inside) or even more of us at the American Embassy (no Ambassador inside), where nineteen Viet Cong had stormed into the compound.

There was an air of unreality over the whole thing. What was even more unbelievable was that it was happening all over the country. Over forty towns and cities were attacked by suicidal waves of VC and previously infiltrated North Vietnamese. But I didn't know that as I lay outside the gates of the US Embassy and cursed the photographer with the big lens in front of me. Which was actually of no use to him at all. It was night time and, more importantly, we were barred from the fighting.

Since we couldn't see what was going on, all the early stories were based on rumour. The big TV morning shows reported that the VC were in the first floor of the embassy when actually they never got further than the garden. Nineteen got in and only one survived. But we all wrote our stories: *US Embassy stormed and held by enemy for over six hours.*

By the time we were allowed through the gates, there were Viet Cong corpses all over the place, and the news began barrelling round the world: a troop of ragamuffin guerrillas who were losers – and losing to All American Might, because that's what President Johnson had told everyone – had just burst into the holy of holies, the American Embassy. For God's sake, Americans said, reasonably enough, are we really winning this war?

How the White House must have mourned press censorship! It didn't even matter that things didn't go as Ho or Le Duan wanted. They'd expected an uprising but found they'd totally misjudged the South Vietnamese. When an ARVN officer got hold of a VC colonel who'd just murdered a mother and her child, he got out his pistol and shot him in the head. It wasn't his fault the picture went round the world, convincing many Americans they were not only losing the war but perhaps not even backing the good guys. Yet another media disaster for the White House.

It was about then I began to get more detailed news about the other attacks around the country and it became clear that Hue, the ancient capital of Vietnam, the 'Perfume City', really had been overrun and moreover was still being held. There was absolutely no point in hanging around in Saigon with packs of other reporters who were still trying to milk the embassy attack when there was a real story out there.

Adrenaline pumping, I walked, almost ran, to the Press Centre and, amazingly, managed to get a call through to Brad in Washington.

'I'm going to Hue, Brad! There's very little news coming out of there. But we know most of the city's taken and the marines and ARVN are fighting house-to-house to take it back. Street by street...'

His sober voice interrupted me, 'Diana, you're not a soldier. This isn't your war. You don't have to go.'

That was the worst thing to say if he wanted to stop me. I fired back, 'I have a duty to the truth.' But he knew and I knew that was only a small part of the reason why I was going. Nor was it just because I felt competitive with other better-connected reporters. It went back much further. Not that I was thinking about the past. Here was the next challenge.

I said hurriedly, 'Sorry, I just have to go. But I'll be back.'

Suddenly we were cut off, or rather submerged in a sea of incomprehensible sounds, like audible hieroglyphics. He didn't even have time to say he loved me.

I grabbed a bag and went out to find which reinforcing troops were going to Hue, when and with whom I would get a ride, where the helos were setting out from and if any other reporter was going too. Probably not. Hopefully not.

It was life as I lived it every day, although I suppose the stakes were a bit higher. But I really did mean to come back and go and live with Brad in California. As Cleo and I used to say to each other in New York, *If darkness comes at noon then midday brings the dawn.* Of course then we fell about laughing.

CLEO

In the middle of February 1968, a male American whose name sounded like Brad telephoned from somewhere round the world and began to sob. The First Drink having been celebrated, alone and in my own flat, I put down the receiver. If it wasn't a wrong number, it should be.

The telephone rang again five or so minutes later.

'Is that Cleo?' The tears had passed. He sounded attractive, authoritative.

'Yes. That's me.' I softened and refilled my glass. Perhaps at last it was the Hollywood producer offering me millions for the honour of making a film of my rubbish novel. Which novel, I wondered, sipping quietly. My latest, about twins who were brought up apart and fell in love with each other, would make a terrific movie.

'I am very sorry...' He paused.

This was not so good. Even I couldn't convince myself that good news came with an introduction like that. *The raven itself is hoarse...* The Shakespearian allusion made me think of Millie and I suddenly wished that she was there beside me. I put down my drink, an almost unprecedented manoeuvre. 'What is it?'

'Your sister...' He paused again and croaked a word I couldn't hear.

'Millie, Millicent?' Of course I knew whatever news he was bringing was not about Millie. Millie was bounded by a protective caul of husband, daughter, church, home, love even.

The man, Brad Wolfe as I came to learn, pronounced another word which was also like a bird cry but more of a whistle as if high in the sky with the wind whistling. I now know he was saying 'Hue'.

He carried on with stranger cries, forcing his way through my wilful deafness and incomprehension until I could not avoid knowing. Di had been killed. He had a letter from her to me. He had notes. He had her address book. He knew my number. They were to have been married very soon. She had been killed in Hue, that high-flying bird's sound again. She had been shot by a sniper in the city, not hit by a bomb. He was keen for me to know that because he said it more than once. 'I have just arrived in Saigon,' he said. 'They brought her back in a body bag.'

I slipped onto the floor as he went on and on. 'I loved her', he said. 'And she loved me.' That was nearly as shocking as her dying. Di didn't do love. She did action. I could believe her dying in action but not in love.

I got up, put down the receiver and with shaking hands poured myself another drink. That drink was more important than hearing every word of Brad's. When I listened again he was saying, 'Shall you tell your mother? She wouldn't want to hear it from the news. Or read about it in a newspaper. Will you tell her?'

I must have made a sound that sounded like 'yes'.

'And her other sister, of course. I'm not sure of her name.'

'Yes, I will.' I definitely said yes to that one. Millie was my only human lifeline. I can't remember what else he said, not very much probably. He'd delivered his message.

I put down the receiver and decided to go and see Hayden, my so-called husband. That was a bad mistake. I didn't go to see him; I went to avoid seeing my mother and to find a drinking partner. It was seven o'clock when I got to the Pheasantry and Hayden was celebrating the end of a long piece on the politics of feminism. I seldom read Hayden's pieces because I suspected they would cause marital disharmony. That's a lie! I just couldn't be bothered. He was clever, he was successful and we had fun together – sometimes. I didn't have a duty to read his pieces as well. He never read one of my books.

'My sister has been killed in a place that sounds like a bird whistling high in the air.'

'In Vietnam, I assume,' said Hayden politely and I was glad he showed no hypocritical signs of sorrow. He had never met Di.

'Hue.' I hadn't noticed the man in the corner. An American whose face I vaguely knew. 'The indentured slaves of capitalism are trying to recapture it.'

'I suppose so.' I picked up a glass and held it out to Hayden who filled it carefully to the brim.

'We can get through this together,' he said. By which he meant that we could drink so much that one dead sister in Hue would make no difference one way or another. This was another of my mistakes.

꿍

'My sympathy for your loss,' added the man in the corner. I saw he was black which was a surprise. There were not many black Americans in England then. Looking at him diverted me for a second from thinking about Di but when I returned to her it was worse. I knocked back another glass.

'I've got to go.' The man in the corner left quietly and Hayden and I got down to some serious drinking.

The point about this unedifying scene is that when I arrived at Julie's flat I was smashed, sozzled, off my head, scrambled eggs instead of brains. I can't remember how I got there, just that I was standing at the door of her flat ringing the doorbell. Somebody must have let me into the building. That was that person's mistake. The porter, I suppose.

'Hello, Cleo,' Julie sighed as she opened the door. That was her mistake, not the sighing, but opening the door to me. A few years later when I became interested in the various pathways to tragedy, I clocked that the most heinous actions are seldom meant in a 100 per cent way, but a combination of bad mistakes and bad luck.

I went ahead into her gloomy living room and noted papers

scattered over a table with her briefcase nearby. She was obviously working late, unwilling to be disturbed, particularly by her difficult, usually angry, usually drunk daughter.

'I've got a message for you,' I said or perhaps shouted.

'Sit down, darling,' she replied in her absent-minded way.

'I'm not your darling!' I became furious immediately, eagerly swapping the grief of Di's death for the anger of a rebellious teenager. I thought (as far as I could think) that I might not tell her about Di's death. What would she care anyway? How could I bear to see her lack of caring? Whatever was the point? I might have gone then and found Millie but instead I stayed. Yet another mistake. A litany of mistakes.

'What's the matter, Cleo?' So she could see I was upset. But I was too far along the road to change my tune.

I looked around the room. 'I suppose you're not offering me a drink?'

'No,' she agreed wearily.

I describe her answer, her weariness, but the truth is that my head was gradually exploding into a scarlet mass of rage and I could hardly see her or hear what she said. Inside that thick redness it felt as if Julie was the cause of everything bad in my world and, without any doubt at all, the cause of Di's death.

'You killed her!' I must have shouted that. How did Julie respond? I've no idea. I suppose she asked what I meant. By then I was standing up, swaying, yelling accusations. Behind me was a bookcase with various unpleasant ornaments on top, probably presents from trips overseas that MPs collect.

'Di! You killed Di!' I must have shouted that. And perhaps repeated the word 'Died!' or 'Dead! Dead! Dead!' Like a child who wants her mother to make everything be all right. I might have screamed, 'Tell me she's not dead! But you can't because you killed her!'

At one level, I still believe that. Our mother made the atmosphere so poisonous that we all fled into danger. Even Millie with her goodness and her own family. Even Millie wasn't immune. Why else did she lose her wits so early. Too early anyway. Well, there was another reason, but that was Julie's fault too.

'You drove Brendan away! Di loved Brendan. All she wanted was a father and you drove him away. What did *you* care as long as *you* got what *you* wanted!' On I went deeper and deeper into the madness.

Now I can wonder what Julie was thinking after hearing of her middle daughter's death. Perhaps she didn't believe me. Perhaps she said something. She must have said something. She can't have received the death of her daughter and said nothing. Perhaps she cried out, 'No! It's not true.' But I was far too lost in my own scenario to see or hear any reaction from her. When I did hear her she was reading from my script.

'Your father ran away from the family because he found someone he loved more than us.' Her voice, cold and bitter, entered my brain like a scalpel. 'I didn't drive him away. He found someone else. If you want to apportion blame, blame the war. World War Two, in case you've forgotten.'

'Liar! Liar! Liar!' I danced hysterically about, the red stuff pouring out of me, my arms waving. 'You killed our father too! You killed everything because you only care about yourself!'

Did she want to ask me about Di then, was it true? Why? Where? When? Or maybe my lunatic appearance deterred her. Maybe the whole scene was as unreal to her as it was to me. She could not have believed Di was dead.

But then she took another slice out of my brain. 'Diana knew all about his other woman. He went to see your sister in New York. Before he...' She paused. The pause caught my attention; the information that Di had known something about Brendan that she hadn't told me, twisted the scalpel.

'I loved Di! Di and I loved each other!' Why ever was I going on about love? Had I caught it off Brad? Perhaps I didn't shout that but

I could see Julie's face again and I could see that she was pleased that she had told me something about Di I hadn't known.

I tottered. Mind and body tottered. Anger swirled and thickened into pure hatred. Even then she could have controlled me; I do believe that, but she wanted to provoke me, she wanted to make me lose total control. For she said in meagre, mincing words, even turning aside a little as if it wasn't very important, 'Of course your father isn't dead. People don't just die. Not even disappeared. He sent me letters for you all, parcels too.' Again that electrifying pause. 'I didn't tell you that. What was the point? Better to get used to his absence.'

At that moment, I knocked something behind me on the bookcase. I turned in a sleepwalking, automatic way, and found I had saved a brass buddha from falling. I held it in my hands. It was heavy and immediately presented itself as a missile. As a way of stopping this hideous dialogue. Although it wasn't so much about the actual words, hers or mine, Brendan had never been as close to me as he was to Di. I guess it was just as much a way of relieving the hideous pressure in my head.

I threw the buddha over-arm which was the last but one mistake because it shot like a cannonball through the room. I had turned myself into a gun, fuelled by hatred and alcohol.

The buddha, fat and smiling serenely, flew across the room and hit the side of Julie's head. She fell. I stared. Blood appeared but not much. I thought I was going to vomit so I staggered to the sideboard, slid the glass door back and took out a sherry bottle which I tipped into my mouth.

Once started, it seemed a pity to stop. I glugged down the bottle like a baby with its milk and by the time it was empty, I was lying on the floor, half under the sideboard.

I suppose I was, to all intents and purposes, unconscious. Certainly time passed without me being aware of it. When I did open my eyes again and saw my mother not far from me, still unconscious, I crawled to the telephone and dialled 999. Leaving her on the floor for so long was my final mistake. In court they reported that I told the 999 operator, 'I've killed my mother but she deserved it.'

What a maniac! I didn't mean to kill her at all. But I expect they all say that. And maybe I laughed a victorious cackle as she fell.

PART TWO

MILLIE

I always knew Cleo wouldn't have meant to hurt Mummy, least of all kill her. Cleo's weapons were words. When the policeman rang up, they didn't tell me at once what had happened. I was half asleep anyway. Still in bed. They just said my sister was in the Westminster police station and needed me to come down there. I assumed she had got drunk and driven into something or fallen over something or anyway hurt herself in some way. It would have been better if they'd prepared me.

'Do you need transport?' the policeman said politely. Perhaps that should have warned me, his extremely polite, almost caring tone.

'No. But I'll have to wait for my husband to get back. He's on a train coming from a meeting in Manchester last night.' Why did I tell him so much? 'I have a daughter who can't be left alone.' Was I becoming nervous?

'Perhaps you'd like your husband with you.'

'No. No. He'll be tired.'

This little conversation stays with me as almost the last time when life was normal. When Eddie came back and I explained, he asked reasonably enough, 'Why don't they get Hayden? Her husband, in case you'd forgotten.' He'd got up early to catch the train. He *was* tired.

'He's probably too drunk.' I forced a little smile, not returned by Eddie. I can't blame him for that nor for anything really. What a family he married into!

I's looked in at Caly's bedroom before I left. She was just waking so I said I had to pop out but Daddy was home. How sweet she'd looked with her tousled dark hair and rosy cheeks.

There are so many bad things about what followed that I can't describe them in any sane way. In the space of an hour I learnt that one sister was dead, my mother was dead and my surviving sister was being arrested under suspicion of our mother's murder or at least manslaughter.

As an example of just how mad I was, I sat in that ugly police reception room, trying to recall which opera ended in a similar level of carnage. The police spoke in one side of my head, in the other side I told myself, 'Verdi ends *Aida* with the star-crossed lovers sealed into a dark tomb. Pretty bad. Meyerbeer rounds up *Les Huguenots* with such thorough massacres that he produced the line *God wants blood.*'

Then I tried Shakespeare who I know better and never lets one down in this sphere. Of course, Macbeth takes the prize, including many named dead, i.e. King Duncan, his two guards, Banquo, Fleance, Lady Macduff and young son and everyone in their castle, Lady Macbeth, Young Siward and Macbeth himself.' I stopped myself moving on to *Titus Andronicus* when I saw the policeman looking at me oddly. Perhaps my lips were moving. He should have been pleased I wasn't screaming.

He was old and paunchy and might have been 'fatherly' in other circumstances. Eventually, he stopped informing me of horrors and said, 'Would you like to go to your sister?' Adding, 'She'll need a lawyer of course.'

It seems strange now that he told me about Di's death. Why would he have known? Can Cleo have told him? Unlikely in her state.

He took me down to a small basement room and there was Cleo apparently sleeping peacefully.

Suddenly angry, I shook her shoulder, disturbing heavy waves of alcohol. 'Cleo! You can't just go to sleep! They say Mummy's dead and you've killed her.'

'Hmm,' went the policeman in disapproval or maybe I'm making that up. Perhaps I shouldn't have been there. Perhaps I was getting special treatment because of who my mother was.

Cleo sat up and said in a surprisingly normal tone of voice, 'I didn't mean to hurt her. Not really. I just threw that hideous buddha, symbol of peace and prosperity, because I was furious. And drunk.' She lay down again. 'Oh do go away, Millie. I can't tell you how my head aches.'

'She's still drunk,' I said to the policeman – needlessly, I would have thought. I looked about in a doubtless deranged way. 'Where *is* my mother?'

Before he could answer, Cleo popped up again, her hair all over her face so I could hardly see it. Her voice was quite different. 'Di's been killed in Vietnam, Millie. Di is dead!' And she burst into tears. She heaved and screamed and contorted her body like some dreadful animal. She didn't look human at all.

I stared at her helplessly for what seemed like ages. Apart from anything else, Cleo never cried. The noise was terrific and I noticed the policeman had retreated to the door. I bowed my head as if sheltering from a storm, and the action reminded me of God and prayers and Mary, Our Mother, who helps us at the hour of our death. I began to say the rosary. I sat on the bed beside Cleo and incanted ten Hail Marys and a Glory Be and gradually she quietened. Heaven knows what the policeman thought, perhaps he'd left, but I've never been so glad of prayer in my life.

By the time I'd got through three of the sorrowful decades, I felt less as if my mind was falling apart but, in all honesty, I'd have to admit that I was still so far from dealing with the situation that I wasn't truly accepting the possibility of Mummy's death, let alone Di's. In fact I put Di on hold for the time being.

I don't know how long I recited fevered prayers, under my breath after the first burst, and Cleo retreated once more into sleep. At some point, Eddie arrived and leant over Cleo's uncommunicative body. 'I've found you a lawyer. A friend of mine. He'll sort things out.' Cleo did not stir.

I prayed some more and then remembered with a panic that I had a daughter. 'Where's Calypso? You've left Caly on her own!'

'Of course not. Helen's going to take her to school.' He sat by me and held my hand. Helen was the nice neighbour who had four children herself. Or perhaps only one or two back then. One four years old like Caly.

At some point, I sensed whispering around me, and realised my eyes were closed and probably I had fallen into a dream state, an evasion of the horror. The whispers seemed to be chorusing death and damnation as only demons can, insinuating their evil little bodies into my brain.

I opened my eyes and saw Eddie and a new younger policeman. They were both staring at me. It was a relief that the demons had fled.

'Would you like to see your mother?' asked Eddie. He was so saintly then, so clear and strong. Even his slight edge of impatience was reassuring. 'She's in a hospital nearby but she won't be there for long.'

It was the middle of the morning when we drove to say goodbye to Mummy, one of those grey February mornings when it never seems to get light, filled with a dripping despondency. My legs were shaking so much that I had to hang on to Eddie as we went to the car. Another new policeman drove with our one at his side. He said, 'We'll go in a side entrance.'

Someone had slipped the news to the press. It was a terrific story from their point of view. A drunken best-selling novelist murders her Cabinet-Minister mother. You couldn't make it up. The fact that it was an accident didn't seem to count. After all, I assume the general thinking went, people are convicted every day for committing murders they never intended, usually when drunk. Why should this spoilt young woman who wrote lubricious novels be judged any differently?

Naturally, I grasped none of this at the time. I didn't really take in the meaning of the crowds as we approached the hospital gates before veering off via some waste ground to the back of the building. Shock is a very beneficial state.

Mummy looked as beautiful as ever. The brass missile had felled her instantly, striking at that most vulnerable point behind the ear. She must have been turning her head. I suppose there was a bump or wound there but her lovely red hair hid it and her face was calm and pearly pale rather than dead grey. There was still some life within her body but I could see her spirit was gone.

I kissed her briefly, then sat down and began to pray for her soul. Essentially, Christianity has a very positive message about death, but happiness and an afterlife, although possible, are not easy to attain. Even though I adored Mummy with a childish, futile love, I knew her faults, so I was glad to be able to help her on her way. I prayed for forgiveness for her and then I enlarged my prayer to encompass all those who had sinned, wilfully or unwittingly. That included Cleo, of course. And myself.

I sat with Mummy for a long time and did my best to evoke joyful memories. But this was not easy under the circumstances so I took refuge in the Vale of Tears. I was so grateful for my faith.

Eddie led me away after a while. I suppose the hospital wanted to prepare the body. It's hard to believe an autopsy was necessary but I suppose it was done anyway.

Eddie said, 'Shall we go back to Cleo?'

My heart beat very fast then. After all I was sitting by Mummy who had died because my sister was drunk and out of control. I felt a surge of rage and hatred but only for a moment.

'We should see that the lawyer has arrived,' added Eddie.

I took several deep breaths.

Outside, the moist skies had turned into cold rain. The police didn't seem interested in us anymore so we looked for a taxi to take us back to the police station. Because it was raining it took ages to find one. The hospital was near a train station and the noise and energy around us built into a concerted roar as if we were standing on the edge of a rough sea. I clutched on to Eddie for safety. Once we did get into a taxi and started rushing along ourselves, I felt sick and had to put my head between my legs. One of the few pieces of advice I can remember Mummy giving me went as follows: 'If you feel car-sick, put your head between your legs, immediately.' That 'immediately', pronounced with resonance, was very typical.

Cleo was lying on her back on the bed with her eyes open. It struck me she looked more dead than Mummy.

'Is it true?' she asked, sitting up.

I nodded but Eddie said firmly, 'Yes. It is.' I hoped he wouldn't remind her of what she'd done and he didn't, although I think he only withdrew the words when he glimpsed my face.

'I see.' She lay back on the bed. 'You'd better tell Hayden, poor thing.' Her voice was husky, like something out of the grave.

'I'll go and see about this non-appearing lawyer,' said Eddie in an oddly calm voice.

I sat or rather collapsed on the bed. If it had been bigger, it really was only a bunk, I would have laid beside Cleo.

After a long pause, Cleo, with her new graveyard voice, said, 'I'm so sorry, Millie.'

That was my moment of hope. All I needed really to carry me through the many terrible months that followed. Cleo was sorry. I didn't try to analyse what kind of sorry. She was sorry, that was enough. It's always enough. At least it's always enough for me. I always forgive people who are sorry, even before I understand.

She talked about Di then. Cleo, who never cries, cried again on that ghastly morning and I was glad about that too. I sat there as she talked on and on, trying to explain, I suppose. I sat with my hands in my lap, not trying to take it in, the words made little sense, but trying to listen and, quite simply, stay there with her.

It's very difficult to mourn for two people at once. Before all this happened I had sometimes wondered how those mothers who lost multiple sons during the First World War managed. Were they able to mourn for them individually? Some lost three or four or five. They must have merged the sorrow together at some point. But two was one too many for me. Now that Cleo had brought Di to the fore, I couldn't just think of Mummy. And yet I hadn't even heard enough to know how Di had died. In Vietnam, I assumed.

At some point, I became aware of an immense hunger and of feeling ashamed. This was no time to feel hungry. But when Eddie came in with a sandwich and a cup of coffee, I grabbed them like a starving child. I would have thought grief would take away your appetite.

I offered Cleo a bite of my sandwich but she couldn't eat. When she was led away to the ladies, Eddie said, 'Roddy Fingal-Twist's here. He will deal with things. We can't stay.'

I must have looked blank – for a moment I believed that Roddy was Cleo's husband – after all, there was no sign of Hayden. Never was again, actually.

'I don't know why you've been allowed to stay with her so long.' Eddie looked at his watch. 'We've got to go. We can't help her with all the legal stuff. Roddy is top notch. She's lucky he was available.'

Ever after that day, Eddie referred to Cleo as 'she' or 'her'. I can't blame him but I feel hurt on Cleo's behalf. As if she no longer deserved a name.

'I've got to get to the office. It's late, and you need to go home and talk to Helen. Helen will support you.'

'I'll just wait to say goodbye to Cleo.' But Cleo didn't reappear so I did just as Eddie said: went home and rang Helen. My hands were shaking so much, I kept misdialling the number so then I went round to see her.

She opened the door and enveloped me in a hug. I stayed there for ages, like a bear in a dark cave. When she gently pushed me out, she said, 'Let's get this clear, I can't possibly imagine what you're going through and it would be too painful to try but I will be here for you and for Caly. Our home is your home.'

Without Helen I wouldn't have survived. As it was, I don't think my mind was ever as clear again. I remember thinking even that first evening, *it's lucky I'm not working because I could never concentrate on a job again.*

Helen and prayer, and Ed and Calypso of course, I was lucky to have so many reasons to live. Cleo had none.

CLEO

Last week I went to the 2018 Women of the Year Luncheon. I was surprised to be invited as one of 400 honoured guests, charity workers, paraplegic skiers, new-brand suffragettes, shining examples for other women.

On my left a small lady in a velvet hat trimmed with a feather, about the only lady wearing a hat in fact, turned to me with a smile. 'Why are you here?'

I only considered for a moment. 'Because I killed my mother.' This was not strictly true, of course, I was there because when I came out of prison I wrote a misery memoir that caught the zeitgeist. That's not true either. I spent nearly ten years writing a novel about crime, punishment and responsibility. Remarkably, and it caused consternation among many right-thinking people, it won the Booker Award. My mother's death had made me famous/notorious and that helped the publicity department.

My Women of the Year neighbour was unphased by my response. 'Are you sure you didn't kill your *father*?' She looked at me with a sharp old lady's gaze. Later I discovered her claim to fame was that she had 'created' 300 hats for the Queen. She seemed to be serious about her question.

'Why do you ask that? Nobody invents killing their mother.'

'I merely thought that killing your father would be more appropriate to the spirit of this lunch.' She gleamed wickedly.

I laughed. We were two old women together, trying to see the funny side of life.

☙

I arrived at HMP Holloway on an icy afternoon in February 1968 with the sun dipping below its grand turreted gateway. I was actually glad to be put away in a place where nobody could see me, and it made everything else scarcely painful at all, even the supposedly horrific withdrawal from alcohol addiction. Relative suffering or, I suppose, relative anything is an interesting subject. I suffered most of all for Di, for her life finished at twenty-eight, and that suffering was so heavy that, on the pain front, nothing else could begin to compete.

I did not think about Julie at all.

I had a small cell to myself and, as a remand prisoner, I was not made to work or do anything very much. I was cut off from my previous existence and for two weeks Millie was my only visitor. Poor Millie, her shock was so great that she couldn't form normal sentences, but I preferred silence so that didn't matter either. We held hands and sometimes she cried. Of course she was mourning for the Mummy she had always wanted and now could never have. She mourned her 'Mummy' and I mourned Di.

It was not surprising that I was so saddened by Di's death. I admired her for being so independent and brave while all I could do was bend and bandy words. Or maybe it was good old-fashioned love, inexplicable as always. And there was that time in New York when Di promised she'd always be there for me. I regretted, when I remembered her words in prison, that I'd joked about her being useless to help me from Vietnam. But, in my heart, I had taken her seriously.

My solicitor came to see me a couple of times. He was Ed's friend and his name, Roddy Fingal-Twist, was the only thing about him that appealed to me. He was noisy when I needed silence, intrusive when I needed my own space, forthright when I needed to hide. He was also tall, balding and wore a blue, too-tight, three-piece suit with no hint of the fashionable flare. I liked flares then.

'I assume you didn't mean to kill the Minister?' he asked me on our first prison meeting, fountain pen in hand.

His use of the word 'Minister' threw me. I pictured a clergyman in a cheap black suit. 'You are referring to my mother?'

'Your mother. Yes.' He frowned. He was mortified that he or rather his chosen barrister had failed to win bail for me, despite me expressly saying that I didn't want it. He kept repeating that the notoriety of the case had been against me. Still was against me. Once an unpleasant warden (as we called them then) flashed me with the front page of the *Daily Express* and a pretty photo of Julie and me. Perhaps Mr Fingal-Twist was warning me of the future. Of the trial. But I was uninterested. I just wanted him to go away.

'I am going to plead guilty to any charge they bring against me,' I told him. 'Manslaughter, do you suppose?' As he looked frustrated, I added, to annoy him, 'Unless you think murder's a better idea.'

He looked down before deciding to ignore my last comment. 'There are, obviously, many categories of manslaughter. But perhaps we should consider diminished responsibility. Were you and the Mi... your mother, close?' He ruminated further. Probably spoke further, before saying hopefully, 'You weren't coping with the late arrival of your monthlies, by any chance?'

I sent him away after that.

Later I met a woman called Rosalee who smothered her mother with two pillows and her body weight, following it up with a hammer blow, but got off on appeal after producing evidence of incapacitating and mind-altering pre-menstrual tension. So Fingal-Twist hadn't been as idiotic as I thought him.

I became the prison hermit, existing on water and small scraps of food which was all that my gullet was prepared to swallow. I had always preferred drinking (alcohol) over food so this was no particular loss to me. I've no idea how long this phase lasted because time had no meaning.

After a while the authorities became worried and a nurse led me out of my cell and put me on her scales. She wrote down the result and patted my shoulder in a concerned way. 'You weigh the same as a ten-year-old child.'

'I've always been light,' I said. 'I won't die.'

'Certainly not, dear.' She was a large peroxide blonde, like something out of an old-fashioned cartoon. She probably weighed four times as much as me.

'It's a pity we can't be averaged out,' I added, spitefully. She didn't understand, unless that was why she sent me to the prison hospital.

'You are severely malnourished,' the nurse there admonished me. I thought of all the suffragettes who went on hunger strike and were tortured by force-feeding in this very prison. 'I won't be force-fed,' I announced. 'I am neither a pig nor a suffragette.' This was more words than I had spoken to anyone since I arrived, and I suddenly felt sickened by the whole charade. What did anyone care whether I lived or died? Not me, for sure. Then I thought of Millie, took pity, and substituted a coarse gown for my clothes – we wore our own – and climbed into a bed as commanded. Since there were no other guests, it was little different from my cell. Just bigger and colder. At night mice came out of the floor and played about the iron wheels of my bed. I saved crumbs for them inside my pillowcase. They were very well-behaved mice and never appeared in daylight.

Like so much in prison, the hospital's attempt to fatten me up turned out to be a random event with no follow-through, so that after four days lying about and drinking cups of tea with milk and sugar – I wasn't actually starving myself – they let me out.

My new cell was on the second floor instead of the ground and I could see a squeezed rag of sky through the window. After I'd been inside for three months, Millie, ever literary, brought me a copy of Oscar Wilde's *De Profundis*, written in jail. '*Outside the day may be blue and gold, but the light that creeps down through the thickly-muffled glass of the small ironed-barred window beneath which one sits is grey and niggard. It is always twilight in one's cell, as it is always midnight in one's heart.*' It was the only book I read for months.

I was possibly wrong about the hospital incident having no follow-up because the day after I returned to the wing, a priest turned up outside my cell. My door was ajar so I could see him standing there, small and neat in his black garb.

He said, 'Father Louis here,' in a hopeful voice.

I said nothing, my normal policy when unwanted people appeared in my eye-line. After the first weeks, I found it too claustrophobic to keep my door closed all the time.

'On the form it says you're Catholic.'

I still said nothing and after a while, he went away. A week later he was back again. 'Father Louis here. May I sit with you for a few moments?'

Why did I let him? Perhaps Millie had prayed extra hard that day.

We both sat on my bed. 'I am not a believer. I am a sinner.'

'So you believe in sin?' Father Louis looked like a humble man but he was actually tough and wily in the cause of his leader – God, that is. 'If you believe in sin, then you believe in virtue. Which probably means that you believe in good and evil which begins to total up to a fair amount of belief.'

'Are you Irish?' The lilt in his voice reminded me of Brendan.

'I was born in Thames Ditton. A London suburb. I don't expect you've ever been to Thames Ditton but it has a large Catholic population and more than one beautiful church. I was one of six sons and two of us are priests. Our mother says we're too small to become bishops because the hat would cover half our bodies. She is very small herself so she takes the blame.'

He really did talk like this while I remained completely silent. If he thought his family stories would elicit mine, he was wrong. At the end of ten or fifteen minutes, he looked at his watch and said, 'I'll see you next week. Thank you for letting me visit.'

I understood that I been tricked. Now I was on his list. Sure enough, the following week, there he was, 'Father Louis here,' as humble as ever but now I saw through it. Yet I let him in.

This time he talked about the rebuilding of the church hall which his parish was undertaking 'at considerable expense'. 'It is a Community Hall,' he said, pronouncing the words with a kind of reverence, 'where the mothers and babies can chat to each other outside of their homes. My elder sisters, Carmel and Theresa, taught me the value of conversation. The church is called Our Lady of Lourdes.'

I wondered if his one-sided conversation would have passed his sisters' quality control system and must have smiled to myself because Father Louis said, almost shouted, 'That's better!' And before I could stop him was making the sign of the cross over my head. He bolted away immediately, as if aware he'd gone too far.

A smile, however momentary, however superficial, has a very powerful effect on the giver. After Father Louis had gone, I was aware something had shifted, a very slight shift, one membrane less in the miasma that I had encouraged to grow round me.

When Millie came, I said, 'Did Di's American fiancé ever get in touch again?'

She was astounded and burst into tears. As I said, we hardly talked and certainly not about anything important. After a while she controlled her tears.

'Oh, Cleo, I didn't think you could bear it but Brad has come back with Di's body. At last. So long to wait. There is to be a funeral here. He doesn't mind it being Catholic, although he's Episcopalian, if he's anything, which is American Anglican.'

Too much information. I stopped listening. I thought of the world out there and found it impossible to believe that it had once been my world. I had no idea how long it had been since Di's death. It could have been years. Millie realised I wasn't listening and began to cry again. I suppose we were both having breakdowns in different ways. I took her hand and we sat in silence until she left.

Next week Father Louis appeared as usual, *d'habitude*, as the French would say. His sitting on the bed and talking had become as much a habit for me as not eating the cereal or avoiding the dirty and broken shower, as not talking to anyone on my wing, even the girl called Violet who was bullied by everyone because she had a harelip – you could call it that then – and whom I felt sorry for, and imagined her light blue eyes hid a surprising intelligence.

'Father Louis here.' He came and we sat on my bed and I, *d'habitude,* looked down at my slippers. They were really ugly, green felt with a rim of evil pink 'fur'. We wore our own clothes in prison but they all came back from the wash looking the same – with a hard, matted texture and colours merging into mud. My slippers, although ugly, had a certain amount of character. Millie had brought them and the sniffer dogs had sniffed them. They were prison slippers. I looked at them to avoid looking at Father Louis.

I waited for him to talk. But instead he cleared his throat. I said nothing. He cleared his throat again and frowned. 'I met your sister as I came in.'

Foolishly, I imagined Di, a ghost visible to a man of the cloth. I pictured her in camouflage, as I'd seen reporters wear in Vietnam on television. I saw her square, forthright face and only just stopped myself asking, 'How is she?'

After a moment or two, I remembered Millie's visit earlier that afternoon. I said nothing. Father Louis's face was less humble than usual. I could tell at once he had something to say, apart from his usual ice-breaking chatter.

'She said that she had meant to say something to you but had lost her nerve.'

'Poor Millie.' Father Louis cheered as I said that. A fellow resident on the wing was peering in curiously, a large girl whose proportions made her dangerous to others when she was in a bad mood. She had never bothered me before or, if she had, I hadn't noticed. I got up and pushed the door half-shut. Priests can feel claustrophobic like anyone else, although I suppose their training in the confessional boxes must be a help.

'I fear the news will be a shock.'

'Go on.' I sat with my hands in my lap. I didn't expect a shock from Father Louis. 'Is it to do with my sister's funeral? My other sister. Will I be allowed to go?' It was the first time I'd ever asked him a question, let alone two, and he seemed cheered again, although only momentarily.

'No,' he said. I decided not to ask which question he had answered. There was a long pause during which I assumed he was praying. I went back to silent mode and once more studied my prison slippers. They looked no better. Eventually he plunged on, with a guilty kind of recklessness, definitely not usual. 'Have you thought about your mother's funeral?'

'No,' I said, deadpan. (I am not making a joke but it's amazing how difficult it is to avoid the word 'dead', although 'deadpan' is really very odd. What is alive about a pan that it should become dead?) 'I will not be going to her funeral.' There was a heavy pause and I longed to return to Father Louis's chatter.

'No. Prison is unwilling to relinquish its inmates.'

'Particularly if they don't want to be relinquished.' I could see he'd lost his nerve too but I was unwary; immune, I was sure to any other news.

He gathered strength after another bowed-head session. 'Your father is in England, with his wife. He read about your mother's death in Australia where they live and has travelled here in order to attend her funeral. He would like to see you.'

I wrestled with the demons hiding in this news. It was not fair that I should be told about these two funerals on the same day, once again linking Di and Julie. I wanted to stay silent. I wanted to shout. I stayed silent, then I shouted, 'Doesn't my so-called father want to go to Di's funeral? Di loved him more than anyone! He didn't care a hoot for my mother. Surely you mean my sister's funeral?'

Father Louis's face became pink as I shouted, more pink than *d'habitude.* It struck me that he didn't know about Di's death. I never spoke to him and nobody else would have told him. He could have read it in the papers, but I suspect he was more attuned to his breviary or maybe the *Catholic Herald*. I was filled with anger but I kept totally still like an animal in the headlights. I would not reveal anything more than those few furious sentences.

He looked at his watch. He had a lot of women on his rota. I was one of many and my allotted time was up. He stood.

'You don't have to say anything to me. I'm just the messenger for your sister.' His heightened colour had subsided.

'Okay.' I watched him walk out of the door and realised that he brought disturbances and decisions and all the things I couldn't deal with. I should never have let him in. At least he hadn't tried to bless me.

Spring had come and my square of sky brightened. Everything was conspiring against my self-willed entombment. I envied enclosed orders of nuns who only leave their cells to go to church but then I remembered that bells summoned them throughout the day and they would be living in a community, jostled perhaps by other nuns as annoying as my wing neighbours. Perhaps it was time to glance outwards. I wiped my window with a damp cloth and caught a glimpse of blue.

I asked Millie when she next visited, 'Have you seen Brendan?' Millie couldn't come to my cell. We met in the Visits Hall, surrounded by crying children and stressed grannies. There were also friends or sisters who competed by the strangeness of their costumes. This was the sixties after all. My favourite was Finola, a trans in today's terminology, who wore frilly yellow blouses and purple ribbons in her hair and was at least six feet tall. When I saw Grayson Perry in drag, I cried 'Snap!' The spitting image of Finola. And of course there were husbands or boyfriends, not yet called partners, some of whom took their clothing to poppycock extremes, although others wore brown sweaters and held their hands out as if for a pint or a ciggie. There was something for everybody in the Visits Hall.

'Dada and Elena are staying with us.' This was not cruelly meant by Millie. She had forced herself to state a fact that she had decided I should know. Or Eddie had decided. Or Brendan had decided.

I said icily, 'You know he had been sending parcels and letters to us which Julie destroyed.'

I *was* being cruel. I watched her wriggle in pain. Brendan must have told her about it already but she didn't want me to say it out loud. Her 'darling beloved Mummy' couldn't have done such a thing. She pulled herself together and looked at me with pity.

'Dada would like to visit you and introduce you to Elena. Elena is lovely. Oh, Cleo!'

Her wail was lost in all the other wails of the Visits Hall. How could I have existed outside prison! It gave me just the right context. It put my suffering, such as seeped through the numbness, into a world of pain and despair. I could join the crowd and walk the same grim corridors and obey the same pointless rules. '*I was merely the figure and the letter of a little cell in a long gallery. One of a thousand lifeless numbers, as of a thousand lifeless lives.*' Oscar Wilde again.

'I am so sorry for you, Cleo.' Millie's grief for me did her credit and I knew there was no point trying to explain how I felt. She saw my extreme thinness – I still ate very little – and assumed it equated with her sort of misery. We sat quietly for a while and it struck me that I, who had always believed words the most important part of my life, now found my principal consolation in silence. Even the silence of the prison, which was exceptionally noisy, felt like silence when no words were directed at me and I didn't speak. I had not written a word since I was brought in, the longest time without the written word since I was three.

There were only ten minutes left of the visit when Millie roused herself perhaps from prayer, and said, 'Brad brought Di's bag back. The one she had when she went to...' She hesitated '...to Hue.'

I sat up. My eyes pleaded. For silence? For explanation?

Millie stared down at her lap, at her flowered skirt which covered her knees. Millie was one of the few women who didn't wear a mini-dress. 'I was expecting, I don't know what, something we could treasure.' She paused.

'What was there?'

'A vest, a pair of pants and a pair of socks. Soap. Lavatory paper. Tampax.'

Of course I laughed, the sound quite horrific. Millie was right to cry. I would have cried if I could. What an epitaph! Vest, pants, socks, soap, lavatory paper and Tampax. In an effort to stop her tears and seeing visitors were already being mustered – 'Time, ladies, please!' – I grabbed her hand and whispered.

'Please tell Brad I'd like him to visit me.' I thought, poor Brad, how can he want such a thing, but it worked, and Millie stopped crying.

I believed at that time that Millie was the most remarkable of all of us: of Julie the grammar-school girl who made it to be minister; of Di, the war reporter who wanted to be a soldier; of myself, the drunken best-selling novelist who became a matricide. Millie looked for the good in everyone, starting with Julie, which was definitely a losing wicket and whose utter disregard for her eldest daughter's feelings could have ruined the life of a lesser person. Brendan's disappearance never stirred her presumption of his innocence, nor Di's lack of interest in Millie her belief in the sisterhood. Then came the big test with her youngest sister – to whom she'd given nothing but love – killing the recipient of her deepest love. Not for one moment did she falter. Not a word of reproach was directed towards me. She believed in love as the overriding force and nothing could ever convince her otherwise. Her closeness to the Church only made her more convinced of the rightness of her path. That was how it seemed then. And in an odd way, it always will be. *Is now and ever shall be.*

MILLIE

The worst moment of those terrible months was when I realised that a constant tension inside me had released and, because I am in the habit of examining my conscience, I identified this as being due to my mother's death. The pain of loving her so much and receiving so little in return had resulted in an almost physical pain which held me vice-like. I was over three decades old, married, with a beloved child of my own, and in all that time I'd felt a searing sense of my inadequacy in her eyes. Of course I had not wanted her to die. I had wanted her to live and love me but once she was dead, I was free. How terrible is that!

I tried to explain it in the confessional but the priest could not understand what I was getting at.

'You did not wish for her death, my child?'

'No, father.'

'You did not pray for her death?'

'No, father.'

'You did not kill her.' This sentence had no question mark after it. Of course, I would not have killed my mother.

'I'm glad she's dead!' I cried out and he heard my pain, my need for absolution.

'Pray for your mother's soul, my child, and say five Hail Marys that God may see fit to release you from your suffering.' He was a good old Irish priest and didn't try to understand women. I chose him from among the priests at the church because I knew he wouldn't have read about Mummy's death in the papers.

I left, comforted. Priests cannot share all our secrets.

By now I had been seeing Dada and Elena regularly. At first they stayed with us, before renting a small flat nearby so Dada could see Caly every day and often pick her up from school. They were hanging on in England until both funerals and the trial were over. Elena, an Italian, resident in Australia and previously resident in the USA, set off for the tourist sights every morning. Sometimes she and Dada took a train together out to Oxford or Salisbury Cathedral or Stratford-upon-Avon, but often she went on her own.

'You're so adventurous,' I told her once when she'd dropped round and found me drinking coffee after taking Calypso to school. 'You make me feel feeble.'

'Come with me then. The sun's shining and I'm taking a boat down the Thames.'

I first dared to look at her on that boat. It was called the *Runnymede* and made us laugh because the decks were black with grime.

'It's a coal tender for sure,' Elena said. She must have been over fifty but she seemed younger with her thick, creamy skin, strong features and dark hair. Somehow the greying streaks made her exotic instead of old.

We were passing under London Bridge when she said, 'Do you blame me for taking away your father?' That was the other thing, she was very direct, very un-English.

'I was quite old when he left.' I realised I couldn't even remember whether he left before or after my marriage. We sat side by side in a cool breeze with a cool sun. The waters passed beneath us in a dark rush and I thought of Lethe, the river that flowed through the Underworld, *The last lost vestiges of the sins of the saved.* I hoped Mummy was nowhere near such horrors. I listened to Elena as she continued.

'He wanted to come to me earlier but I said, "No, no. What about your children?" I couldn't refuse when he came again. I could see his unhappiness. But perhaps none of this would happen if he'd stayed. I ask that to myself often. Often.' She had a way of repeating words. As she stared at me with big dark eyes, I saw now that there were lines on her face, not spiders' webs as on English skin, but deep and quite straight. Creases. I couldn't think how I had missed them before.

'Mummy found it difficult to love anybody.'

'Ah!'

'Mummy had an exceptional career. She helped so very many people. She did much good in the world. Politics was her life. The Labour Party was her life. Her family.' This obvious truth had never been so clear to me.

'She should not marry. She should not have children. Not children.'

I had nothing to say. I could hardly wish myself away. 'I was born in 1938 and then the war came so she had two more. Women did in the war. If their husbands were around or came back from wherever they were. Strange, I suppose.'

'The war show Brendan another way.'

'You mean he met you.'

She looked proud suddenly, shaking her head a little so her thick hair swayed forward, hiding the creases in her face. 'I sent him home to you. I have told you.'

'I don't believe he was ever really with us.' I had not thought this before and it gave me pain, not for myself but because I imagined that Mummy must have been aware of it. I wanted to say how pretty she had been. How dazzling!

'I wrote to him once a year. Just once.'

I was on Mummy's side now so I said firmly, 'Once was enough.'

We were interrupted by an announcement from an ancient man with a strong Scottish accent who appeared on the deck with a loud hailer: 'We will shortly terminate at Tower Bridge where optional disembarkation will take place. The return journey will take place in fifteen minutes. You are liable for a further payment if you remain on board. Disembarkation on the return journey will take place at

Westminster Pier with easy access to the House of Commons.'

Easy access to the House of Commons, whenever had I heard that? Never for me. I was switching back again, yet ashamed to reproach Mummy in death.

We stood together at the rail and stared admiringly at the Tower of London. The top turrets were not yet gilded as they are now, so it looked more historic, less Disneyland. Not far away there was huge demolition and construction work at an inland dock. The noise was terrific, throwing up vast waves of brick dust as walls crashed to the ground.

'I think that's St Katherine's Docks,' I told Elena. 'Once there were great Victorian warehouses and before that medieval slums, but they were bombed in the war. I don't know what the plans are for it now.'

'Italy was not much bombed,' commented Elena. 'You could thank Mussolini for it but I do not. No. Since the war, I choose to live in two countries where there was no bombing, no bombing: America and Australia.'

I realised that I didn't want to know about her life before Dada or indeed her life with Dada.

Nobody got off at the Tower and nobody got on so we were soon heading upriver again, this time the wind in our faces. We went to the back of the boat and sheltered behind the cabin. I had brought a book of Marvell's poetry which I took out and began to read. Elena closed her eyes.

When the Houses of Parliament were in sight, she opened them and said, 'Brendan is very nervous about visiting Cleo. Is she so fierce?'

'Murderers tend to be, you know.' I stopped abruptly, horrified at myself. 'Sorry. It has all been a strain. So sorry.' I took a breath. 'Cleo is most like Mummy. But she's never had her confidence. Very talented but she doesn't rate her success as a novelist.'

She looked at me intently with her dark eyes. 'Of course the death was an accident?'

'Of course.' Why did she think Cleo was in prison? Elena was another strong woman. This is what she had wanted to ask all along. It's what everyone wanted to ask. I considered. Why should I not be honest? 'Cleo hated Mummy. They avoided each other. When they met, they were at war. She did not plan to kill her.'

I put my book of Marvell poems in my pocket. Shakespeare is much sharper than Marvell about the wildness of human love.

She stared at me without speaking so I carried on. 'Earlier, you asked me if I blamed you for taking away Dada. No, I never thought of blaming you. I didn't blame Dada either. I didn't understand enough then. Now I understand more but I still don't blame you. Only God can pass judgement.'

CLEO

I pleaded sickness twice before I deigned to see Brad.

I can't describe him because I couldn't look at him. He just seemed very American and very distressed, quite unnoticing of the Visits Hall madness and, now I come to think of it, he looked at me no more than I looked at him. We might as well have had glass and bars between us like some US penitentiaries. Like a soldier, he had come with a message, and like a soldier he delivered it,

'Di's funeral is tomorrow.' I pictured soldiers raising their guns and firing a salute over her grave. She would have liked that. He continued, his voice so absolutely American in this pit of Englishness that I began to listen to the cadences instead of the words. But I couldn't avoid the message. 'We don't know if you would have got permission to attend it but we decided, I decided,' he glanced at me then, 'not to ask because the publicity around you would have made it a media circus instead of a dignified conclusion for your very special sister. I am truly sorry.'

He looked sorry. Maybe truly sorry but truly firm too and, of course I saw his point. It was the Julie factor again, the non-pacifist, bloody buddha. I should stop making feeble jokes about that innocent effigy; it is rude and unworthy of me, although, because I am unworthy, looked at another way, it is absolutely worthy of me.

Finally I stared at Brad and concluded he was the most clean-shaven man I'd ever met. I imagined Di running her fingers down his smooth face, golden brown as if he'd been in the sun a lot, and realising here was the man for her. I imagined them making love. She had sex with all sorts of men but something must have told her Brad was special.

I heard tears in my voice. 'I am sorry. I loved Di.'

'She loved you. She wrote to you.' He hesitated, as if he wanted to ask me something. 'You were the only one she wrote to.'

I saw a gleam of hope on his face. 'Would you like her letters?' It was all I could offer and I did so willingly. He sighed. Oh he was a nice man! It's quite possible he would never have asked for them. 'Millie will help you search. In my flat. Please stay there, if you want.'

It felt odd imagining what someone else might want. Exhausting. I slumped back in my chair and hoped he'd go. I put my hand over my eyes.

'Thank you. I'll get us tea.' He was a man of action, not words.

He put the cups on the table, so that the handle faced my fingers. 'You gave Di's bag to Millie.' I thought about the sad contents. Not much of a swap for my letters.

'Yes. I did that.' I noticed the expression on his face changing. Then he felt in an inner pocket and laid something on the table. 'There was this too. I'm sorry. I just wanted something of hers.'

It was a man's hairbrush. He pushed it towards me. I recognised it across the decades, the brush made by the Italian Partisans for Brendan. I pushed it back. 'I'm glad you've got it. Really, her name should be on it too.'

'Yes. You're right.' I can't remember what else he said. Maybe he talked about Vietnam, told me he was staying in the army. Maybe he talked about Di's bravery. But he knew he didn't have to say that to me so perhaps we just drank our tea. I think he called Di 'driven'.

☙❧

Not many days after Brad's visit, Brendan himself came to the prison. My post killing numbness, my hermit's protection, was wearing even thinner. I still wasn't eating much but smoked heavily instead. I began to gnaw at my nails, not worrying if I tore the quick. I could feel little pimples on my face. Luckily there wasn't a mirror in the cell.

Poor Brendan! He literally didn't recognise me when he came

into the Visits Hall. I had no problem looking at him, a big man, fairer than I remembered, sunburnt skin, a bit hunched, an echo of someone I'd once known; maybe it was my childhood Dada as he'd come back from the war.

'Hi!' I waved at him. His face wrinkled with misery, aged years in a few seconds.

'Oh, Cleo!' Did his shocked response to my appearance mean he loved me? Did it matter if he did? He clasped my bitten hand and I was afraid he was going to cry.

'Sit down,' I instructed him.

He sat down, squeezing his thighs uncomfortably under the plastic table. 'I'm sorry.'

'I'm sorry.' We spoke together. It wasn't a bad start really, but somehow pathetic and I wanted to cry too.

'You can buy cups of tea,' I said. 'Over there.' I pointed. I was reminded of Brad. I needed him to go away for a moment or two. He looked like Di. It was two days since Di had been buried. I forced the image away from me.

He came back and slid under the table with more ease. I've often been told that human beings are the most adaptable of creatures and there he was, legs under the table, tea on top of it, me staring with my pale, spotty, possibly accusatory face, although I wasn't planning to accuse him of anything. Who am I to cast the first buddha (still at my silly jokes).

'I bought some biscuits,' he said. I hadn't noticed the biscuits. 'You're much too thin.'

I blinked. How dare he! 'Is that the doctor speaking?'

He smiled. Did he not recognise the caustic tone of my voice?

'I'm sure it is. What do you weigh? Don't they feed you in this place?' He looked round disapprovingly, as if hoping to find someone to blame and shame. His tears had gone back to source.

'It's my choice,' I said. 'The food's disgusting but there's plenty of it.'

'I could have brought in some fruit and cheese.'

'You can't.' I looked at him and saw his eyes were hazel and set wide apart. 'Have you never been in a prison before?

'Why ever would I?'

'How would I know?' How would I know anything about him? I could see he would prefer to go on talking about my weight, perhaps prescribing vitamin C for my immune system and E for skin and eyes and D for bones and teeth. I relented. 'I suppose you want me to tell you what happened? How I killed your ex-wife. I suppose you two did divorce, even if you never told us.'

'No, although thanks for the offer.' We were eye to eye now. 'You were drunk, you threw a heavy object which happened to hit your mother a glancing blow, instead of the wall. Eddie says his friend the solicitor says you shouldn't be convicted and even if you are, you won't have to serve more than a year as you've already been in prison for months. It is unfortunate that the foolish judge did not allow you bail. I am afraid it was Julie's post-mortem stab at retaliation. But I must not talk ill of the dead. If you want to know, I do blame myself, certainly, for my absence but not as much as you might think. I lived a miserable existence without Elena for all those years and I did it for you lot.' He stopped abruptly.

I was surprised that he had bothered to tell me this. To be honest, I was moved. Not hugely but more than if a stranger had told me his story. But I said, almost jokily, 'And look how we've repaid you...' My voice tailed away. 'Look how *I've* repaid you.' I suspected we were both thinking of Di but I was still not ready for her. 'On the other hand, Millie is brave. She should have been called Grace or Charity or Virtue or Angel.' I was determined to carry us further from Di. 'And now there's Calypso for you and your wife to admire. I assume she is your wife.'

'Did Julie tell you nothing?'

'I tried not to talk to her and she returned the compliment. No, she told me nothing.' I hesitated. 'But, you're quite right, I didn't plan to kill her.'

We were silent then. Out of puff. We'd never talked so much all the time I was growing up. I felt Di still hovering over us. Did I blame him for Di? Di was underground now.

He leant forward so our heads were close. 'We don't have to talk about everything this afternoon. I shall come again,' he put his hand out to me, 'if I may.'

I said nothing but once again I let him take my hand. He stood up. I noticed that the bullied Violet, with her provocative harelip, was at the next table with a large grey-faced mother whose fat fingers lay like slugs on the table. No harelip, however.

'I did want to keep in touch.' Brendan stood over me. 'I sent letters, parcels.'

'I know.' There seemed no point in describing how that information had played its part in Julie's death. I might have had 'anger management problems', but I didn't go in for cruelty, not with important things, anyway. Not intentionally. Manslaughter. Unintentional. Womanslaughter, actually. I'd never have killed my mother if she'd been a man.

He sat down again. 'I am so very sorry you could not be at your sister's funeral.'

If there'd been a missile at hand, copper saucepan, a concrete block, perhaps I'd have thrown it at him. But that's the thing about prisons, they protect you from yourself and others from you. It's the system. There was an argument for keeping me in HMP Holloway forever.

'You're angry.'

I'd forgotten his hazel eyes. Like brackish puddles with black pebbles at the bottom. 'Yes.' I put my hand over my eyes and mumbled something about how much I admired Di, how I read her pieces about Vietnam – had he read them? – if not, he should. How she told me what it meant to her to be part of something important, how my death wouldn't have mattered, didn't matter, bring on the Death Penalty (it had only just been abolished, incidentally), but Di's death did matter and I ended by saying, with my eyes on those brackish puddles, 'You know how much she admired you and yet you left her.'

Brendan was silent for such a long time that I came out of my reverie and looked at the clock on the wall. There were only five minutes left of visiting time. Already disreputable huggings and undercover fumblings had begun. 'Stand apart on table five!' commanded a warden from the desk. Since she was too lazy to walk round the room, nobody took much notice.

'You'll have to go soon,' I told the eternally silent Brendan.

'I can't answer you,' said Brendan slowly and deliberately as if he was daring the session to end. 'But I hope that I helped Di to do what she wanted with her life, not sent her to her death. I'll blame the Viet Cong and the NVA for that. She chose to go to war. To that war.'

Everybody was going now, chased out like rebellious sheep, but Brendan sat like a rock.

'You have to go now.' A warden stood over him, swishing her metaphorical cane.

'Yes.' He stood up and straightened his shoulders. He leant towards me. 'You'll be all right,' he said, 'You're tough. Just don't try and lay blame.' He held my hand, then left quickly as I was hustled away.

I thought of his words as I tried to get to sleep that night – a fiendish paranoid-delusional slob was playing 'Love me, Love me tender' over and over again – at top volume naturally. Then I remembered Di and that insane saying *If darkness comes at noon then midday brings the dawn* and I felt a little consoled.

Julie deserved to die, even if I hadn't meant to kill her. Well, perhaps death was a bit extreme but I *did* blame her. Only Millie never blamed anyone. Or so I thought.

The next day I carried on the conversation with Father Louis. We sat as usual side by side on my bed. He no longer rattled on because, of course, I'd begun to speak.

'Would you say blame is part of discerning the difference between good and evil?' I spoke provocatively, puffing on my cigarette so he became hazed in a pall of smoke.

'No, I wouldn't.'

I quite liked that and watched approvingly as he batted the smoke away. 'Surely I must be blamed for swigging back the alcohol like there's no tomorrow – there wasn't one for Julie - losing my temper, and killing my mother?'

'Certainly that is what you did, my poor child.'

'Don't poor child me.' Actually, I wasn't angry at that moment and respected the little priest at my side, so I bowed my head. 'Sorry, I shouldn't be rude.'

'I don't blame you for it.'

That made me smile, then laugh. Father Louis smiled too. 'I suppose I find blame unhelpful. I prefer understanding.'

'But if no one ever got blamed, how would we fill our prisons?'

'Ah, you're talking about punishment now.'

We went on like this for some time, a kind of sparring which we both knew served as a substitute for my taking responsibility for what I'd done. On this occasion it ended when Louis – I was beginning to drop the 'Father' – said in his most cajoling voice, 'I went to your sister's funeral you know. Very beautiful it was. A very beautiful service.'

I was immediately on my guard. 'Di didn't believe in God or Jesus or Mary.'

'Did she not. Is that so.' There were no question marks. He always became more Irish when he felt his faith under attack. 'It was in a lovely church, where your eldest sister got married, I believe.'

I stood up, puffing out smoke like a cross dragon, walking up and down. Why should he be at my sister's funeral when I couldn't? Did I have to have her rites of passage filtered through his narrow mind? Religiously narrowed mind?

Louis looked up at me mildly. 'I was sad you couldn't go. So I went for you. I con-celebrated the Mass.'

'What?'

'I joined the parish priest on the altar and we said the Mass together. I was honoured.' He looked at me enquiringly but without nervousness.

'I see.' I sat down again.

'Millicent invited me. Afterwards I went with her family and Diana's fiancé to the crematorium. That is always a painful moment.'

'Crematorium!' Where was the grave with the soldiers pointing their guns to the sky? 'They're called Millie and Di.'

'Mr Wolfe wanted to take her ashes to America.'

This is the worst thing about prison. Any news comes to you from outside, second hand, relayed by anyone who has the time and the kindness to visit you. You are set apart, non-active, a non-participant, a receiver, not a giver. When I wished to be disconnected from the world, more wicked because of me, this made no difference to my life. But then, in that moment, while I listened to Louis's telling of the end of Di's story, I was acutely aware of my passive role. The choice seemed to be one long scream of rebellion or to learn patience. I had always despised patience.

'Thank you for going to my sister's funeral,' I said, as Louis stood, preparing to move on to his next suffering soul.

He gave me his innocent stare which meant, as I'd learnt, 'Shall we pray together?'

'Not today, Father.'

Later that same day when I was lying on my bed filled with self-pity, Sherril, the fat bleach-blonde nurse, filled the space.

'You've got to have a supplementary diet,' she said, quite nicely, considering the extra work. 'And vitamins. Doctors' orders.'

I sat up. 'What doctor?' I knew it must be Brendan making a fuss and the warm feeling that accompanied this thought surprised me.

'That would be telling.' Suddenly I was special so perhaps she enjoyed that. Most of prison life is a series of repetitions. 'You're probably being fattened up for your trial.'

I had not thought much about the trial. When Roddy Fingal-Twist came, I passed the time with an interior monologue on his fashion failures (too-short trousers, too-long waistcoat, too-prominent cufflinks). Sherril must have known something because the following morning he appeared (suddenly nothing but visitors), this time sporting a red flannel waistcoat and red carnation in his button-hole which occupied my thoughts through his first sentence. By the time I returned from describing him to myself as 'Roddy Red-Breast' and 'Carmen Miranda', I'd missed his first sentence. Eventually I realised it had contained the date of my trial. It seemed that no one had taken seriously my guilty pleas: I would be charged with murder by the Crown Prosecution, and the Defence – I had not yet met my barrister – would make sure this was reduced to Manslaughter. I know I should have listened and understood but there was not a will and there was not a way. The date set was July 14th.

I told myself that I was pleased to have more time in prison.

CALY

Once a week Mummy went out to 'a Shakespeare matinée'. So she said. I was too young to know about Shakespeare or about a 'matinée'. They were long, interesting words that came with a long, sad face that suggested questions would receive no answers.

After school on those days, I went next door and played with Mary and baby Xavier. I enjoyed that part. We ate spaghetti or baked beans or boiled eggs, followed by rice pudding with Mars-bar sauce but at the back of my mind was Mummy's face and the funny, slow way she moved on the Shakespeare matinée days.

Of course she hugged me when she came to pick me up but she felt like a stranger. By the time we got back to our house, things were a bit better. Once, or perhaps more than once, she ran my bath, and threw in a handful of pink bath salts saying, 'Here you are my darling! A special treat so you smell like a film star!'

Another day, she took my dirty clothes and put them in the fridge. I found them there in the morning when I went to get the milk out. 'Mummy,' I shrieked and began to laugh, 'Just look what *you've* done!'

But she didn't even smile. 'How stupid!' she said, looking as if she might cry.

'I love you, Mummy!' I said and hugged her until she put her arms round me and gave me a proper hug back. Daddy had gone to work early, as usual.

As time passed I stopped noticing the difficult days so they weren't difficult any more, just different, and I always enjoyed going next door where baby Xavier was soon displaced by baby Francis.

Nobody ever said the words Aunt Cleo and prison in one sentence. Or the words at all, if it comes to that.

CLEO

A new boss-woman called Charlie came onto my wing who entertained herself with the scandal and gossip of others. She was a tall, scrawny women with needle marks up her arms and legs, but that didn't hinder her terrorising skills. Her main source of information was *The Sun*, supplemented by titbits from friends of hers among the staff – she seemed to have haunted Holloway since she was eighteen and knew everyone. Before the memorial, I had believed her antics were quite harmless. Calling me 'Belsen' was her unimaginative idea of fun. Quite probably, she didn't even know about the real Belsen.

I was lying on my bed when she came into my cell one afternoon waving her filthy paper. 'I knew you wouldn't want to miss your Ma's memorial.'

I closed my eyes.

'Fucking killed your fucking ma, didn't you Belsen! With a heavy object! Wouldn't think you had the strength. Must have been a teeny-weeny heavy object. *'Julie Flynn, valued member of the Cabinet who was killed by her daughter...'* she began to read. I blocked my ears, psychologically speaking. There was absolutely no point in trying to stop her. She didn't find reading easy so she'd give up soon. But I'd underrated her determination in pursuit of entertainment, for she summoned one of her slave girls whose education had progressed beyond primary school.

'Go on, Suze, give her the whole works. Can't let dear old Belsen miss out on her Mum's big day.'

Poor Sue, I watched her bent over the paper and thought, as she struggled obediently, that she was suffering more than me. Then I considered the movement for solidarity among women, growing apace in the late sixties, and decided there was not much evidence of it in prison. The women were bossy, selfish, high-handed and bullying unless they were weak, demented and cowardly. More of the latter. They were all stupid. Then I guessed what they would say about me: stuck-up, stand-offish and selfish; all things told, a bit of a nutter. I suppose they were right.

Sue was still stumbling along to giant cackles from Charlie and her acolytes gathered behind them, so I closed my eyes and reflected. Julie had been a feminist, in a direct line from Sylvia Pankhurst, so would I rather have been born to Ms Pankhurst? I tried to remember what I knew about her. A decade ago at my good girls' school, I had written a paper about her which had won an A*. Sylvia was daughter to Emmeline Pankhurst – who was just as famous – and sister to Christabel, all of them suffragettes of course. Sylvia visited this very prison here where I now lay, eight times. Perhaps my cell had been hers. But, making my earlier point about lack of female solidarity, they fell out dramatically during the First World War when Sylvia became a pacifist and her mother and sister supported the war. Moreover, Emmeline refused to talk to Sylvia ever again when she wouldn't marry the father of her child (a son). In short, they were a thoroughly dysfunctional set of female relatives, although, it has to be admitted, none of them resorted to murder. Instead, Sylvia went off to Ethiopia where she did good works and was eventually given a full state funeral by Emperor Haile Selassie.

Dredging my memory for all this drama blotted out most of Julie's memorial, although the few words that sneaked through, 'Prime Minister' and 'Representative of the Queen', made me realise that she could be proud of her send-off, even if the Head of State herself hadn't turned up in person as Haile Selassie did for Sylvia Pankhurst, pronouncing her 'an honorary Ethiopian'.

I was beginning to run out of Pankhurst A* material, when the smell of sausages and cabbage drew away my tormentors. Since I scarcely ate, this was a peaceful time of the day, good for avoiding the slings and arrows, but, when I went to close my door, I found *The Sun* (it should be called *The Fog*) discarded on my floor. There she was, Mother Julie, staring up with her red curls, her quick, bright eyes, her pretty smile and, quite against everything I thought I thought, I began to cry.

It is possible they were tears for myself, my own sad state, but the truth is they were not, they were tears for my mother who I had, single-handedly, cast into outer darkness when she was still quite young enough to enjoy more health and happiness and help more people in the world. '*Loved by her constituents...*' the words sprang out at me. She had been loved by others but not given love to her children, nor apparently wanted it from us. No wonder I cried!

And as I cried, I wondered why she had behaved as she did. What had gone wrong? I realised that with all my hatred I had never tried to understand her; I had just wanted her to understand me. And now I had made that impossible.

MILLIE

I often wondered fearfully how the horrors of those months in 1968 might affect Calypso. Of course I didn't take her to either funeral, or to the very public memorial, and she was too young to understand about the trial; at least I trust she was. We never told her where Aunt Cleo had gone, except to say she was 'on holiday' or 'at work' and she soon stopped asking. But I was in a state of shock all that time.

Motherhood is a selfish state, the love so intense, that nothing else matters if one feels the loved one under threat. Although I was as kind as I could be to Cleo – visiting the prison at least once a week which was itself a misery of sympathy and regret – my heart was tortured by worry over Calypso.

It is well recognised now that children understand far more about any situation than grown-ups want to believe. Back then, it was assumed that if children weren't told something, they wouldn't know it – a composite of wishful thinking, laziness and arrogance. But I could remember how I felt as a child, the slights I endured from Mummy which never diminished my adoration. I was like a spurned lover, the more cruelly used, the louder I cried for more. So I *could* imagine how Caly's four-year-old mind saw my panics and tried to understand them, leaving aside the simple fact that her grandma and her aunt had abruptly dropped from her life. Di she hardly knew but, still, another ghostly spectre. I used to think it might have been helpful if she could have visited Cleo in prison, but Cleo would never allow it. To begin with she was half deranged, I can see that now. Then later she wanted to protect Caly. Protect? Or shut out?

The person I shut out from my closest self was Eddie. We had always made love with passion and understanding. Our bodies seemed made for each other, his so straight and dark and strong. When his fingers stroked my thighs or pulsed my breasts until they ached for his mouth, I would cry out 'Oh! Oh! Oh!' I only had to kiss his face or lower my mouth to his chest and stomach and he would already be longing to take me.

Our bodies had brought us together at the beginning and kept us together as we discovered our differences and strived to make adjustments to each other's needs. I doubt I'd have left my job (which he'd always wanted) if I didn't have the warmth and excitement of our lovemaking. My pregnancy seemed a wonderful outcome and when no more pregnancies followed, I knew at night time, in the dark (we were traditional in that way as well), my body would still open joyfully to his.

I wonder if this seems childish now or I sound subservient to Ed. But it never felt like that. Our marriage seemed perfect and I forgot the very earliest days when I had secretly considered him 'boring'. He could never be boring, he was my husband, father of my child; I was so lucky.

Then came the nightmare year and it was not that I didn't want to escape into Eddie's arms but that I couldn't. I would lie in bed vibrating with the tensions of my thoughts and when he turned to me it felt like an assault. I wanted to curl into a ball and disappear, if I possibly could, into a sleep, a sleep created by pills, but better than never-ending wakefulness. It was unfair, I knew, because he was behaving so well, so nobly, finding the lawyer for Cleo, supporting me in every way. I could feel his hurt but I couldn't do anything to make him understand. I would say feebly, 'Wait. It will get better.' But I recognised that was not enough. Neither of us had the habit, now I would say the gift, of talking about our feelings.

But he saw how I cared for Caly, how I touched her and held her close and he was jealous. I didn't really get it at the time but, even if

I had, I couldn't have done anything about it. Calypso was a child and she had to come first. My body told me that I must look after her and that Ed would survive.

He did. In a way.

CLEO

Shame was a new experience for me. Sam Levy wrote me a note saying he would like to visit and I wrote a note back saying it was not possible. Of course it was possible but I couldn't let him come because I was ashamed of myself. The burden of shame was so heavy that even I, a master of fiction and disguise, couldn't disguise it from myself. Up till then any shame I'd felt had been childish: when I'd written an embarrassing paragraph or when I got so drunk that I insulted someone without even knowing it. Or the shame of marrying Hayden for no greater reason than we were drinking partners and in the same witty-clever-show-off circle.

Sam wrote again, '*I do not sleep at night for worrying about you. You should take pity on an old widower who has asthma, an arrhythmic heart, doubtful hips and shaky legs. Or perhaps you want to hasten my end?*' He may not have said exactly that but a plea along those lines. Once again I said no.

By then I had my sentence. Four years. Perhaps my miserable, skin-and-bones body or my tragic telling of the story of my crime – alcohol-fuelled with the furies bottled up in childhood – even my dear father abandoned me – soothed the jury's need for vengeance and awoke their sympathy. If the judge had told them a different story, I would not have blamed him, I will never blame anyone ever again. No blame. Only shame (so I thought then). But he handed out the four years, recommending a minimum of two if I behaved myself. Quite an average sentence, I was informed, for someone convicted of 'Involuntary Manslaughter'.

I suspect, if I'd thrown that blameless buddha a few decades later, I would have been given much longer. Just think of the fun the bloggers and trolls, plying their miserable trade on Instagrams and Facebooks, would have had with me. How the righteous leftists would have reviled my privileged sinfulness! How the even more righteous rightists would have mocked this misguided daughter of a socialist star!

In 1968 it was only *The Sun* and the *News of the World* who had a go, ubiquitous in prisons but easy to overlook in the world beyond bars; no one I knew would read them. Nor would the big wide world. Di's Brad would not see them in Washington, Sam Levy would not read them in Hampstead.

'*I have had my hernia operated on,*' Sam wrote to me for the third or more time, '*but feel recovered at last. Are you ready for a visit yet?*'

I let him come. It was autumn. Holloway Prison is (or was) in north-east London, an area spoilt by war, poverty, cheaply built housing. The gracious white villas remaining kept themselves to themselves in streets barricaded by one-way systems. I felt sorry for Sam coming down from his golden-leafed heights to the tawdry tackiness of the Visits Hall. In deference to him, I took off my spongy prison slippers and released my hair from its elastic band.

'My dear.' He recognised me with no difficulty. I thought he looked quite perky, considering the bodily woes he had listed, plus the unlisted but operated-on hernia. His hair seemed no greyer, his glasses no thicker, his shoulders no more bowed.

I stood up. 'It is so kind of you to come. Did it take you ages?' I did feel suddenly happy to have him there.

He sat down, looked around, before nodding his head. 'I've seen worse.'

'Where's that?' I asked. I looked round too. I saw the room through his intelligent old man eyes. I saw a druggy woman with her arms round a little boy. The boy wriggled and shouted, 'I wanna biccy, Nan!' At the next table sat a young man in a velvet jacket with his long black hair tied back in a pink ribbon. A pair of twins ran away from their mum crying, 'Mum! Mum!' then ran back to give her a kiss. A pair of lovers, male–female, leant together, noses touching. 'Break up there!' commanded the warden at the desk.

'It's not so bad,' I admitted. 'Just people.'

'What's your cell like?' Sam asked.

'I'm calling it "room" now,' I said. 'Where did you see worse?'

'I am not come to talk about me. What do you do all day? Do you need books? Writing material? Is there a library here? Have you made friends? Or a friend? One friend is enough.'

'I've just moved onto a new wing.' I'd cast myself as the bad girl when I'd forced myself on him, the bad Catholic who drank like a fish, wrote shocking novels and married unsuitable men, the nemesis of Rebekah, his good daughter-in-law, Lennie's wife. *My* Lennie. But it had been a joke in order to entertain. I hadn't been wicked then. Now I was in prison, a convict, where did that leave us?

Sam stopped asking me about books and leant back in his chair. Apparently, he was waiting for me to say more. I tried to oblige. 'There was this king-pin woman who tried to bully me.'

'I don't see you as a victim.'

'No.' I decided not to tell him about the shampoo poured into my tea, the toothbrush rammed down my throat, the heavy feet on my toes, the sudden slaps and pinches. None of it was important. I'd told no one. Just requested a move to another wing. Which happened. We weren't so over-crowded in those days.

'How's Lennie?' Why did I ask? Masochism, I suppose. Masochism had become my friend.

'They have a baby boy called Samuel. Known as Sam.'

'After his doting grandfather.'

Neither of us smiled. In the old days we had talked so much that our words mingled into conjoined sentences. But already we seemed to be at the end of our conversation. I had assumed by Sam's calm manner and reference to having seen worse that he was not at all shocked by my situation, but perhaps I was wrong. Because I had been eating a little more lately, I might have underestimated the physical change he saw in me. Or, worse, he saw me as truly bad.

'There is a library here,' I said, placatingly.

'You go?'

'Not much.' Never, actually. Pause. 'I was always more of a writer than a reader. I wrote from my life and my imagination.'

'So, what do you do all day?'

'Sometimes I have visitors. My father came.'

'Your father!'

Now I had shocked him. I don't think I'd ever mentioned my father. 'He's gone back to Australia now. With his wife.'

'Ah.' I watched him putting this fact to one side. The conversation stalled again.

'So, is Lennie happy with Sam Junior?'

'Oh, yes. But with his job no. He is discontented, he tells me. He sits where you used to sit and begins by saying cheering things to a lonely old man but then his expression darkens and he is sad or cross.'

'Not with you?' I tried to disguise my selfish gladness that Lennie should be discontented.

'No, never. He is a good boy. I find these times are disturbing. You see what goes on in so much of Europe and the world too. Student riots, as they describe them, as if that makes them less important. But they try to improve the world, these people, students or not. They don't want to live under communism or dictatorships. In America, they see the Vietnam War and racial inequality. Lennie thinks about these things. They unsettle him. He wants to help, perhaps go to France. He tries to understand the difference between New Left activists in one country and communists in another. But his wife tells him, "You have a good job, a safe job, you are a married man with a baby, with duties and responsibilities." Sometimes she adds, so he tells me, "And what use were these heroic students when the Jews were being starved and tortured and killed?"'

'Ah. Ah.' Sam sighed and stopped. He looked at his pale fingers and twisted them together.

I was astounded. 'Does Lennie really tell you all this?'

'More. She tells him, "You have spent too long in America. So, which one are you going to sign up for? Anti-capitalism? Anti-imperialism? Anti-racism? Civil rights? Environmentalism? Feminism? Liberalisation? There's plenty for you to pick from!"'

'That must be hard for him.'

Sam didn't raise his head. 'He moves in family circles who are not friendly to his thoughts. With me, he is simply thinking out loud.'

'I am sorry,' I lied. How cruel we become when under the sway of the Jealous God. I wanted Lennie to hate his wife. I wanted them to hate each other. To hell with their baby!

'Yes, Rebekah is a good, strong girl.'

'They will work it out.' I considered what Sam had reported. I had paid no attention to what was going on anywhere but inside my head. I hadn't read a paper since I came to prison. I didn't want to know about the big world outside, the world of 'antis' and 'isms'. It seemed that Rebekah and I agreed about this. I reconsidered New York and what Lennie had been doing there. He had been there a long time. He had spoken to me about playing the piano so I had perceived him as a floppy-haired maestro, but I knew he was a member of Vietnam protest committees. I could have joined them too but, although I went on a march or two, it was more about networking and copy for my writing than belief. Mostly, I made up foolish stories about unimportant people like Dr Timothy Leary. What a charlatan! I should have walked in protest against *him*.

I noted how quietly Sam waited for me to speak. 'Lennie had a beard in New York,' I said, 'and he lived in a horrible room at one end of a defunct factory. Perhaps he was aligning himself with the workers. Or the students anyway.'

Why did I carry on loving Lennie when I knew him so little?

Well, maybe that's the answer: I could never then have loved someone I knew well. Or even someone that loved me.

Sam looked at his watch. I looked at the clock on the wall. Around me people were beginning the frenzied farewell kissing and cuddling. The warden on the stage, unusually energetic, came down and walked among us. Babies and children caught the tension and began to cry. I stood up. It was always better to leave before we prisoners were herded away like a bunch of branded cattle. I would have to stand and wait in the corner but I could wave off my visitor in a gracious hostess way. Should I say, *Please come again*? Of course I should.

'Please come again. If you can face it.'

'May I bring a book next time?' It was a deal he wanted.

'They'll take it away but I might get it later, assuming you haven't hollowed it out and inserted a pistol.'

'I promise not to.'

'Actually I'd rather you brought me a notebook and a pencil. Not a ring-binder because I might uncoil the wire and stab someone with it.'

Sam's visit inspired the penitent murderess, skulking in her dark hermit's cave, to discover a peephole through which she glimpsed the outside world. I understood in a fearful way that the hole could widen until the cave disappeared and I would be out in the light again.

MILLIE

I visited Di's grave in Kensal Green. It was the autumn of 1968. Cleo had been convicted and sentenced since the summer and was now serving her time stoically. I could not help her, although I still visited Holloway regularly. Really, we had nothing to say to each other.

Kensal Green is bounded on one side by the thundering Harrow Road and on the other by the dark and oily waters of the Grand Union Canal, with a view beyond of gasometers and Wormwood Scrubs prison. Maybe you can't quite see the prison, but I felt its presence. A male prison, of course. I had promised myself to walk along the towpath after I'd paid my respects and, as I wended my way through the gravestones, some great and majestic, some crumbling back into the earth, I pictured the canal, just as I had the Thames earlier, as the River Lethe, the most convenient pathway to dusty death.

I told myself that death is the end for everyone and, in Christian teaching, it is filled with light and hope, not at all 'dusty' as poor Macbeth imagined.

I reached Di's grave which was halfway between canal and road, and took from my bag a fine pot of white cyclamen which I stood in the brass holder in front of the white marble. Brad had insisted on paying for everything, the gravestone, the service, the small reception afterwards and the cars to transport us. As we travelled from church to crematorium, he and Eddie had discussed the celebrities which lay at their rest in the cemetery, including writers Wilkie Collins, Anthony Trollope and William Makepeace Thackeray, although they were more impressed by engineers Brunel, Siemens and Babbage.

Brad and I had had many polite discussions about how everything should be arranged. He wanted a cremation so that he could take what he called 'Diana's remains' – surely her spirit remained – back home to America, and I wanted burial, which the Catholics still believed best, although cremation was no longer forbidden. So we had compromised with a Requiem Mass, a cremation and a burial of half her ashes in Kensal Green and the other half transported by Brad to a destination of his choice.

Brad would have been the perfect partner for Di. I truly believed that and it made me sadder than anything. He was strong and sometimes seemed stiff like the soldier he was, but it seemed that his suffering over the Vietnam War – mental suffering, as he had served in a cause he could not believe in – had softened him. I imagined how they would have lived in the house he had bought for them in California, near the beach but with mountains not far away. He described it to me once and we both cried. It was terribly moving to see this nearly middle-aged man crying. They could have climbed and swum and helped the odd people that Di would have collected round her. Maybe Diana, that brave and lonely hunter, would have softened too and even given birth.

I stood for some time at Di's grave – the ground was wet and it felt wrong to sit on her memorial stone: *Remember Di Flynn who gave her life for her beliefs 1940–1968*. Brad's choice of inscription. I, of course, would have had a Shakespearean quote, perhaps Gertrude's remark in *Hamlet: 'Passing from Nature to Eternity'*. I like the simplicity of it. I shall suggest it to Caly as suitable for my own grave.

I stood so long, swathed as I was in a flowing coat, that I began to feel like one of the stone guardian angels who graced many of the older, grander tombs. Half consciously, I watched leaves falling from a turkey oak nearby. They were still mostly green with deeply serrated edges. It seemed to me that they let go of the branches reluctantly and their descent to the ground was not graceful. It was as if they fought against an unwanted death. Then I began to think about darling Mummy.

I have always tried not to think about Mummy in the same headspace as Di. Cleo once remarked on a similar plan. But that autumn afternoon, the shiny oak leaves reminded me of her and I had to walk quickly out of the cemetery to avoid bringing the two deaths together.

I had determined to put off any real thoughts about what happened on the day of her death until Cleo came out of prison. I would never tell Cleo what I had seen but I did not even want to think about it. Not yet. Not then.

CLEO

Violet hanged herself in the night. We all heard the noise, the yelling, alarm bells, the struggles to cut her down, to carry her out, doors clanging open, crashing shut, even the distant siren of the ambulance. Then the women started screaming and banging their doors. In the morning some were subdued and others elated.

'I didn't think she had it in her!' crowed Lisette, a new girl on the block. It was true that women tended to cut themselves and generally do self-harm, while men went for the jugular. 'Probably she'd had enough of looking such a fright,' continued Lisette, masticating soggy toast.

Violet was the girl with the harelip and the mother with slug-like fingers who visited her every week. I'd recently discovered she had two children looked after by her mother. But they never came to visit.

I'd convinced myself prison was an okay place to be. I could think in relative peace; I could blot out the everyday female shrieking, banging doors, jangling keys, blaring trannies. I could write, once Sam bought me a pad and pencil, and I could read when I eventually found my way to the library. But Violet's suicide knocked me. Death was different from bullying, sexual assaults, depression. Suddenly I was lonely.

Soon after Violet took her life, I made a friend. Eve had stabbed her grandmother with a kitchen knife when she was sixteen. I was shocked to learn she was facing a fifteen-year sentence, even more when I heard she couldn't read or write. So I became her teacher. She learnt to read so quickly I could scarcely keep up.

Word got around in Holloway and soon I was the wing scribe

and teacher and general well-educated dogsbody. Want to write to your Auntie May, call Cleo. Want to read (and even understand) your lawyer's letter, call Cleo. Want to send a sexy come-on to this mate of your brother who looks gorgeous in the photo and will be out of Wandsworth about the same time as you (assuming neither of you get into trouble), call Cleo. The calls on my time became so great, I pinned a note to my cell door, *'By appointment only'* but, as my would-be clients couldn't read, it had little effect.

I'd never been useful before, just annoyed and annoying in equal parts. And entertaining, perhaps, although that was more for my books. If my books hadn't been witty, they'd have been trash. And now there I was helping the undeserving poor so successfully that I got little thank-you notes, partly to show off new skills but also because they were truly grateful. Soon it got about that I hadn't killed my mother at all but it had been pinned on me by another sister who was jealous of me. Stories in prison are legion and it's never worth trying to substitute the truth. I, who had lived through fiction, found myself completely out-fictioned. Few of the women had a hold on reality and little wished to find it. They liked me, so I couldn't have attacked my mother because most of them were supported in one way or another by their mothers. Mothers were tops.

My fan club's ardour found physical expression when Eve decided on the date of my birthday. I came back from the library one afternoon to find my room filled with garish decorations, packets of revolting pink and fake cream biscuits and a sponge cake, strangely decorated.

'Happy Birthday dear Cleo, a fucking Happy Birthday to you,' sang Eve and her cohorts. There was Tess who only had one eye (her father had punched out the other), Mabs who was old and not quite there but could now read simple books; there was Lil who was very pretty and tended to attract the butch girls more easily than was good for her but liked writing poetry about birds and butterflies.

There were others, eager, excited faces, most with dreadful backgrounds, a few of whom had done dreadful things, most just revolving in and out of the prison door, all united in giving me a good time on my birthday.

'In! In!' shrilled Lil, taking my pile of books from me.

'It's a fucking surprise,' commented Mabs with an air of concentration as she said the word. I suspected surprises were not generally positive in her life. She took hold of my arm and led me to the cake. 'I spelled out your name in Smarties.'

I realised that it didn't matter that my birthday wasn't for another three months. The candles could not be lit of course, matches not being prison issue, but Eve nudged me commandingly in the back, 'Blow! Blow!' So I blew gustily amid shouts of delight and congratulation.

'All in one go,' said Lily admiringly. 'I can never do that.' And we all cackled. This was shaping up for a great party!

I admired my new friends for their keenness to learn and their determination to carry on. They talked about children who needed looking after, of men who they loved or who had abused them or both, of attempts to get out of the cycle of crime which had gripped them since childhood. They got that we were kindred souls. I was part of their hopes for a better future.

Because she'd come into prison so young, Eve had no children and her mother and the rest of her family refused to see her. Once Eve could read and write, she began to compose poetry. One day I brought her Palgrave's *Golden Treasury* from the library but she pushed it away angrily.

'That's for the likes of you,' she said. She was sitting in her cell, doing her nails

'It's much harder to write poetry than to read it.'

'No, it's fucking not!' She sounded so furious that I took a step backwards. Her eyes seemed even darker and her skin, which I probably admired too much because she was the first black girl I

223

knew, suddenly seemed a barrier to understanding. 'Take it away!' She was shouting. Because it was 'unlock', three girls gathered across the wing, ready for drama.

'Sorry.' I left hurriedly, hugging the book and keeping my head bowed like a monk over a missal, so that the tears in my eyes were hidden.

It took weeks for Eve to tell me her story. We were walking side by side in the exercise yard on a hot autumn afternoon. Our release from our stuffy cells made me think of Di's love of the great outside, her escape to Hampstead Heath where she made friends with a rough sleeper in his filthy shelter. By chance, I'd witnessed him being taken away by the police, him cursing, them brutally hustling. Di hadn't wanted to know about that. I saw the man's life as an interesting story, she saw it as reality.

Eve's mother had been one of the first Jamaicans to come to London, meeting Eve's father and marrying just before their daughter's birth.

'I had a fine childhood,' Eve told me, 'five younger kids. Once Dad left, I looked after them, no time for school. But it was my mum who sorted everything, she had too many jobs to count. My mum was the centre of our world. I had a boyfriend too. Noah was respectful, a churchgoer. Then one dark morning Gran turned up on a visit from what she called home, but Jamaica wasn't my home and she thought she was fucking queen. Sat in the best chair all day, ordering this and that, demanding fags and drink and special foods, ugly roots and that, hard to prepare. Mum couldn't say no to her, gave her bed over and came in with us kids, or more often worked all night. I could see her just fading away while fucking Gran grew fatter and wanted more and more of everything. She found friends too who took their cue from her so that there'd be three or four ordering this and that. I had to look after them as well as the kids. I was young and strong but I could see my mum just fading.'

Eve stopped there in her story, as if the rest was obvious. I knew it anyway. One evening she'd picked up the kitchen knife and lunged across the table and that one hate-filled stabbing had done for her gran. We were more alike than anyone could have guessed. Do the stars or even something grander bring people with similar stories together?

We stopped our perambulations then and I looked up at the sky. It was a deep blue with white puffy clouds sailing across.

Eve looked up at it too. 'Ten years must pass by before I see that from outside a fucking cage.' She didn't sound bitter, just expressing a fact.

Suddenly my time inside seemed short and I felt guilty. Was her knife-stabbing worse than my buddha-throwing? Had she meant to kill her gran? Murder most foul, not manslaughter by a drunken fool. Should there be so many prison years between her sentence and mine? I couldn't ask her that so instead I said, 'Why won't your mother see you?'

She stared at me as if I'd gone mad. When she saw I was serious, she answered firmly, 'Loved her mum, didn't she. Gran was in Mum's house. Gran had travelled over to see her.'

'But didn't she love *you*?' I could hear the childish whine in my voice.

'She had to think of the other kids. She got a lot of the blame on the street, even if I was the one that done it.'

She was using the same matter-of-fact voice. 'Had to move away. She's up north now. I don't know where. Started a new life, didn't she. She sent someone to tell me that. My mum's a survivor, she'll be alright.'

'But what about *you*?'

She became more thoughtful. 'If I thought I'd smashed her life and the kids I'd go right down, wouldn't I. Don't know exactly where they live now but I imagine them happy. Sort of keeps me going.'

We had begun walking again and, it was true, her step had

become lighter as she thought of the happiness she imagined her family enjoying.

'But don't you want visits? Something to look forward to?' Her unselfishness infuriated me.

'I lost that when I picked up that knife. The Good Lord tells us...'

I always stopped listening when she started quoting from the Bible. We were walking back into the dark, heavy walls, when Eve decided to tell me why she wrote poetry.

'My mum, was a poet, see. All day long she made rhymes and songs and hymns. Whatever she was doing. Sometimes she'd just hum a bit and then go for the words, like they kept her going. She was the poet of the family, she gave us words, along with food on our plates. Just humming until the words come along. She could read, you know, taught back in Jamaica. If she could see me now, you teaching, me learning, she'd thank the Lord. She'd give praise and before you know she'd have some new words to say about it, all moving along like music and maybe rhyming too. She had a gift for that.'

We stopped at a gate, a bunch of us jailbirds, waiting as a warden took a big bunch of keys and let us into the main part of the prison. The sky was shut out, but Eve's eyes were bright. Again, I was infuriated.

'But she *could* see you, know what you're doing, what we're doing together!'

'Thought I told you.' She turned her face away from me and a big Jamaican woman, newly in England before she made it into Holloway, pushed between us.

Eve side-stepped away from both of us and, as the gates were unlocked, pushed ahead quickly. I hung back. I had work at that time, helping in the kitchen, so I took out my anger on the pots, heavy metal things that clashed together like ugly cymbals.

That night, alone in my cell, I considered Eve, my friend, whose experience of matriarchy was so much crueller than mine, but who held to her love, writing poems every day for her mum.

I thought, they must have loved each other, Eve's mother and Eve.

MILLIE

In despair, I took a job. My mind was too addled for higher academia – or not addled in the right way – but I found a niche in the school where Cleo had studied (or not studied). It was a girls' private day school; odd, perhaps for the daughter of a committed member of the Labour Party, but not unusual in those days. They knew Cleo's story, of course, and redirected their sympathy to me. I taught Religious Studies. It was a school with solid standards and later Caly went there too.

It was the right course of action but it increased the misunderstanding between Eddie and me.

'You're going out to work! Now! In your...' There was a pause while he tried to subdue annoyance with kindness, '... your state of mind?' He wanted to hold my hand and comfort me. Pity was the default position that worked for him, at least to some extent. But how could he do that if I built a career? Unlikely as it seemed.

'I'm sorry, Eddie. I didn't go looking for a job. It just came to me'

'No. I get that. You don't get up till eleven. You sit and read Shakespeare on the sofa. You sit and read poetry in the garden. You sit in the kitchen with Caly.'

All this was true. 'I know. Darling. I'm very sorry.'

'How will you find time to visit Cleo? Your visits exhaust you for the day before and the day after.'

I sighed and half shut my eyes. I hated making him unhappy. 'I might only do two days a week.'

But I didn't. I managed three and my life became marginally more possible. I still visited Cleo but sometimes I missed a week.

Teaching Religious Studies set me a little apart from the way

England was going. There had not yet been the sex abuse scandal which did so much damage to the Church, to the Catholic Church in particular. But religion was out of fashion with intellectuals – perhaps it always had been and I hadn't noticed. 'Belief' survived as a not-very-holy relic of what once had been.

Even Eddie seldom joined Caly and me at Mass now. He said he was exhausted from his long working hours in the city and his Sundays were sacred for replenishing his energy. He used the word 'sacred' to annoy me.

Sometimes I wondered if he blamed the Church for taking me away from him, which was ridiculous because it was what supported me. But then he wanted to be the one to support me.

Of course my Religious Studies curriculum was not confined to Christianity. In fact I loved learning about other religions and at one point was drawn to Buddhism for the calmness it seemed to promise. But after Caly's First Communion, I saw that only Catholicism could give me a sense of that community of souls and of ordinary humanity, from which followed a welcome loss of self. I was always good at putting others before myself.

CLEO

A weird thing happened when I was well into my prison sentence. Settled, you might say. Reading, writing. Given up smoking again and even eating a little. Yes, settled. Out of the blue, we were informed, usually knowledgeable rumour mongers equally amazed, that Holloway Prison was closing down for a complete rebuild.

Literally from one day to the next, I found myself transported in 'the sweat box' (more like refrigerator on a freezing December dawn) to a large fifteenth-century house in the country. There, a hairy woman with body odour pointed out to me that I was no danger to society and that I was now in an 'open' prison where I could go out to work as long I came back in the evening. Me, go out to work! I had never done such a thing in my life.

The shock was terrific. None of my wing mates came with me, lost as they seemed in the entrails of the system. Lost too was Father Louis and, worst of all, Sam Levy.

Once he'd tracked me down, he wrote a note. His handwriting was dark, elaborate and foreign: '*My dear, with great sadness I must curtail my visits. I am told that I must catch a bus to Charing Cross, a train to Maidstone, Kent, and at least one more bus to your new home. It is too much for Brother Ass.*' I had once told him Saint Francis's description of his own inadequate body. '*With regret, I must limit our conversations to letters.*'

Poor darling Millie made the journey whenever she could. She'd given up visiting every week when she started helping out at my old school, but I still knew she was my staff and comfort. I hope she gains a Millie-million brownie points when she finally glides up to the pearly gates. Then at last I'll have done her some good.

I was summoned by the Governor, Miss Plume, a tiny bird-like woman, very well-coiffured, who called us 'her girls' not in a particularly friendly way. When asked if I had any questions, I set off in challenging tones, so that I could feel my escort squirming: 'I'm writing a book. Can you find me a half-day job inside prison?'

'Not on the subject of your crime, I may assume, Flynn?' The room smelled strongly of a cloying scent, mimosa, I guessed. Miss Plume carried it with her wherever she went. Despite her delicate appearance, she had Queen Elizabeth's *I may have the body of a weak and feeble woman but I have the heart and stomach of a king...* pinned up on the wall and she dished out punishment with a liberal (non-liberal) hand.

'Certainly not, Miss Plume, Governor,' I lied in a servile way. From the beginning, my encounters with Miss Plume had the flavour of fiction, a TV sitcom, perhaps. I never could make her seem real and doubtless exaggerated her absurd qualities.

'Well, Flynn,' I detected a little smile, 'You will have to bring the pages to be checked that there is nothing improper.' What I didn't know at that time was that she was a fan of my novels, in particular the first and worst (now worth a good sum online).

'It will be a pleasure, Governor.'

'In that case, I'll put you down for gardening duties.'

Was I to be a war-time land-girl up to my elbows in frosty mud and ordure? An image of a cabbage, greyish-green and smelling of rot, a swede, like a tomb raider's rock, spinach, green as slime, carrots like a questing cock, passed before my eyes. I have always hated vegetables.

As if reading my mind, Miss Plume leaned forward, queen to subject. 'Fortunately for you, we have a hothouse where indoor plants are cultivated. I shall put you down for that. You may find harmony in nature.'

I smiled sweetly, thinking, of course, *Fat chance.*

She fixed me questioningly with her small bright eyes and for a scary moment I saw Julie staring out at me. Ever since I had admitted to myself my guilt in ending her life, she had left my thoughts mostly alone, for which I had been duly grateful. Probably the first time I had been grateful to my mother for anything. Perhaps it was Miss Plume's likeness to Julie that made it impossible for me to see her in reality.

'I would like hothouse flowers,' I murmured to Miss Plume.

'Then that is a decision made. F L Y N N, Trestle.' She spelled out and nodded to a secretary, huddled behind her making notes. 'I strive to know all my girls personally, as you see.'

Perhaps I deserved some luck at this point. At that time I didn't realise that the Governor had set me up with a job where I could write in a warm peaceful environment, and bury anything I wanted to hide from her in the earth. This addendum was not her plan; she was happy for me to scribble beside the geraniums only if I brought the results to her. But after I was first summoned to deliver my pages of writing and found my patron took a great deal more interest and pleasure than any of my editors in a previous life, I knew that I must write two novels, one for Miss Plume and one for myself.

Her story would be of girlish pursuits – mostly of men who behaved badly – combining a touch of morality, perhaps a frail sister who needed self-sacrificing care, with dangerous adventures, i.e. in Hollywood with an older film producer who promised her a role in his latest movie... Actually, as time went on, I became rather more involved in this ridiculous tosh than I meant to. Lizzie, my heroine, had an appealing way of biting her lower lip when anxious, which drove Alexis, the film producer, wild. He said, in his gravelly, nicotine voice, 'Are you a girl or a spirit I've conjured up to destroy my life?' He was married with a busty film-star wife so it was a reasonable question.

The front was upheld that the reader who checked the work was Miss Plume's secretary, Miss Trestle who resembled her name. But the Governor would call me into her office with references that showed me her creative interest. 'I think such a man, so rich and powerful, should have a cigar, as large as Churchill's, and a magnificent silver car, and a team of personal assistants with clipboards.'

Naturally, I was happy to oblige. The Governor's imagination proved her a true romantic who, despite her presumed virgin state and being entirely surrounded by women of various sexual orientations, stayed faithful to Man as the target of her love. (Her other love was milk chocolates with centres such as violet, rose, orange and strawberry. She once offered me the box and, thinking it unpolitic to refuse such an example of favour, I was hard put not to vomit.) By now she becoming very unlike my mother.

So the tosh book saw the light of day and meanwhile my own, which started life as *comédie noire,* with excoriating references to the prison way of life (Holloway, not Plume-world with all its benisons) and much fiendishly painful introspection, continued at night in my cell, to be transported and buried as and when. This was, after all, an 'open' prison, so that I was not watched constantly and hardly at all, once I'd had my training, in the hothouses. There were actually three glass bunkers and produce was sold in neighbouring shops.

The other 'girls' working there were extraordinarily lazy. I had always thought of myself as inclined that way, why ever not? All writers are naturally lazy, except for the few hours when they create. But the task of writing two novels simultaneously, plus looking after hundreds of plants, spraying, pinching, watering, was, to say the least, testing. To keep my strength up, I even had to eat.

'You have roses in your cheeks,' commented Miss Plume, as she handed me back a chapter of *Invisible Joy*. She was such an old-fashioned romantic that she kept Boots Lending Library romantic novels circa 1958, e.g. *The Sheik* and *Sons of the Sheik* by Ethel M. Dell, in her drawer next to her chocolates. Which detail I must have imagined.

Sex was not her bag, I believe, and, under my present circumstances, I tended to agree. Nights in the dormitory were a special torment. At any one time a proportion of my neighbours had their hands under the sheets pleasing themselves or another with accompanying sound effects. The strain of holding on to the secret life which a writer needs so badly if she is to flourish, eventually became too much. In March, when the geraniums were branching out, I began to shriek randomly so that I suddenly found myself in a solitary room which I was told was a place of punishment. A breakdown perhaps but bliss too! Every time the wardens suggested I was cured and would be allowed back into society, I went at it full throttle.

Very soon, news of my 'disruptive behaviour' came to the ears of Miss Plume and, further bliss, I was escorted to a garret under the eaves of the old house which I liked to think had belonged to a thirteen-year-old maidservant in 1780 or a visiting poet who had overstayed his welcome.

As a thank you to Miss Plume, in the next chapter of *Invisible Joy,* our elusive heroine, Lizzie, goes to a ball and, like Cinderella, wows everyone with her charms. I described her dress in great detail, emphasising its diaphanous, see-through material which allowed her delicate limbs to shine through like fish in water. No! It can't have been that bad. Even I didn't deal in such obvious caricature.

My rule was to keep the books on parallel, both on page 56 or 106, like racehorses running neck and neck but, all at once, to my shame, *Invisible Joy* began to streak ahead. After much uncomfortable soul-searching and communing with the geraniums, I realised that I had never tried to write a serious book before, to confront 'issues' as they would say now, and that the experience was horribly depressing. Perhaps I was doomed to write tosh for the rest of my life.

By now it was April; most of the geraniums had been sold and the tender plants we had been nurturing in the hothouses were nearly ready to plant out. This demanded a change in my serious novel-burying routine and gave me a reason to slow up for a bit. 'Why,' I asked myself 'would anyone be interested in my maunderings about the meaning of life?' I remembered that a caustic reviewer of one of my novels had commented that I seemed to believe that 'profundity was in a light trill of words leading to a sober full stop.' Then, I had scoffed, sure in the knowledge that I had no high aspirations but, at the same time, quoted to myself Keats' phrase that poems should come 'as naturally as the leaves to a tree'. I was confident in nothing but my ability to write – content unimportant.

But now I was *trying to say something*. I took to my garret bed and listened to the mice scurrying round in the roof. They were having fun, at least. After several days, I was summoned back to the garden, under threat of being sent back to a closed prison. 'Do you not see,' said the head gardener, an ex-sergeant major, previously my friend, who had taken horticultural courses and treated the plants like his troops, 'that by your lack of care, you are *killing* them. One by one. Leaf and root.'

I looked into his dark, worried eyes in his worn, leather face and did not say, 'I am a murderess so of course I will kill them.' Instead I went and found the hose-pipe. A couple of hours later, I looked up at the sky and saw the sun was out. I sat down on a step and breathed in the fresh spring air. Second breakdown over. A bird tweeted – or even several. *Fuck it*! I thought, more cheerful than I had been for ages. *Just fuck it*! Then I found a spade and dug over a large patch of ground.

'Well done, girl,' said the ex-sergeant major.

God helps those who help themselves. The very next day I had a visitor. He arrived before the letter that should have announced his arrival.

The visitors' room in that place was nothing like Holloway's grisly theatre. It even had a small terrace with some of our geraniums in pots. He was sitting waiting when I came in, pulling off my gloves, still in working dungarees. I had assumed my visitor was Millie.

'You! What are you doing here?' I smelled the fertiliser in my hair.

'Papa insisted. He told me he'd written.' I'd forgotten he called his father *Papa*. 'This isn't so bad.' He waved his hand around.

'Your dad said the same when he came to Holloway and that was like a scene out of Ibsen, when everyone's on the verge of death, suicide or murder.' I felt the idiocy of this and blushed. Words always came to me before anything else. This was the long-lost love of my life in my prison. How was I supposed to react? I felt my hands shaking and shoved them into my pockets.

'Do you want me to stay?' He'd grown his beard again. With many men beards look like a disguise but with Lennie it seemed to expand his personality.

'The only person who visits me is Millie.'

'Your sister?' I always forgot that we scarcely knew each other. My love blinded me to that. I knew his father so much better.

'Please stay.' I sat down, on a chair a little way from him, so, with any luck, the fertiliser wouldn't overpower him. My nervousness was making me acutely self-conscious. Even words were not helping. 'I work in the garden,' I said pathetically.

'I never saw you as a garden kind of person.' He smiled which was surprising. And nice. I relaxed slightly. I didn't remember him smiling much.

'I suppose you read all about my crime in the papers.' Going from one extreme to another, I adopted a challenging expression.

'Not really.' He stared at his fingers, not very big and rather white. I remembered them.

I had earth under my fingernails, despite the gloves. My emotions tumbled around and suddenly I felt angry with him. 'Your wife must be horrified. Honestly, I can't think why you've come.'

'I told you. My father asked me to. He's not well. He wanted to know how you're getting on.' He was mumbling.

'So, what do you think of me as a gardener?' I jumped up and posed like a strong-arm man. I was embarrassing myself but couldn't stop.

'You seem fine.' He spoke without looking up.

I sat down again and we both became silent. The thing was I had no idea what he thought of me, never had had any idea, to be honest. I studied him with a sideways glance, a small man with wild dark hair, a neat beard, dressed in a pink denim shirt, faded jeans and sneakers. He wore a leather thong round his neck. He looked quite American, a bit old-school hippy, not very married man with a child and a job in his uncle's firm. I began to feel calmer.

'I'm sorry about Di,' he said more loudly than before. 'Your sister,' he added as if I wouldn't know. He was nervous too. He had come all the way to find me. 'She took over that flat of mine in the old glove factory down by Brooklyn Bridge. Do you remember?'

I had not known or forgotten that he'd met Di. 'It's a long time ago,' I murmured. I pictured the snow and Washington Square. 'You were playing the piano. What happened about that?'

He stood up so abruptly that he knocked his chair over which he didn't appear to notice. The chair hit one of the flowerpots, breaking off the branch of a pink geranium. I resisted going to help it. Concentrating on myself, I hadn't noticed up till now just how anxious he was. Even more than me.

'Are you all right?' I said, forgetting how I despised people who asked that question in tones expecting the answer 'yes'. I wanted to touch him but he was too far away and I thought he didn't want that.

'Fine, thank you.'

I stood up beside him and, like two statues, we stared out over the garden, my unlikely domain.

'I guess you're an old friend,' he said, still not looking at me.

I wanted to correct him and say 'old lover' but instead I laid my hand on his arm. It was shaking slightly. Very thin.

'My father's dying, I've left Rebekah and I need help.' He took a step from me and seemed about to sit down in the chair which was still upended on the floor. I swung it up quickly and he slumped into it and put his head in his hands.

After a while, I began to talk to him, about the prison at first, just random happenings, the difference between life in Holloway and in this country mansion. I told him that Millie was so good and that she continued to visit me whenever she had time and that I missed Di terribly. I had never said those words out loud before and I wasn't even sure that he was listening and perhaps that was why I felt able to talk, that and his obvious suffering. I didn't say anything about Julie. I didn't want her name between us.

Eventually, I ran out of steam and Lennie came out of his trance and said in a normal voice, 'Papa thought we could chat about things, although he pretended he needed a report on your state of mind. He wants me to go into analysis. Because of his background in Germany and Freud living just up the road, he's quite into such things.'

'But I'm in a terrible muddle myself,' I replied, and found myself gasping for air. When had I admitted that?

'Even analysts are. So I'm assured.'

'But they haven't...' I stopped abruptly.

'You don't need to talk about that.' We looked at each other for the first time since he'd arrived. 'Not now.'

It was quite extraordinary how comforting that look was. It set the foundation for everything that followed. It was about trust and openness and of course about love. In our many talks over the following months – Lennie got into the habit of coming at least once a fortnight – he told me about his growing up, the huge pressures from his mother to make up the loss of her entire family in the war,

His father was different, absent in his books, leaving human contact to his wife. Neither of them, as he saw it, allowed latitude for what he called 'star-gazing'. He became a great admirer of Delius's music, he told me, because the composer believed in 'drift', that is allowing life's currents to carry you along. A Yorkshire boy, Delius's currents took him to working in an orange plantation in Florida as well as studying in Germany.

'But in my home', cried Lennie, sounding about ten years old, 'everything had to be practically directed. Even music was for a performance and philosophy was to make the world a better place.'

Things were made harder by his sister who conformed to their mother's ideal and made his own reluctance seem cruel. So as soon as he'd finished university, he escaped to New York. I think he'd forgotten that I was one of the people he left behind. Delius led him to the piano and he found a kind of freedom. But when his mother died suddenly, he had been horrified by his selfishness and returned, determined to make up for what he then saw as his cruelty. At his lowest point, he blamed his own absence for his mother's death.

'I married Rebekah to please my mother,' he smiled bitterly and added, 'Even though she was dead and I'd never believed in the afterlife.'

When Sam sent him to me that day in the open prison and we had our first talk, one word kept coming into my head: 'war'. In different ways, the effects of war on our parents had tortured our lives into agonising shapes. I found peace with alcohol and threw an item of peaceful connotation with angry intent, and he married Rebekah. I suppose Rebekah deserved sympathy.

After Lennie's first visit, I went to Miss Plume and told her that unfortunately the artistic inspiration for *Invisible Joy* had abandoned me. She was devastated and immediately ordered me back to the dormitory. Incidentally, I think the truth about Miss Plume is that she was a slightly odd woman who felt sorry for me and tried to help me as best she could. Hardly surprising that she eventually lost patience. Or perhaps she realised I needed to fight my own demons.

So I returned to my 'serious' book, no longer a *comédie noire*. It progressed so slowly that sometimes I felt as if I was plunging backwards into a deep hole. I could only write it in my cell and by the time of my release, I had exactly ten pages to take with me. But I also had Lennie.

MILLIE

By the time Cleo got out of prison in 1970 I had become accustomed to her being part of another world. All the same, I was shocked when Lennie moved in with her. He had a wife and a young child. I still believed marriage was forever. Odd I suppose when Daddy had fled his marriage so completely. Perhaps I believed marriage *should* be forever.

On the evening that Cleo told me, a London summer's evening when the roses smelt nearly as strong as the exhaust, Eddie came in as usual. I was sitting on the sofa as usual. Caly was upstairs doing her homework as usual. As usual, Eddie said, 'How was your day, darling?' He was so handsome as he took off his jacket and tie. It was all such a pity.

He used that strange tone of voice that we'd both adopted, love overlayed by layers of unexpressed sadness. How could I get over the sadness? He might have said, 'Do you still love me, darling?'

I might have answered, 'Yes, I do love you but my feelings are bound up in ropes of anxiety. Maybe you could cut through them, like Prince Charming finding Sleeping Beauty.' Instead I said, in our mutual tone, 'Lennie's moved in with Cleo.' Had I ever been able to express myself freely?

And he asked, although he knew the answer perfectly well, 'Who is Lennie?'

And I said, 'She's known him for ages.' Then I paused before adding, 'He's married with a young child.'

And Eddie said, 'I need a drink. I can't tell you how much money I made for my client today.'

So I poured him a gin and tonic and myself a small white wine and we sat together. I didn't blame him for not wanting to talk about Cleo ever again. So I let him read the paper and after a bit I went to cook supper, liver and bacon, his favourite.

Caly found me there and said, 'I didn't really have any homework. I was just pretending. I love homework, you know. It makes me feel so grown-up.'

And I laughed. And she went off to find her dad.

CLEO

I had been out of prison for six months when Lennie asked me to go along to his papa's funeral. I said, 'No, my dearest, bearded, male, person. I would be the scarlet woman. People would mock and spit at me and I couldn't blame them. I love you.' I was proud of my new ability to speak that out loud. 'But my wondrous love does not blind me, I regret to say, to the reality.'

Lennie said nothing. We were lying on our bed in our little flat in Notting Hill. I continued, 'You know how I loved (there I went again) your father. I thought he was the nearest person to you that was within my reach. Then he became my dearest friend, actually my only friend. He taught me all sorts of things that I failed to put into practice; he even attended my first, maybe my last' – here I gave him a flirtatious look – 'ridiculous wedding, but he never gave up on me and then he sent you to me. Of *course* I would like to go to his funeral, to pay grateful homage but...' He interrupted me, pulling on my naked arm and turning me round to him.

'I want you to come.'

'I presume this will be a full-scale Jewish wedding, sorry, funeral, and I will not only be the scarlet woman, but the Catholic scarlet woman who has stolen the son away from his family, from his wife, his child, his son moreover, and that is not to even mention the murder of her own mother, the well-respected Labour minister, cut down in her prime. How can we want such an *unnatural* women in the midst of...'

He interrupted me again: 'Stop messing around. I am not joking. I need you there. I want you at my side. My father would want you to be at my side.'

'No, he wouldn't. He would understand what I am saying.'

Over the twenty-four hours before the funeral, we had more than one conversation like this. We were argumentative lovers at the best of times. Since we'd been living together, I realised that there is nothing worse for a writer than to have the object of her love within constant reach. Lennie, after all, was still in breakdown mode, unable to work or settle down to anything, while I had enjoyed nearly two years of prison to measure up to my problems, find myself wanting and decide I had paid enough of a price already. This made me keen to do the thing that I most trusted: my writing. But Lennie could scarcely avoid noticing that writing took me away into another world where he didn't exist, so, quite understandably, he created interruptions.

I'm not saying Lennie's invitation to Sam's funeral was merely another in a continuing string of interruptions, but he used the same tone of voice, a bit sad, a bit childish, in which he suggested we went out to a movie or for a pizza when I had claimed a couple of hours' writing time. This was still my 'serious' book incidentally, which continued to give me trouble. Sometimes I thought I should never have given up on my alternative prison novel, *Invisible Joy*. Buffy, who had come back into my life and did not at all like the sound of a book about guilt and responsibility. 'You'll tell me next it's written in blank verse,' she groaned, finding succour in a G and T. 'What's wrong with a good old murder story?' Buffy was never sensitive.

I suppose I said yes to Lennie in the end because he was the stronger character—or maybe I loved him too much, because I absolutely knew that I should *not* go. I hadn't met his sister since we came together; I had never met his wife nor his son nor any of his other relatives or friends. We were a hermit double-act, dependent on each other and not yet fit for other society. I suppose that's actually why I agreed finally: I didn't think he'd get through it without me.

I was wrong. A hot July day: two young persons, sweating in

unnatural black clothes, set off from Notting Hill. A couple of hours later one of them returns, fumbles for her key, opens the outer door to the house, walks up two flights of stairs, opens a flat door, staggers to the bed on which she falls, screaming. That was me.

The moment I saw Rebekah, a pretty, intelligent-looking woman with a soft round face, and her son, Lennie's son, a tiny serious boy with dark curls like his dad, I knew it was all over. Done. Finito. Caput. A love affair that began on a CND march, continued in a prison and finally strove for the long-term (well, anyway, *more* long-term) was over, done, finito, caput. As repeated in my head while I lay heartbroken (I could feel it bleeding) on the bed.

With my history, how *could* I be the one to take a parent from his child, even if said parent had departed before I arrived on the scene? 'The wedded couple might get together again without you on the scene', as Millie felt moved to confide in me.

Actually, she said nothing to me, but I could see it in her eyes. In fact I didn't even need the absent Millie's conscience: my own hammered against my chest as if a parade ground of regimental drummers were beating out one message, '*Leave!*' So I left, and didn't watch Lennie greet his wife nor admire Sam's bio-degradable coffin (no flowers) nor listen to the moving address from the rabbi that Lennie had known since he was a child, although he had seldom taken his advice. He told me years later, 'Everything he suggested made sense but that made me more inclined to look elsewhere. Only dead fish swim with the stream.'

Lennie's background was too strong for me on the day of his father's funeral. He loved his father and the love spilled over to Rebekah and his son, Sam. I said the name out loud. Sam senior, dead, Sam junior, alive.

I lay on my bed and howled. The next generation was destroying the present. After a couple of hours, with red, bulging eyes and gasping throat, I thought, *That's what Julie did, sacrificed the next generation to satisfy her own needs*. But at least she was trying (and succeeding, don't let's forget) to do good for others. So then I cried again until my eyes were so waterlogged and soft that the eyelashes felt like barbed wire.

Why did it always have to come back to my mother? I remembered what I had worked so hard to forget, the moment when I held that buddha and released it drunkenly in her direction. Had I truly wanted to kill her? That I couldn't remember. Anger made my heart pump; I could feel myself puffing up like a toad, filled with ugliness and despair.

At about ten that evening, I heard Lennie let himself into the flat. I had bathed and washed my hair and looked, I hoped, normal. He must not think I was hysterical. *Keep calm*, I told myself. *You are a war baby. You have survived prison. You can do this.* I sat at my typewriter, although if he had checked, he would have seen the paper was blank.

'Sorry I fled.' I followed him through to our little sitting room. I made my feet go one-two in a sturdy walk. I glanced back at my typewriter.

'I've been sitting shiva,' said Lennie. 'There were a lot of old friends there.' He went into the bedroom, taking off his jacket and tie and shoes and then his yarmulke which he put into the pocket of his jacket.

'That's good,' I said, following him through.

'Yes.' He lay on the bed and I hoped it wasn't still wet from my tears.

'Do you want to know why I ran away?' I stood over him and was uncomfortably reminded of the less-nice wardens standing over my bed in my cell, so I perched near his feet.

'This doesn't have to be about you.' He spoke wearily and warily. 'You were upset to see Rebekah and the boy. I understand. You were probably right to leave. You would have felt out of place.'

'I would have *been* out of place. I told you.'

'Okay. If you say so.' He shut his eyes. Perhaps he was mourning his papa. Or perhaps he didn't want to hear what I had to say. 'Can't it wait till the morning? Please.'

It was a reprieve. A deep sigh of relief made me gasp. I had changed from toad to fish. I couldn't speak. I just stared, before clasping my hands together as if in prayer.

'We can mourn tonight and talk tomorrow,' said Lennie slowly, eyes still closed.

'Yes,' the fish gasped in gratitude.

One more night together.

We made love in the very darkest hours when our London street was absolutely silent as if we could be in the empty countryside, without even a bird. We stroked each other tenderly as if we were new lovers instead of about to part, pausing on the special places and smiling as we made our lover pant or cry out.

We whispered words secretly into hair or shoulder-blades or arm or leg. They were hopes or promises or wishful thinking. 'We can still be friends.' 'You are my love.' 'I will be with you always.' 'We are one.'

Very unoriginal. And we never did 'talk' that morning.

Lennie collected his things while the day was still blurred and tinged with silver. I lay in bed and watched him move about like a ghost. I half shut my eyes and thought I could wipe him out altogether by just closing my eyelids, clicking them shut like the drawers he was opening and shutting. But of course I didn't.

He brought things in from the living room and piled them on the bed and I was grateful he was including me in his going away. But he didn't have much so it didn't take long, although long enough for me to drown in tears.

CALY

Aunt Cleo was my get-out clause, my get-out-of-prison-free card, my ticket to the moon. She made anything seem possible whereas my mum, my darling mum, could make a border of tulips seem threatening.

My friends at school liked her though, the ones who had problems at home felt safe with her and told me, 'You're so lucky to have such a special mother.' Or if they didn't always say those very words I could feel it in the way they looked at her. She was beautiful too, like a Victorian beauty, dark-haired and pale-skinned, rather heavy. She taught Religious Studies to older girls and they liked her too. They knew she had her own belief as a Catholic but she was quite fair-minded, so I understood, about other religions. She told them once that if she hadn't been born in England, she might have been a Buddhist which they liked. Frankly I can't imagine her anything but Catholic.

When I think of my mum I always think of her at home or in the garden. But Aunt Cleo could be anywhere. She was so quick. She reminded me of Ariel, a sprite, whose body was only pinned down to the earth by words. When I was still very young, she took me on amusing trips, to the isle of Islay in Scotland once; the journey took much longer than our stay there. Another time she hired a launch and a driver and went up the Thames for miles. It was raining and cold and she really enjoyed herself. She also took me to lunch at a huge hotel in Piccadilly where the waiters treated me like a princess. She ordered a tiny glass of pink champagne for me but she drank water.

The most dramatic trip was when we went by hired car (she doesn't drive) to see HMP Holloway. It was a great big red-brick building. I sort of knew it was where she'd been once upon a time but she didn't say anything and I was too embarrassed to ask. We didn't get out but she sat for ages with her head pressed to the window.

'So what do you think, Caly, darling?' she asked me eventually. She sat back in the seat and waited for my answer.

'Hideous,' I said firmly.

'That's exactly right.' She smiled in a pleased sort of way.

CLEO

Famously (or perhaps notoriously), Evelyn Waugh said that writers have a splinter of ice at their heart. He doesn't speculate how it got there but definitely approves of the effects. Checking with Wikipedia, I see it was not Waugh but Graham Greene who pronounced this. Makes more sense when I look at Greene's cold blue eyes against the protuberant Waugh eyes of a suffering drunk. Contradictorily, once I was no longer a drunk I had much more sympathy for the breed. Well-rounded, happy folk never need to alter their state with wickedly distorted grapes or potatoes or hops or rice or whatever man's ingenuity suggests when life is just too too hard. Nobody *wants* to be a drunk. It's just the least bad option.

Drink kept me going, certainly in the wrong direction and with disastrous results, but that 6pm glug had been my friend, thank you very much (one brief incident apart). It enabled me to turn the ice splinter on others, not myself. Preferably in my novels rather than in what is optimistically called everyday life. Once I had left drink behind, I had to create a new self, which I was forced to do anyway because I was in prison. Then along came Lennie. Oh my darling Lennie! Six months we lived under the same roof before his dear papa died and the funeral split us apart.

It was June 1971 when I found myself alone. That year shoulder-heaving, prickly Ted Heath was Prime Minister and Great Britain went decimal. Big deal. Long Kesh, where militant Irish patriots were held without trial, came into being. Not a good idea. We were still wearing miniskirts. 'We' being women of all ages. Even the Queen pinned on Orders of the British Empire wearing skirts above her knees. I was still trying to write my 'serious', perhaps upped by then to 'apocalyptic', novel. What was it about? To be or not to be?

Buffy read 20,000 words and invited me to lunch. She had never invited me to lunch. We went to the Ritz. In those days, publishers liked showing off successful authors, even ones as tawdry and controversial as myself. No one else had a jailbird (and what a crime!) on their books. At the next table Ringo Starr was being wooed by an agent who wanted to help him start his new life away from the Beatles. Both Buffy and I found it hard to concentrate on my novel.

As she absentmindedly sipped her way through a bottle of Puligny Montrachet, I amused myself seeing how long I could make each breadstick last (ten minutes).

Eventually, Buffy addressed me. 'What is it about?' After a bottle of wine, she could ask the question with a convincing air of interest, even curiosity. But, on breadsticks, there was no way I could answer.

'At one point I wondered if it was your political thriller,' she continued, dredging for hope. 'The tragic underdog, discarded into prison, emerging with a score to settle. Dostoevsky crossed with John le Carré.' She was on a roll (not bread – ha!) so I let her carry on.

She spoke and I considered politics which naturally led on to thoughts about Julie. When Buffy paused to light and puff a cigarette – she now used a holder so she could target smoke more effectively at the opposition – I pronounced with a faux negligent air, 'The Personal is Political.' This was a newish slogan at the time, first appearing in *Notes from the Second Year: Women's' Liberation in 1970*.

'Ah. I was right then.' Buffy, not getting the reference to Women's Lib, smiled with her scarlet gash lips. 'My directors will be pleased. They're always saying I need more politics in my books. But please don't diminish the fucking, darling. You were becoming quite good at it before you popped into you know where. I suppose you had little opportunity there, except for the single sex variety which would cut down readership numbers. Not that I'm against it.' She took another puff. 'Did I ever tell you about me and darling Serena?

What a woman! We happened to be up the Empire State Building together...'

Sometimes I asked myself whether my publisher was sane. With my past experience, I should have blamed the empty bottle of wine. But why ever would she think I was interested in sex between her and whoever, wherever?

'... of course I could be wrong. It might be just the moment for a modern lesbian novel, darling. The ones written in the thirties are all so heavy-handed...'

'Gay,' I said.

'Not at all. Oh, I see what you mean. Isn't that just for men?'

'No. Anyway I'm writing a political novel. Sort of.'

'A scandalous story of betrayal at the heart ...' She paused as the waiter came and lifted the empty bottle. Her eyes swivelled longingly before regretfully declining his invitation to a second bottle. 'I have a meeting shortly in which I shall present your new masterpiece. Does it have a title, Cleo dearest one?'

'*Matricide.*'

She was already standing. 'You don't mind if I leave you. I'll pay on my way out. *Matricide*? Doesn't sound very political to me. Oh I see. I see.' She winked complicitly and launched herself between the white tablecloths.

I watched her across the room, scarcely weaving at all, stopping to drop ash over a fellow publisher. Then I sat back and ordered a double espresso. The Ritz dining room is lit with golden chandeliers reflected in a multitude of mirrors. I raised my eyes to the ceiling where pink clouds drifting across blue sky lightened my heart. I dropped my gaze to the end-of-lunch diners. One man caught my eye. He was short, stocky, balding; he held a cheroot in one hand and was saying goodbye to his guest, a younger man.

The splinter of ice emerged and I pushed back my chair and walked slowly, casually over to him.

'I hope you don't mind me introducing myself. I'm Cleopatra

Flynn, Julie Flynn's daughter. I think you were a friend of hers.'

The man blinked. I saw in his Welsh dark eyes and by the way he ducked his head that he felt horribly trapped. 'I wonder if I could have ten minutes with you when you have a moment.'

He was a politician. Politicians never say 'no' to a member of the public. 'I am so sorry to bother you.' I was charming. I tried to be charming.

He stood up, took a card from his waistcoat pocket and handed it to me. 'My secretary will arrange it. Do you want to tell me what it's about?' The lilt in his voice counteracted his direct manner.

I stopped being charming. 'Not really.'

The thing about being a writer is that you have a licence to do anything. You just say to yourself and anyone else who cares that you are writing a book. Full stop. Reason enough. I didn't take to drink when Lennie and I parted but I encouraged the splinter of ice until it became a veritable iceberg and, at last, stripped of soft diversions, I could write my serious/apocalyptic book. In this project Vernon Jones MP, Shadow Home Secretary, alias the man in the Ritz, turned out to be a great help.

We never became real friends, but once he understood that I was going to write (seriously) about crime and retribution, he helped me in every way he could. As the patron of a prison reform charity, he arranged for me to visit men's prisons which, with my record, would have been impossible without him. He explained how the political system worked which I had tried so hard to avoid knowing during Julie's lifetime. He introduced me to lawyers so that I could understood how that worked too. I had encouraged my imagination to flourish at the expense of my intellect. He became my teacher and guide.

Oh the glory of words! Words, wonderful words. Words, words and more words. I sold my flat in Notting Hill and built a glass house on the south side of the River Thames. The house and my book grew.

Eve became the centre of my thoughts. Eve who had stabbed her grandmother and was still in prison. Eve who was born to a monstrous mother. Eve who cared for her brothers and sisters as if she was their mum and accepted her punishment as the will of God. Most of all the Eve who still loved her vile, selfish, stupid, cruel mother.

When she'd let me, I began to visit her in her new prison outside London, her only visitor. I brought her things, like pretty cards with kittens or flowers, books that I knew she could now read, poetry which she didn't send away.

I told her, 'I'm writing a book about prison. And other things.'

She responded quickly. 'Not about me, I hope.'

'It's a novel,' I said. 'Fiction. But there will be a good woman at its heart. When people think about prison, they think about violent men, murderers and rapists. What they call, "dangers to society".'

She looked down. She was wearing a furry jumper tied at the neck with two tassels. Everyone tried to look cheery in the Visits Hall. She began to play with the ends as if they were little animals, baby hamsters perhaps. I knew she was thinking that she was a murderer too.

'Whatever you did, you are not a danger to society.'

She nodded, knowing that to be no more than the truth. She raised her head. 'You write what you think best. That's the only way. Come and see me now and again like a breath of fresh air.'

I was absurdly pleased to be called 'a breath of fresh air'. 'Yes, I will. Can't forget my prison friends, can I? Who's teaching the girls reading now?' Eve was too modest to tell me that she played that role now.

One winter's night soon after I'd moved into my new house, when I was sitting with my hands in my lap watching the sharp lights around Tower Bridge and the *Cutty Sark* reflected in the river, there was a tap on my door below. Although it was over a year since I'd seen Lennie, I knew it was his hand tapping.

Without stopping to brush my hair or worry that I was wearing a dressing gown tied with a scarf and my hideous prison slippers – the latter survivors like myself – I went quickly downstairs. He stood there like a beggar, a mendicant, a travelling holy man, a homeless, hopeless man. I took him into my bedroom which was also downstairs and we took off our clothes. Speech seemed far too complicated.

His body seemed dry, cold, old, uncared for and uncaring. He held on to me as I wrapped myself round him. My tears fell on him and I let them fall. He should know what I felt.

He stayed all night long and, gradually, he became alive. We made love once and then again, our bodies separated as a man and a woman so that I no longer supported him.

When a pale light came through the large, uncurtained window, he went over and stared at the river, patterned with the ghostly tips of waves and the streaky wakes of boats. A tugboat guiding a barge went slowly by as we watched.

'Amazing, isn't it!' They were the first words I'd spoken.

'Amazing,' he repeated, and sighed. I knew then he had not come to stay.

CALY

It was a fearful blow when, soon after my sixteenth birthday, my parents summoned me into the drawing room – a lovely, light-flowing room where there were parties and friends, a Christmas tree or birthday garlands – and told me they were separating. No divorce because they were Catholics. Mum made that point; Dad looked less convinced. It was 1980, I was at an academic private girls' school, not a convent, and there were children whose parents were divorced. I suppose Mum teaching Religious Studies made it a little bit embarrassing. Previously, I had regarded Mum and Dad, who had such a weirdly hands-off relationship, with trusting love, tinged with pity and a certain amount of comfortable disdain. Divorce seemed uncharacteristically dramatic.

'You must be joking!' I cried out as soon as they had stumbled through telling me. I looked from loved face to loved face. What a child I was! My mother looked beautiful and helpless. Dad looked miserable. I noticed his face was an uneven blotchy red. 'I am so sorry, darling.' He opened his arms to me but I didn't go towards him. A girl has pride, I told myself.

'I think I'll go to my room,' I said. They gave me no explanations and I asked for none. But the next day, in an act of rebellion (and self-preservation) I skipped school (for the first time ever) and went round to Aunt Cleo's.

'Darling! Darling! Darling!' Apparently, Cleo had seen me coming which was not difficult because she lived in a two-storey house almost entirely made of glass. When I was younger I'd asked her why and she'd replied, 'Surely it's obvious, Caly darling, to a girl of your intelligence, "Those who live in glass houses shouldn't throw stones."'

'But I still don't understand,' I said. I was very literal in those days, 'Is it a joke?'

She'd given me a kiss, 'Anything but. More like a warning to myself. You'll understand when you're older.'

The house was built on a forgotten bombsite south of the river, actually on the river, not far from Southwark tube station, in one of those areas which are now filled with vast glass towers. Cleo was ahead of her time.

I still loved and admired Aunt Cleo nearly as much as my parents, although always in a quite different way. She was exciting, famous, notorious, funny, outrageous and made spectacular ice cream, covered with home-made dark chocolate sauce which seemed to be her own staple diet. It was obvious I'd go to her with my shameful secret – I assumed my parents' separation was secret.

'Come in darling! What a relief to see you. To be frank, anyone would do. Do you know what the very worst thing is about being a writer?'

One of Cleo's charms was (is, actually) that she made me feel involved in her life and indeed quite often asked for my help. 'Go on, guess!'

'Well, it can't be interruptions,' I said, trying to be clever, 'because you're pleased to see me.'

'You've got it! Unlimited time! That's the very worst thing for a writer. People in proper jobs have interruptions all the time, which means they're in a constant state of tension, absolutely the only way anything gets done. Writers fight against lassitude, long for deadlines, hope for their beloved niece to come and interrupt them. What is it, darling? You look like Sisyphus after the stone had rolled down on him for the umpteenth time, or maybe Job when the plague of boils had shrivelled his gizzard and other areas unmentionable but possibly more important. And painful. Tell your old aunt.'

By now we had reached the upper floor where Cleo worked, a

large area filled by a view of the river and a chair, small desk and computer. I haven't mentioned it, but England was enjoying or anyway living through a spectacular summer. It hadn't rained for months, the London sky was always blue, tinged with a metallic sheen, surfaces were hot to the touch and the pavements decorated with a tracery of black blobs where dirt had glued itself beyond the sweeper's brush. The London plane tree was turning a brassy colour even though it was only July and, in the parks, dried-out leaves began to speckle the thin, pale grass. On the tube there was a smell of hot bodies, as areas of skin, normally hidden, were displayed, pink and hot and sweating.

This description might sound as if I didn't like the heat. But I did, I loved it. Best of all. I loved catching a bus to Hampstead Heath Ladies' Pond with a bunch of friends and sploshing in the brown water with the ducks; then, streaked with slime, flopping on the bank with only our pants on. The thing is we had all finished our O-Levels so the sun seemed glorious. No longer did we need to hide away in our rooms, revising as if our lives depended on the results; we were free, almost ecstatic in our childish joy. The dirt, the smells, the weary trees, the naked flesh were all part of this exciting world I was tiptoeing towards.

My parents' news came down like a hammer on a blossoming plant.

I stood in Cleo's room and surveyed the broad expanse of water, shining silver and black, gold and crimson, living green, a magnificent snakeskin. Behind it, so close to my eye, stood Tower Bridge, human-made, fragile, yet ancient. Usually the sight seemed filled with possibilities, and I would press my nose to the glass, but that day the bridge seemed tarnished, without meaning, and the river monstrous.

I came over to Cleo who was sitting on the chair which she had swung round to face me. She had bare feet, showing off silver nail varnish, wore a short, flowered dress with her hair tied back in a bunch. I wore baggy shorts and T-shirt and stood with my legs apart, my arms folded. I was accusatory, cross, defiant, pathetic.

'Mum and Dad are separating. They would be divorcing if they were Anglicans.'

'Ah,' said Cleo with a bright sharp look. 'The Robin Redbreast has struck.' She saw my bewilderment. What had my parents' disloyalty to me, each other and their faith to do with a bourgeois bird?

'I get it, said Cleo, holding my gaze so that I noted how the river's reflection darkened the pale blue of her eyes. 'No mention of Robin then. Or Robyna, I believe. What a name! No wonder she has to steal other people's husbands. Poor Eddie has made a mistake there. But men do. Women, too I suppose, now that we're all feminists.'

She talked on for several minutes, trying to give me time to take it all in, I suppose, although I'm sure she'd not mentioned Robyna by accident. Cleo's mind works in coils but like a maze there's a destination in the middle – if you can find it. On this occasion she built a rubbish riff on feminist chimps who wear skirts so that the male can't see their pink swollen bottoms when they're on heat or whatever it's called. But now these admirable feminists are wondering if they should wear trousers.

It worked in one way, at least the image of the chimp feminist trying to decide whether to wear a skirt stayed with me, long after I'd come to grips with my father's weakness.

'Do you mean Dad has a girlfriend?' I said, as she tailed off (there's a pun for you, Cleo).

'Lover, I'd say. Girlfriend suggests someone nice and cosy who keep you company while you smoke a ciggy in front of the telly and like to remind you now and again about sex, although probably...'

'Please, Aunt Cleo.'

'Sorry. So neither of them told you. Cowards! Why don't you sit down.'

'There's only one chair.'

'What's wrong with the rug.' She sounded quite irritated. Perhaps

I had interrupted her while she was creating a great new character, but I don't think so. I think she was cross with Eddie.

I sat on the rug and tried not to cry. Then I did cry. So she got off her chair and came down and hugged me. Her hugs were completely different from Mummy's because she was so much thinner. It was like being caressed by scarves and ribbons instead of wrapped in a shawl. I can't remember what she said, perhaps nothing at all. What she didn't say was anything falsely consoling. She didn't suggest it was nothing or that Daddy still loved Mummy, although he did, or that he would come back to her, although he did on and off for the rest of his life, or that Robyna was a nasty piece of work, although she was – worst of all when she pretended to suck up to me by saying that Mummy was a heroic woman but 'not of this century'. Thank *you*, Robyna!

No, Aunt Cleo simply sat with me until I finished crying and by then the sun had moved from the east and was pouring across the river from behind us, turning it into a brilliant shimmer of light. So we sat together staring and saying 'Wow' when a boat created new electric patterns until suddenly there was a bang downstairs and Cleo leapt to her feet. She dashed joyfully to the door.

'Lennie's here!' I heard her cry of welcome.

MILLIE

'Of course he still loves you. He still loves me, as a matter of fact.' I know I shouldn't have added that bit about me to Caly. Children, even when they're sixteen and wear skirts up to their bottoms and hair down to their waists, they still see you as Mum, the one person who puts them first. At least that was the basis of my attitude to my darling daughter. And look how well it had worked up till then! A lovely confident, clever girl – sailed through her O-Levels – unselfconscious, unselfish, sensitive…

She was lying on her bed when I came in and sat up immediately book across her like a breastplate. *The Millstone* by Margaret Drabble, I noted.

'Honestly, Mum.' How well I understood her feelings. She was too kind to say out loud, 'Go away. You've made this mess but I don't want to hear.'

But I felt like speaking out. Just for once. 'Dad is a good man, a very good man, but…'

'Mum, please!' Caly shook her head like a pony beset by flies and her hair flew around like a mane. 'I understand.'

Of course she didn't understand. It was quite complicated and, I'm afraid, dated back to that terrible time when Mummy and Diana had died and Cleo was in prison. I just couldn't have sex with Eddie. I tried but I suppose not hard enough. I felt bound tight in barbed coils of terror and sadness, so how could I relax and make love? How could I go to Diana's funeral one day, with dear sad Brad who's become a friend, if long-distance, then Mummy's miserable little funeral, followed by her *huge,* grand, memorial service in Westminster Abbey – it really was – then off to see Cleo, like a tiny zombie, as ethereal as a cartoon ghost, in that Hammer House of Horrors prison, and after all that be expected to pop into bed with Eddie for a bit of mutual pleasuring.

I suppose I could have given *him* pleasure but our making love had always been so very easy and open, no pretending. We both wanted each other and knew how to make each other happy. I suppose we learnt together. During those happy days, Eddie once told me that I only had to touch his arm for him to feel it in his cock. And I must admit that his lips brushing my cheek made me want to pull him onto the floor.

'The important thing is that you don't feel unloved.'

'I don't. Okay?'

Suddenly, I grasped what she was trying to tell me; this was my problem, not hers. It was several weeks since Eddie had gone. She was over it. Actually Eddie was not fully gone because he'd been back several times on the excuse of pickings things up, then stayed for quite a while 'to check everything was fine'.

Fine! He actually said that. Eddie was never too good with words but, since giving up academia, very good at making money. Part of me being 'fine' was agreeing that I had plenty of money, which I had. 'I will never boot you out of the house,' said Eddie. 'The house?' My home. Obviously I had some learning to do. One of the things I learnt was to recognise when he was speaking with Robyna's words. It quite amused me actually because her language was so crass and unimaginative. Obviously she'd never read a book in her life.

Calypso, my bookish darling daughter, holding Margaret Drabble as a shield, dealt me a far more severe blow than anything Robyna could have achieved. She showed me that my job as a mother was over. Even though still a schoolgirl, she thought independently and, although doubtless grateful of any support and encouragement, didn't really *need* me. Not in the way I wanted to be needed. It was my need I was bringing to her. For a fleeting moment I imagined Mummy and could have wailed.

Instead, I took a deep breath and a step back. All the same I couldn't quite bear her to turn her back on me quite yet. I know I had her love but I wanted her attention.

'I think I might try and do something at the university again.' Where had that come from? I'd felt happy when my school teaching had contracted to a day and a half. I volunteered for various Catholic organisations, I did a little bit of academic reviewing. But I did read around my old subject as well as my usual Shakespearian reading.

'Oh, Mum, that's wonderful!' Calypso's smile of approbation made my heart turn over. 'Could you really go back to the university? Just think, you'd be able to read Shakespeare for a *living*!'

Only later, I thought that her eagerness to see me into a bright future, although enjoyed out of love, also helped to absolve her from too much sorrow on my behalf. She was not going to be my mother, after all. She did not blame me for the divorce, but she did not blame her father either.

Not long after this, she told me that she had decided not to do the A-Levels previously planned, English, History and French, but to change to the sciences. 'If I get the grades I need in O-Levels,' she added modestly. We both knew she would. She had always been a clever, hard-working girl, keen to win. But this change from arts to science was another move towards independence from me, her Shakespeare-obsessed mother.

Probably this slight barrier between us was why I never said what I had wanted to say about Eddie.

Your Dad wants to wipe out the bad things. He wants a woman without a sister killed in Vietnam and another who killed their mother and a wife who didn't spend two years going off to prison every week. He wants normal. Like Robyna.

CLEO

Sometime in the eighties, my MP friend, Vernon, took me to lunch in the Polish Club in Exhibition Road. He had left politics and only came to London occasionally. He said he enjoyed the club because the Welsh were like the Poles. When I asked why, he answered in a don't-you-know-already voice, 'Too clever by half. Disliked. Often exiles but longing for home.' I always enjoyed Vernon's company.

When we sat down and the waiter arrived, he offered me a drink.

I smiled, 'You know I don't drink.'

He put his hand flat on the top of his bald head, a rather odd habit he had, and said, 'Of course. Do you know why I gave you my card that day in the Ritz?' He didn't wait for my answer. Even ex-politicians are like that. 'Because I could see you hadn't taken drink. For sure your tragic personal life and your success as a novelist made you interesting but it was your teetotalism that really impressed me.' He paused. Another thing politicians soon perfect is the pause without giving an opportunity for interruption. 'Later on, I wondered why you never asked me about your mother.'

'But I did!' Now he had surprised me. 'Every time I referred to *a* "woman in politics" and you answered me with information, I learnt more about my mother.'

'Is that so?' It was his turn to be surprised.

'I learnt how hard it was to be a pretty woman without a husband and hold your own in the Houses of Parliament. I learnt about the sly insults, the veiled threats, the insincere overtures, the overt bullying, the fawning patronage, the special pleading that came the way of a woman like her.'

'I never said anything remotely like that.' Vernon sat back in his chair and laughed. 'Anyone would think you loved her.'

'No. But I was her daughter.'

My side of this conversation was part of the truth. Vernon did teach me about a woman's lot in politics but he also taught me that it was too late to understand who my mother was, even when, which he had quite forgotten by the time of our lunch in the Polish Club, he told me about her growing up.

Briefly, and it is all I shall ever know, Julie had been the only daughter of an Irish mother and a German who had fallen out of a Zeppelin during World War I and become a prisoner of war. Names unknown. They lived in a small house near the docks in Liverpool and one day my grandfather got on a ship and went home. Nothing more was ever heard of him and soon a stepfather, a dockworker, name unknown, took his place and there were six or seven more children.

Apparently, so Julie told Vernon, her father was an educated man who had taught her to read when she was three, whereas her stepfather could not even read. After she'd left school, she helped her mother with the children while working part-time in a convent where she continued to gather scraps of education, but, as soon as she could, left home and came to London. Very soon she met Brendan. That was it. Apparently Vernon was the only person she even told as much as this.

The story hadn't surprised me. It fitted in perfectly with everything I knew about her, so much so that I even played with the idea that she had invented a story both nebulous and precise which suited her self-image. However in the end I believed it was true because it explained that she had learnt to abandon little girl relatives at a very young age. It had worked once so why should it not again?

When I reminded Vernon of this conversation, he looked thoughtful and said that there was something odd about the whole thing, that she hadn't been running from the children, as I suggested, or at least there was something else.

'Bad?' I questioned him.

He refused to be drawn but wouldn't deny it. 'I suppose you could find under what name she married and trace her back to Liverpool.'

'I wouldn't put it past Julie to change her name,' I said, smiling.

'Oh, you young things are so cynical.'

'Sorry. I forgot she was your friend.' I smiled again.

'Proudly so.' He paused. 'But that doesn't mean she told me all her secrets.'

'Well, if she wanted her secrets, then she can have them,' I said firmly. 'I've done enough already. And I'm *not* young. Not many years before I'll be half a century.'

The expression on Vernon's face stayed with me and several days after our conversation, it crossed my mind to wonder why Julie's family had never claimed her when she became famous. Perhaps there had been something 'bad' in her past.

I put this thought away quickly. I very much didn't want to know Julie's secrets.

MILLIE

Eddie and I had a conversation. Sort of. At his request we drove
to Richmond Park. 'It will be easier to walk and talk,' he said, and
I suspected Robyna's voice. He drove while I lay back and recited
inwardly and with irony, *Shall I compare thee to a summer's day? Thou
art more lovely and more temperate* etc. It was a summer's day, the
eighties, five years since he'd left the family home. Despite the irony,
I couldn't help hoping for a reconciliation. How stupid can you be!

We walked silently at first. We had never been good at intimate
conversations, baring our souls, as I thought it, an occupation
better kept for God. But I did recognise that I had to try and
explain, although what I should try and explain was not clear to
me. I tried to take courage from the beauty of the day, the ancient
flourishing oaks, the undulating waves of green, the spiky bracken,
the sinuous paths trodden by visitors, royal from 1630, public a
couple of centuries later. How many sorrowing lovers had walked
the same way, hoping that the bright air and sun would heal their
wounds! *I wandered lonely as a cloud* etc.

I realised we were making our way to the Isabella Plantation,
a Victorian garden, principally of magnificent azaleas, planted
within woodland. It had been Calypso's favourite place when we'd
come to the park occasionally for a picnic – usually we went to
Hampstead Heath which was much closer. Caly called it the 'Secret
Garden' probably because she'd loved reading Frances Hodgson
Burnett's novel of the same name.

Indeed the moment we were within the gardens' railings Eddie
began on what at first seemed a Shakespearian soliloquy because
he didn't look at me as he spoke but stared fixedly at a long-dead

azalea flower, but which, once he turned to face me, became a full-blooded rant.

'You know it's amazing and wonderful to be the centre of attention. Robyna may not be as beautiful or as clever as you but she loves me 100 per cent whereas I'd put you at 10 per cent tops. I suppose I just never noticed because of the sex and being young and hopeful. But once the sex went out of the window, what did you offer me? Can you think of one thing? Not even 10 per cent of love and attention. Nil per cent financial input. Oh your teaching... Sorry. 5 per cent input given your pathetic wages. Caring for the house might be 5 per cent, caring for Calypso plenty of percentage but that wasn't me. Me! When did you think of ME? Me, your husband. All you cared about was your dead mother and your sister who were scarcely part of our lives. Well, maybe 4.5 per cent.'

While he ranted, I listened and wondered where all this percentage business came from. Could it be Robyna speaking? She was something called a 'systems analyst'. Perhaps such people spoke in percentages. It is possible I am exaggerating Eddie's use of percentages but, ever since he'd worked in the city, I'd noticed a preference for numbers over words.

'I am sorry about my family,' I replied in what I hoped was a dignified voice. 'At that dreadful time you were so strong and kind. I could not have survived without you.'

'You say "at that time" but that time never ended. It is still with us because you were always obsessed with your mother and her death made sure her power over you lasted for ever. You couldn't or wouldn't make love with me because it desecrated her memory. You turned your back on me, literally, night after night.'

Retaining my dignity, I said quietly, 'I loved my mother.' But inside my breast, my heart was fluttering and jumping. Was this the moment to tell the truth? A truth so bad that I had not even dared take it to the confessional. I loved my mother but, for one brief moment, I had hated her too.

I began to cry. Eddie looked at me astounded. I suppose my collapse into tears was unexpected. He didn't know I was crying to cover up the truth. 'I am so sorry, Eddie.' That was true. 'I know you have had to put up with so much.' That was true.

Eddie is and always was a good, kind man. We shared a great deal: our belief in a spiritual life, our love for Caly, our striving for a higher good.

'I should have got a proper job,' I sobbed, although knowing it wouldn't console Eddie. On the other hand he could always deal with my collapses.

He put his arm round me. 'You are a fine woman who has had to cope with serious tragedy.'

My sobs decreased. But the truth was as hard to tell as ever and, quite possibly, it was too late and it would mean nothing to him.

We walked on, holding hands, and after a bit sat down on a bench. We were like two old people who had weathered a storm, and I like to believe there was a little more love between us, 25 per cent perhaps, I thought with a wry smile to myself, even if the truth stayed outside the garden.

CALY

Aunt Cleo invited me to be her partner at the Booker Prize dinner. 'She said, 'Of course I won't win, darling, so you won't have to watch me making a fool of myself on the stage.' Of course she did win. And she was very witty on stage until she got to the thankyou's when she overdid it about my mum. I found that totally embarrassing.

It is the top UK literary prize and, even though I'd turned my back on all things arts and had just started to read Forensic Science at Cambridge, I was mightily impressed. £50,000 too! 'Not bad for a jailbird' as my friend Girish commented. Girish (which means Lord of the Mountains in Hindi) is Indian and a brilliant scientist and was keeping me up to the mark.

Cleo didn't want to go to any of the parties so we sloped back to her place. She was very quiet. Perhaps she was thinking about her award-winning book. It's very dark. Not grim like some dark books, say more Russian-soulful which sounds like a pretty puerile critique because Cleo doesn't believe in the soul or the spirit. At least I think she doesn't. You never quite knew where you are with Aunt Cleo.

The central figure is a girl in prison. I suppose it's the goodness of the girl that makes it readable. Storm clouds with a silver lining. Wow! Just as well I left Eng Lit behind me. Girish says my brain is definitely more scientific, whatever my mother may tell me.

Anyway, Cleo's book which is called *Matricide* (catchy eh?) tells the story of this beautiful Caribbean girl who lands up in prison. I cried so hard when I finished reading it that Girish asked jokingly whether my mum had died. I hadn't told him about my grandmother's death. Why would I?

MILLIE

It was watching her win the Booker on the TV that sent me over the edge. When she received the prize, she began thanking people, beginning with a cutaway to her mad-looking old publisher with scarlet lips and a cigarette which she was waving around as if it was a balloon and ending with me: 'My dearest friend without whom I would never have got through the most difficult period of my life.' More, 'One of the most truly good, unselfish people and I've known her since I was born. Thank you, dear sister, Millie.' Luckily I wasn't there so there was no cutaway for me, or my tears would have wiped the screen clean.

I still lived then in our beautiful big Islington home; over nearly two decades it had trebled in value. No Eddie of course and very little of Caly who had just started at university. I switched off the television and leant back in the sofa, the same old beige corded sofa where I had used to recover with a cup of tea after visiting Cleo in prison. Sometimes I poured whisky in it or had a gin and tonic on the side but I had to be careful because I would soon drive to pick up Calypso from school. Only very occasionally I had wept, guilty tears, that seemed red hot as they burnt their way down my cheeks.

After Cleo's speech, I allowed myself to cry and didn't even begin on the tea.

Caly would be gone the next day and then, I decided, glass in hand, I would go over to Cleo's house. The weather had been cold recently, the sunset a bloody red and I could imagine how it would look, reflected in the Thames. I pictured William Blake's lapping flames of hell. Maybe they would curl out of the water and reach out for me where I sat with my sister who talked of me with such love and admiration.

I put aside my glass and went up to bed. Knowing it would be impossible to sleep, I lay fully clothed on my bed, so tense that when the phone rang, I clutched my heart as if I'd been stabbed.

'Wasn't it terrific, Mum! Could you believe it! I've got an aunt who won the Booker! I hope you watched it ... What?' She broke off. I imagined Cleo who expected nothing good of life, smiling and holding onto my daughter. '... so do you mind if I go home with Cleo? She can't face the parties and all that stuff. She says we can have angels on horseback with Welsh rarebit which is a grander name for cheese on toast accompanied by hot chocolate, spiced with cinnamon. I'll have to go straight from there to Euston...'

I would never stop Caly spending time with Cleo. It was the one gift I could offer her. A little mitigation when the Grim Reaper or even our Heavenly Maker comes to call the card. Caly talked on excitedly, even after I'd said it was fine. All the time I could hear background voices congratulating Cleo, never Cleo's voice, but I felt happy for her.

I decided to go to her the following day.

CLEO

I watched Calypso sleeping, tucked up under a fur blanket on my sofa. She seemed so very calm, cheeks flushed like a younger child, eyelashes fluttering now and again. I was glad I'd chosen to take her to the Booker. She'd remember it as part of our history. A good day. An innocent day.

I could have asked Lennie to come with me. Rebekah wouldn't have minded. She accepted that we were linked and that I presented no threat to her. I did not even wish her dead or only very very occasionally. Yes, Caly was a good choice, a choice for the future perhaps.

MILLIE

I got off my bed long before it was light. I undressed, washed and carefully brushed my long hair, not all that much grey and still thick, pleated it against my head. I dressed again in a smart crimson dress with velvet collar and cuffs. It was quite child-like so perhaps I was pleading for mercy.

I waited until ten, then drove slowly, heading directly south before turning east and following the river on my right until I crossed at Vauxhall Bridge. I could already see Tower Bridge to the left. The other side of the river was a muddle of dark streets, underpasses, battered old buildings plus a smattering of modern blocks. I knew the roads well enough and didn't have to worry about becoming lost. At first I'd grumbled to myself about Cleo finding a place to live far from normal habitation but then I began to see it suited her.

Just before I reached my destination, I turned on the radio. A man pronounced reverentially 'It is hard to recognise a new radiant voice when it comes from such a grim source.' I immediately switched over to Radio 4. The man might have been referring to Cleo's novel and it wasn't worth risking it. Not today.

On Radio 4, a man's voice pronounced soberly, 'With the economy in recession once more, there are real fears of a second Winter of Discontent.' I turned off the radio and a few minutes later, crawled into the little yard behind Cleo's glass house. I sat for a moment before getting out of the car and knocking on the door. She didn't believe in bells.

'Hi there!' Cleo wore huge furry moccasins and a striped gold and purple kaftan. I noted with pleasure that she'd finally got rid of her prison slippers. 'Come in. I've just put the kettle on. How did I ever exist before coffee!'

'You drank.'

She laughed. 'What an idiot I was!'

I'd never seen her so happy. Happy and Cleo just didn't go together. It couldn't be winning the award. Cleo never cared about things like that. Perhaps she had been happy for a while and I just hadn't noticed. I walked in.

'Brilliant about winning.'

'Over ten years it took me. And a prison sentence.' She laughed again. Her pale curly hair was tied in a knot at the top of her head, with a plumed pen stuck through it.

We went into the kitchen and as I took off my coat, I thought how different we were, her with her royal robe and me with my schoolgirl's dress.

The light in the house was always amazing, even on a cold winter's day. There were no red flames as I'd imagined but shimmering streamers of silver and blue coming off the river like melting ice. She made coffee and we went upstairs into her extraordinary living room. She lay on the fur rug facing the sky and water while I sat primly on the only chair.

'You couldn't be much further from a prison cell,' I said. I was trying to get myself going but the view was seductive as the silver streaks became tinged with the pale yellow of a winter sun just rising through the clouds. The water was suddenly black, then grey and tinselled again.

'You can't possibly write in here,' I said.

'I *think* in here. It's excellent for thinking. Sometimes I cry when I think of Di. But mostly I think about what I'm writing.'

My heart began to squirm and wriggle and flutter.

"Are you okay?'

'Oh, yes. Thank you for taking Caly along last night. She obviously had a terrific time.'

'My pleasure. For a forensic scientist, she's very sympathetic to writers.'

'She loves you. We both do.'

She looked at me curiously. 'Are you sure you're all right, darling?'

In the Bible there are scenes where little devils jump out of a sinner's mouth. I could feel them inside me jostling each other for space and chattering rudely. I thought once they get up to my head, I'll open my mouth and let them jump out in words. My head became burning hot and my eyes seemed ready to roll out of the sockets.

'I wanted to tell you something about the night Mummy died.' The words came out with a great puff of breath. Cleo immediately sat up and faced me, sitting cross-legged.

'No, Millie,' she said gently. She held out a hand to me.

'I have to.' I squeezed my hands between my knees and leant forward. 'You know how I loved Mummy, adored her, to be more accurate. When I was growing up, my whole attention was centred on her, like a plant looking for water, a sunflower turning its face to the sun.'

'I know,' said Cleo, as I paused.

'I should have grown out of it, but I didn't. I had a husband and a child and my God. That should have been enough. I was so given so much, so much.' I paused again and this time she said nothing. Cleo would have made a good therapist. She listened with such attention.

'I don't know why I went to see Mummy that particular evening. Although I did quite often actually. Sometimes she turned me out, if she had a lot of work, other times she let me hang about as long as I kept quiet. I usually went late when Eddie was working at home and could babysit Caly. He told me I was mad but he didn't stop me. Sometimes I just slipped out without telling him and then slipped back in without him noticing. That night he was away. I left Caly alone.' I paused. 'That was wrong. She was only little.'

We both sat silently for a moment. She didn't ask me which

night I was referring to. I felt some pain in my hands where I was squeezing them between my legs and when I removed them I saw they were white. I held them together loosely but they soon started squeezing each other again. I continued.

'I had my own key to Mummy's flat so I let myself in and went to see where she was and what mood she was in. These visits always made me nervous, my heart beat too fast and my eyes were partially covered with little black spots. I think that must be why I didn't take in at first what was there in front of me. I didn't see you at all. You were half under the drinks cabinet and it was dark in that corner. When I saw Mummy, of course I went over and crouched beside her. I assumed she'd fainted and took up her hand. She stirred then and her eyes opened.

'Oh Millie, do leave me alone.' That's what she said, murmured it but distinct to me. Irritable. I didn't see any blood then and I moved back obediently, as usual trying to please. She closed her eyes again and her head fell back in a quite strange way, so after a minute or two I approached again which was when I realised she was unconscious. That there was something wrong with her. It was very odd. I had always been in thrall to her and now, suddenly, she was in thrall to me. It was for me to act, make a decision. Naturally, I didn't know it was a matter of life or death. Or perhaps I did.'

I stopped talking. My head was whirling with the effort of remembering and being honest. Did I know Mummy's life was in my hands?

'It was then I saw you. Of course I was crouched down at the same level. There was a bottle by you so I was pretty sure what was wrong with you. But all the same it made everything more confusing.

'I began to picture Buñuel films where nothing is quite what it seems. Emergency services and telephones where people dial 999 existed on a different planet to me. I went over to you and held your hand, as I had Mummy's. You didn't stir at all. Your whole body was slumped forward but I could smell the alcohol and, although your hair covered your face, I knew you were not sick, just drunk.' I paused. 'Sorry, Cleo.'

Cleo said nothing. I stared for a moment at the river. The sun had gone away again and the water was bottle green. Altogether changed.

'So I left you and went back for the third time to Mummy. She hadn't moved so I felt her pulse which was moving along quite briskly. I suddenly imagined that she was going to spring up angrily and tell me what a *bore* I was and couldn't I see that she was resting and that she had Cleo for company... It was all quite quite mad. I can't exactly pinpoint the scene, although it does remind me of the guilty Macbeth's crazed meeting with the witches when they parade all sorts of ghastly horrors in front of him but eventually convince him he is safe. I really did think you two would both spring up and start conversing, while casting sidelong glances in my direction. I'd really lost it. Oh, yes. I didn't have a clue. It wasn't that I've ever been jealous of you. You always hated her so much, or said you did, but just that I couldn't cope with it. I think I actually was deranged, if that means not understanding in a normal way. I was not normal.'

I stopped abruptly. My hands ached again where I'd been twisting them together and my head felt like a great big stone ball. No features. Not even a mouth.

Cleo cleared her throat. 'So I suppose you ran away.'

'Yes.' The stone cracked open a little.

'So you think *you* killed her, not me.'

'Yes.'

'There's no reason for *you* to kill her. *You* loved her.'

Cleo stared at me. Her pale eyes seemed to have black stripes down the middle like a cat's. After a while, when I said nothing, could say nothing, she said calmly, 'I see.'

I tried again. 'It was just in that moment I hated Mummy. Then when I got down to the pavement, I realised that leaving her felt like a huge release. I stood there breathing deeply, just giving myself a moment, before I went back to her and rang for an ambulance. But the next thing I knew, I was walking towards the car and I had got into it and driven home. I was in bed when the police rang.'

I wanted to shout *Mea Culpa Mea Culpa* then, or something dramatic. I'd carried the burden of sin for so long that just telling it in a dull voice, dull with my own dullness, didn't seem enough. I felt dull and stupid and being sinful was almost better than that. Of course it wasn't, but the dullness was a new sort of pain. Did Cleo's silence mean that she didn't understand the importance of what I was saying? 'My darling sister!' I wanted to cry out, 'Please forgive me! I have wronged you! Give me penance! You were in prison and when I came to you, I knew it was I that was the guilty one!'

My head was no longer stone but a pulpy mass of sin. But that also was a sin because it was not me that mattered. I stood up to relieve the pressure.

'I'm sorry, Millie.' Cleo spoke at last, far below me on her fur rug. 'I don't blame you. I can't, even though you ran away. Doubtless you can find the scriptural reference for when the disciples abandoned their Lord, in extremity, I believe, and about to die. But they didn't believe they'd killed him. Perhaps you want me to reproach you and give you penances and encourage you to beat your breast. But I can't. Julie was a bad mother but I don't blame her anymore so why should I start blaming you? I love you. My advice to you is to go to your priest and get absolution from him. You didn't kill Julie. But ask for penance for running away. Explain it all to Eddie, if he'll listen. Don't tell Calypso. Caly's fine. Honestly, I don't think there's much more to say.'

I stared down on her. 'Really?' I was so feeble that all I could say was 'Really?' and feel my legs shaking. Strange ideas like throwing myself through the glass window into the Thames came and went.

'Look, darling Millie, I've only got one sister left and you're her. She. I'm not about to lose you to your conscience.'

CLEO

Millie's confession shouldn't have surprised me. I had never been fool enough to believe that people matched their public casing. So my immediate reaction was sadness that she had born the burden – of sin, as she saw it – for so long. It sent me back to thinking that Julie had buggered us all up for ever and ever.

One night, a night without Lennie, I woke out of a dream in which I opened my eyes and saw Millie bending over Julie, then standing up and walking away, with a hard, determined expression on her face. Not like my dear Millie at all but in line with her feelings of anger as she'd described them to me.

I woke up sweating because the dream had seemed so real. I lay awake waiting for the light to show me my river and bring me back to myself. The hours passed slowly until only a thin blue mist clouded the water. I got out of my bed and stared outwards but, even when the mist dissolved and I could see ripples and a police boat passing on the far side of the river, I felt no better. I was convinced that I had briefly come out of my drunken coma and witnessed Millie acting in the way she'd told me, while I lay like an empty sack under the drinks cabinet. It seemed to me that I had purposefully blocked the memory. By failing to croak out 'Millie darling, call the ambulance' or just tug on her skirt as she passed, I had killed my mother for the second time.

The first question was: should I say anything to Millie? I had closed the subject finally and lovingly by announcing that I wasn't prepared to lose her to her conscience. Should I open the grisly scene all over again, like a crime scene which never can be resolved until the last detail, the last twinge and tweak of guilt has been documented and punished. Would it make Millie feel better if I took some of the blame she judged to be hers? Would she believe me? Or if she did believe me, would she be willing to blame me? Maybe she wanted to blame herself? Maybe she needed to feel that that moment of anger had been important and relevant? Perhaps she needed to feel she'd punished our mother? My head tangled with questions until I literally became ill.

Lennie found me writhing in bed, scarlet in the face and trembling uncontrollably.

'What is it?' He lay down beside me and tried to hold me still.

In my delirium, I told him what it was. I went on and on, raving like a lunatic so that he only picked up that it was about the evening Julie died and missed the subtleties which, after all, was what it was actually about.

In the end, he gave up trying calm me with understanding or words and took off my clothes and began to stroke me as if I wasn't ill at all but merely hysterical. Not such a bad estimation. Then he took off his own clothes and began to make love to me until it was impossible for me to do anything but make love back. Then we slept.

In the morning, I woke up late and sat up as he brought me a cup of coffee.

'What was it with you, last night?' he said as he had the night before. His eyes were on the river, rosy with the morning sun. 'I thought you were okay about your mother.'

'I dreamed that I watched Millie come into the room, see that Julie was dying and then run out without helping her. Then I lapsed into my habitual drunken coma.'

Lennie looked at me with amazement. He put down the coffee, gently tugged his beard, a habit that I found lovable but irritating, and stared some more. 'All that was about a dream?'

'Well, Millie told me that was what happened. She was very upset.'

'Then you dreamed you saw it happening?'

'Exactly'.

'You *dreamed* it?'

'Last night it seemed real. I believed it was real and I had all these options swirling round my brain.'

'So you got upset?' I didn't answer. 'But you're smiling now.'

'Because you're here. Because we made love. I don't know. Maybe I'm tired of trying to sort it all out so I decided to smile.'

Lennie sat on the bed. 'Do you think you can write this morning?'

Now I looked at *him* with amazement. 'Why ever not?'

He stood up. 'I rest my case.' He walked to the door before pausing. 'You dreamed that you'd seen whatever Millie did or didn't do to your mother and last night you worked yourself up into a frenzy because you couldn't work out the difference between fact and fiction. Worse still, you didn't know how to command the action. Let it go, my creative genius, let Julie go.'

CLEO

Of course I did lose Millie. But it took a long time.

As the eighties and the nineties turned into the millennium and I wrote books, one every two years or three if heavily researched (never interesting to write *about* one's books because they themselves contain all that is of interest), Millie drifted away. She had always had a child-like side of her nature, the side that was determined to make 'Mummy' love her. Most children are very one-track, I consider, which is why they hang on to fantasies (think their little friends or even Father Christmas) for as long as they do. But Millie's child self was educated by Shakespeare and other more esoteric reading, so that she could imagine horrors or voids that few children would conjure up.

Caly told me about her mother's nightmares and her lassitude, describing her staring eyes and wondering words as 'Ophelia without the water'. We were both frightened and took her to a doctor who diagnosed early onset Alzheimer's – she was still only sixty – and put her on pills. It was a sad day when she had to give up teaching. She had forgotten the name of the Pope, Millie herself told me. Eddie, like the devoted ex-husband he was, often stayed with her, and there were always friends who took pity. She was never angry, just a little vacant and given to pronouncements such as 'I want to go home' which made me weep.

Caly became successful. After years of training, she became a research scientist and seemed to travel the world giving prestigious lectures at prestigious conferences. I suppose she slogged away at her lab in Cambridge too, with her 'team'. But I was never very bright at understanding that sort of thing. I looked her up on Wikipedia recently to remind myself of her area of expertise and, even when she explained perfectly clearly, I only retained the information for two or three days. I told myself consolingly that if I retained too much information in my head, my imagination, from which I made my living (and which was also my joy and salvation) would be ever more squeezed.

Lennie was another joy. After twenty years or so we came permanently together. Rebekah sent him off, commenting romantically, 'It's a nuisance to have someone loafing about miserably.' He did become a pianist but only in an amateur kind of way. He made his living as a clock-mender. That sounds like something out of Dickens, and sometimes, when he took to wearing little round glasses and bending close over a spring or a spandrel with a bezel in the background – I loved the words for clock parts – he did seem out of another age. In fact his speciality was mending antique grandfather clocks which seemed to suit him very well. He had a shed along the wharf filled with elegant old grandfathers, as if a homage to his family's past. He made some money but I was the real bread-winner.

We lived together in my glass house and, all totalled up, must have spent weeks of our life being happy while we stared at the river. Lennie's son, Sam, came often. He was a good, practical boy like his mother, but I think he enjoyed time off with us. Despite my worldly success, he insisted on calling us 'the ancient hippies'. So untrue. I lived greedily off the life around me. All writers do.

I suppose I'm our family survivor. But I did kill my mother. Well, with a bit of help from Millie. I scarcely thought about Julie anymore. As the years passed, she seems more of an enigma than ever but one I had no intention of trying to solve.

Then, when London was gearing up to celebrate the millennium and we were looking forward to a massive firework display on the Thames, I received a letter from Brendan announcing his arrival. He wrote 'I am coming to die.'

I showed the letter to Lennie who thought it was as odd as I did.

'What does he want? We meet him off the plane with wreaths and a needle?' said Lennie.

'If he wants to commit suicide, Switzerland's the place,' I agreed, only half joking. 'He never used to be so dramatic.' I hesitated. 'As far as I can remember.'

We were chopping vegetables side by side and it always made me cheerful, even a little heartless, particularly when the morning's writing had gone well. We hadn't seen my father for thirty years, only keeping in touch with the odd letter or card, so he, like my mother, had drifted from my mind.

'It's lucky we don't have a spare room,' I remarked later when I was walking with Lennie to his workplace. My breath went ahead of me in white puffs. 'He must be eighty-five or so. I never really knew his age.'

'Perhaps he has a terminal illness,' said Lennie, his pace quickening as we neared his beloved clocks. 'As a doctor, he'd know.'

I blew my breath towards the sky and the puffs turned into plumes and feathers. 'Elena must have died ten years ago. Perhaps he wants looking after.'

Lennie glanced at me before producing the large key which opened his door. It had once belonged to an eighteenth-century French grandfather and Lennie loved it with all his heart. He turned the key carefully through three circuits. 'What would you think of that?'

I decided not to answer. We didn't have another message from Brendan so we could make no preparations. About halfway through January on another cold day when I kept looking at the Thames hoping for ice-floats as I'd once seen in New York on the Hudson, there was a ring on my doorbell and there he was.

It was the middle of the morning so I had been writing and Lennie was tending his clocks.

'Hey, Brendan.' That was an odd way to welcome him, I suppose, but it felt okay, friendly and unsurprised.

Although he was so old, actually nearly ninety, he didn't look much different. I remembered thinking the same when he came to me in prison. His hair was still thick, his shoulders still broad, even if his hazel eyes were hooded now.

'Ah, Cleopatra, my dear.'

He came in and took off a heavy sheepskin-lined coat. Then I saw he was thinner and bent but still I was struck by his sameness.

We went upstairs and sat facing the river. He seemed quite relaxed.

'How long is it since Elena died?' I asked to get things going. I am always a little brisk in the mornings if I'm interrupted in my writing.

'Twelve years,' he said. 'Cancer.' He turned to stare at me. 'You look well.'

'I'm a survivor,' I said, smiling. But he took it seriously.

'Yes. I wanted to talk about your mother.' For the first time he looked uncomfortable, even disturbed. Honestly, I expect I did too.

Then he went back to staring out of the window and changed the subject. 'My hotel room looks over the river from the north side. I'm staying in the Savoy. I thought why the fuck not.'

Presumably this decision was linked to his imminent death with no need to save the pounds. But the 'fuck' was a surprise. I hadn't seen him as a 'fucking' sort of man.

'That sounds great.' There was a pause. 'You don't look ill.'

'I waited for a good day to come and see you.'

So he really was dying. I tested my emotions and was surprised to find that I had a visceral sense of approaching loss. Not huge but definitely there. 'I'm sorry.'

'I'd love a whisky.'

'I don't drink. But I'll check what Lennie has in the cupboard. Probably only wine.'

I heard him sigh as I went down to the kitchen. Maybe it was harder than he thought to talk about Julie. I considered saying, 'Give us both a break and leave that woman out of it,' but when I handed him the glass, his face was determined in a way I remembered from childhood so I kept quiet.

'Thanks.' He sipped delicately. 'I'm not supposed to drink. I suppose you gave up in prison.'

'Yes. I didn't fancy the hooch. Bread, fruit, sugar, tomato paste, maybe prunes and marmite for kicks. Tasted like old underwear.' I wasn't going to say, 'Look where drink led me.'

'I get your point.'

Brendan's voice, which had always had a touch of the shamrock, was now overlaid with an Aussie twang. I waited for him to speak. Somewhere in the steel grey river under a steel grey sky, I could see a streak of white. Could it be ice forming?

'This is an amazing house.'

'It's always under threat now. Developers can't believe a silly old writer is sitting here with one of the best views of the river.'

Brendan continued sipping. I looked at my watch. I always wrote till one and then re-wrote and corrected in the afternoon. It was nearly midday. I listened as our nearest church clock struck twelve times. Brendan placed the empty glass at his feet.

'You see the thing about Julie is that she was born at the wrong time. Forty years later and she'd have been a career woman with no problems.'

Was that all? This whole build-up and he was groping to give me a little lesson in feminism. He must have seen the scepticism in my face because he started again quickly. 'I'm not saying she wasn't a difficult character and definitely an inferior mother...'

I gulped, 'Inferior!'

He ignored this interruption '... but I had a lot to do with it.'

So I was to hear *his* confession before he died. Millie before her mind wandered away and Brendan before he took off for a better place. 'You see she got pregnant before we married and I persuaded her to marry me. She hated the idea. She wanted to get rid of it or, if that couldn't be managed, hand it over for adoption. That was quite normal then.'

'You mean, abort Millie, who adored her,' I said, trying to be unkind. Really this story seemed so old hat as to be both pointless and tasteless.

Again he ignored me. 'To be honest, I forced her.'

'Then she had two more kiddies,' I said meanly, trying to hurry things along, before turning back to the river where I felt sure the ice, it was ice, was spreading.

'She lost hope.'

A knot was beginning to form in my chest, hard and painful. I took a few deep breaths. 'Then you went off,' I said, still trying to get this meeting over. Perhaps there'd be still a quarter of an hour for my writing before lunch.

'Yes. I couldn't bear being with her. She was so angry. The war was a godsend for me. I felt as if I could start a new life.'

'And you met Elena. That was handy.'

He stood up and walked up close to the glass. I did that often. It felt as if you were part of the river. He turned round and said in the same quiet voice he'd used all along, 'I tried to make it work. I waited till you were all grown-up before I went to Elena.'

'You loved Di. That's true.' He didn't deny my inference that Di was the only one of us he loved. I saw the guilty pain in his face. But it was because he had loved Di and she had died. The hard knot beat heat into my head. 'Do you know, Brendan, you're an old man, apparently dying soon, so you want to own up but you can't put anything right so what's the point? I'm not a priest to give you absolution. Frankly, it's just raking up coals and causing me pain, which is not exactly helpful, in fact some might say it's thoroughly selfish. Are you saying, for example, that I should have thrown that poor innocent buddha at *you*? Not Julie. That *you're* the guilty one? Well, I'm sure you can see that's unlikely to make me feel any better about my role in family life. I was an angry, out-of-control drunk. You say I look well, so why don't we leave it at that.'

Fired by my words, I stood up and found we were side by side, faces close to the glass. Once more I searched for the streak of ice. But I couldn't see it anymore, everything seemed to have become lighter and brighter. I looked up at the sky and, as I watched, noting its thick texture, a few white flakes began to descend, so slowly and gently that they seemed to hover in front of the window.

'It's snowing,' said Brendan.

We both stared, as if each snowflake meant something special, telling us a story before it fell, twirling slightly onto the water.

I felt an arm, warm round my waist, not clasping, warm and steady, undemanding but, there was no other word for it, loving.

I didn't look up at Brendan's face but I didn't move away.

We stayed like that, watching the snowflakes fall, faster and thicker, until I heard Lennie's voice from below.

'Cleo! It's snowing! We must go out at once. It's just so beautiful!'

CALY

No one had ever looked at my grandmother's personal possessions after her death. I suppose under the circumstances, it was hardly surprising. Once the police had finished with them, they'd just been thrown into boxes and sent into storage. The flat with its furnishings had been rented and her secretary took anything relating to government. But all the same, I was surprised how little she'd left behind.

A letter came from a storage depot, on the river in south-west London, saying they'd had a fire and although Mrs Flynn's possessions were undamaged, they had decided to get rid of smaller, long-standing, fire-risk items, including clothes and papers. They advised that they had a charity willing to take the clothes sight unseen. I immediately agreed to that. I shuddered at the thought of poor Mummy even getting to hear of their existence and Cleo certainly didn't deserve to deal with suits and dresses, still presumably scented with Julie's perfume, even after all that time locked in a box, waiting to be released, like a genie from a bottle.

But I was curious enough to go and collect her other belongings myself. I was in a hurry as usual, rushing in a taxi over Hammersmith Bridge and telling the driver to wait outside the building. I was on my phone when we arrived, assuring my PA that I would not be late for the lecture I was giving on parasites and vectors at midday. She could see where I was on her phone and didn't quite believe me.

The boxes were waiting, I had arranged that. Only three of them, none of them big. My heart did do a bit of an emotional leap then. The driver helped me carry them into his cab. I could see he sensed a story so I determined not to say a word.

In fact I'd been to Amsterdam and back before I found time and a pair of scissors to open them. It was evening. Spring. When London looks least like a great commercial machine and more like a collection of gardens. My flat is small, in North London, not far from the house where I grew up. I travelled so much that I'd never done it up much but I liked the view reaching over gardens and roads to Hampstead Heath.

I put on rubber gloves and opened the first box, which was filled with still-sealed letters. They were addressed to Millicent, Diana and Cleopatra Flynn. My grandfather had died in London a few years back and I recognised his handwriting. I found I had absolutely no wish to read them or to try and guess why they were unopened, but I couldn't help noticing that they had Australian postmarks and were dated in the late 1950s and 1960s. I shut that box. It would have felt like trespassing.

The second box held signed books. I supposed the rest had been disposed of. There were not many. I shut that box too, although thinking I might check through in case there were any I wanted before they hit the charity shops.

The third were bathroom items, creams, shampoos, hairdryer, her perfume bottle, Ma Griffe, nothing interesting. Yet so personal that again I had that sense of trespassing on someone else's story. They were fifty years out of date of course, so seemed old-fashioned, which jarred with my memory of her as the glamorous grandmother. Trying not to think further, I tipped them into a black bag and added them to my garbage bin.

Ah hour later, after I'd had a ready-cooked fish pie with a cup of coffee, I came back and put all the letters in another black bag and added it to the bin. If I'd had access to a bonfire, I'd have burnt them. That would have been more fitting. Either way, I had learnt that it was never wise to look back.

A week or two passed while I did, glory of glories, some lab work, so that my mind was a crossword puzzle of theories and analysis.

Meanwhile, the box sat there, in the corner of my living room, out of place in my orderly life. So on a Saturday, I put on my rubber gloves again and took out all the books. They were a disappointing lot. Signed, certainly, but usually by the giver, not by the author. There was a first edition of Mary Wilson's poems, signed by the author '*with admiration*' but that was the pick of the bunch. Most were political biographies given by well-wishers.

I separated Mrs Wilson, carried the box to the door to take out later and then, on impulse, reached in and took out one other. It was elegantly bound in navy blue and gold and, on inspection, I found it was the *Oxford Book of English Verse*, chosen and edited by Sir Arthur Quiller-Couch and first published in 1900, although endlessly reprinted. It was dedicated to '*The President, Fellows and Scholars of Trinity College, Oxford, A house of Learning, Ancient, Humane, Liberal*', which rather intrigued me. So, although I seldom read poetry, I put it aside to check out later. I suppose I had some idea that my mother might like it.

Once again time passed, until, on another empty Saturday, I picked up the book again and opened it at random. Two pieces of paper fell out. I knew my grandmother's handwriting from when I'd cleared up Mummy's house, also one of them was written on House of Commons writing paper. Even I wasn't strong enough to find a black bag for these. Neither had a date nor a heading. The only difference was that the one which turned out to be the first was written in a neater, smaller style. I sat down and began to read it.

'*He was so big. But not big in the way O'Sullivan was big, big bully, big brute, big stupid, ugly selfish. That's enough about him. My stepdad, forgotten just as they all are. My family. So-called. It was easy to leave them even before Brendan came along. I never looked back, not once. I don't, even now want to know if any of them are dead or alive, how all those kids got on with their lives. Brendan blotted them out. I didn't have to tell him the whole* story. I'd done enough for them. My anger puffed out smoke and flames. It was lucky for them, I didn't go back. I told no one. I breathed the breath of an escaping prisoner. Why I am writing this now? Because I'm on my own with three children? Because it reminds me of the past? Because my anger builds again? My name was Elise Hirsch. Then it became Elsie O'Sullivan. Never my real name. How brave I am now I'm Julie Flynn! Julie Flynn now and no one will ever know. No one will ever find me. My stepfather was nothing, a nobody, but he was bigger and stronger than me. Why am I writing this? Because there's a war on and Brendan might never come back. Does he guess I used him like a rope ladder? My escape mechanism. Never my lover. How could I ever love a man again? Julie Flynn is writing this, not poor, pathetic, Elsie O'Sullivan.'*

The second page was the one on House of Commons paper.

'Just came across this outpouring. I can't imagine why I kept it. Tomorrow I expect to be summoned to Downing Street. I'll be a dedicated, hard-working minister. I suppose that's why I'm writing this. To make the point to myself. I am a somebody. A minister in the Labour Government. I am somebody important, not a poor, snivelling child, crawling yet again from under a drunken man, with heavy belly, flabby buttocks and semen still dripping from his disgusting penis.

I have made myself somebody.'

I burned both papers. It was obvious they were not meant to be seen and I regretted opening that book. It was impulsive, irrational and out of character. After I'd burnt the papers in the sink, I found that my hands were shaking so hard, I needed to pour myself a drink and sit down.

Unfortunately, I couldn't get the reference to the still dripping semen out of my mind. As a scientist, a microbiologist, I am used to analysing information in order to predict possible, probable or certain outcomes. The idea that my grandmother's notes presented to my mind only came under the 'possible' heading but I still found it distressing and even obsessive. Had she become pregnant by her stepfather's semen, run away, found Brendan and, with or without his knowledge, given birth to Millie, my mother, a child of abuse or, let's face it, rape?

I was four when Julie died so remembered her as a small, very pretty woman, with an extremely disturbing aura. In her presence my mother changed from calm and loving to something I couldn't understand or describe, still can't actually, auras not being my thing, then or now.

This was the possibility I confronted in as scientific a way I could manage. It struck me, in this investigatory mode, how unlike to either of my grandparents Mum looked. Cleo took after Julie and Diana, I had always been told, and have now checked photographs to confirm it. Di resembled her father. Mum was dark and rounded, once beautiful, (beautiful again now she's left her demons behind). Could it be that she took after the O'Sullivan family, a blue-eyed, black-haired, white-skinned Celtic girl?

It seemed to me that the 'possible' moved nearer to the 'probable', even though it would have made her very young when she married Brendan. At this point in my thinking I had to fly to Atlanta where I was taking part in an important pharmaceutics, microbiology and biotechnology conference. When I returned to England, my thinking had shifted. It was helped along by a visit from Aunt Cleo. She was one of those older women who always seemed youthful. I don't mean she didn't have wrinkles – she'd always been thin and her skin had crumpled like a rose petal – but her mind and approach to life was as vibrantly youthful as anyone I know.

'I'm over the hump, Caly, my darling, so I've come to celebrate. And what a hump it was! An enormous camel's hump, although not quite a dromedary when two humps rise in horrid sequence. All the same I've been agonised for weeks. Dear Reggie. Sometimes I just love the men in my novels. I'm sure I've mentioned Reggie to you. To die? To flee? To die heroically? To die as a coward? Not to die at all? Thank God, no. Rather, sorry God for I am playing God. This morning I gave Reggie life. Oh, Caly, what a joy! To save the life of such a man... I haven't left the house for weeks and now here I am!' She threw her arms round me.

I was the only person, so I believe, to whom Cleo talked about whatever novel she was writing so I was more aware than most how fiction, the making up of stories, dominated her every breath. Mum had told me that she was always the same, even as a little girl, and I suddenly had an instinctive understanding, very unscientific, that it was her unhappy, angry, unloving mother who had made her like that.

'You haven't forgotten Millie's birthday, have you, darling?' said Cleo as she left.

'*She'll* certainly have forgotten,' I replied.

After I'd closed the door, I realised that Mum, too, had escaped into a world of make-believe.

An hour later when, despite a brisk walk to buy my supper, I still hadn't got the subject out of my mind, the obvious struck me that Julie herself, in a more thorough way than any of her daughters, had discarded the reality of her existence and created a fictional character to replace the old, unwanted model.

In all fairness, you couldn't really blame her.

MILLIE

It's my birthday. So they keep telling me. They joke about eighty. Oh what a horrid cake! As if I cared. I hate cake. Now they've left me alone. Where am I? I want to go home. Where is home? This is home. So they keep telling me. Better alone. Better. Better.

I am in a garden. Cleo was here. I think she was here. But not at home. Did Mummy die? Mummy, did you die? You should know. Of course you died. Cleo told me.

Cleo said, 'Mummy died, Millie. You know that.'

But why should I ask then? I *think* I know she died. 'How long ago did she die, Cleo?' Cleo is my friend. She comes to me and smiles and says, 'Hello, darling Millie.' Sometimes she sounds like Mummy.

'How long ago did Mummy die?' I *think* I know but how can I be sure? So I ask Cleo. 'When did Mummy die?'

'In 1968, Millie. Half a century ago. You went to her funeral.'

I feel Cleo moving away. I'm not blind. At least I *think* I'm not blind. But sometimes the outside world seems very far away. Things inside my head seem much closer. Well, obviously they are closer.

They tell me to look at the flowers in the garden so I do. They tell me to touch them. They think that will make them real? But why should that make them any more real than the flowers inside my head? People are very stupid. Four wedding bouquets. That's a thought. Makes me laugh.

Oh dear. Oh dear. Laughing used to be fun. Now Carmen will be cross. No. I like Carmen. I *think* I like Carmen. I think I'm wearing a pad. That's all right then.

I'll shut my eyes in the sun. Or is it the light in my room? No need to panic either way. If I shut my eyes it makes no difference. I can see what I like then.

Cleo left me a tape recorder. She put it down beside me. 'This is Millie talking. This is Millicent talking. This is Millicent not talking.'

Cleo said, 'I'll leave it turned on so you can record your eightieth birthday. Sorry I can't stay longer.'

Carmen said, 'How lovely!'

And Cleo from the door said, 'To stop you drifting.'

I *think* she said 'drifting'. She didn't *mean* to be unkind. But what is wrong with drifting? I *think* thinking is drifting. Everybody thinks. Perhaps she means 'drifting into the past'. Yes. The past. Now I *think* she means that.

Cleo is my sister. I also have a daughter. I know I do. I'm sure I do. A darling daughter. I love my daughter. Certainly. Certainly. I wonder where my daughter is. I must ask Cleo.

I love Cleo. Even after what she did or didn't do to Mummy. I certainly don't want to drift back to that. Perhaps that's what she's afraid of.

Darling Mummy. I wonder if she's alive somewhere. On earth, I mean. Nothing is sure. Was there a birthday cake somewhere? An ugly birthday cake with my name on it and candles. Or am I drifting again?

'I am not drifting, Cleo.' I said that into the recorder. At least, I *think* I did.

'Carmen, dear, did I just speak?'

No answer. Not here? 'I'd love a small slice of that birthday cake, Carmen.' Beggars can't be choosers. I enjoy marzipan. I *think* I enjoy marzipan if it is what I *think* it is.

There I go laughing again. And now I don't *think* I'm wearing a pad.

'Carmen!' She will come. I like Carmen. 'Sorry, my dear. Too much laughing on my birthday.'

'*She hath often dreamt of unhappiness and waked herself with laughing.*' *Much Ado about Nothing.* If my memory has gone, how can I remember that?

CLEO

I don't why I suddenly decided to pay a visit to Kensal Green Cemetery.

One cool April morning, I found myself walking beside the canal that leads from Harrow Road to Ladbroke Grove. I was a South London woman who considered anything with an N in the postcode alien territory. On the other hand I often made little forays into the unknown when researching my novels and I told myself it felt like that. Curiosity, nothing more.

Nor was the date significant to either my mother or sister, neither the anniversary of birth nor death. Curiosity, I repeated to myself. Late-flowering curiosity. In that spirit I described to myself what I saw on the banks. The water: brown, a torpid mixture of colours left out when the rainbow was created. The boats, battered, brutalised by the weather, yet some garlanded with spring plants, not fresh as in 'now is the month of May...' but weathered old troopers, survivors of the winter and, just occasionally, shown up by a young starlet, a red geranium clinging to its pot.

One boat was notable for its owner, a leather-faced leprechaun bent assiduously over undecipherable bundles on the bank. Animal? Vegetable? Mineral? Perhaps all three. But behind him on his boat an outsized tiger lounged complacently on a velvet chaise longue, spotted with pigeon poo and striped with cat wee. The ducks were more discreet, black and white moorhens on their nests, a white swan its purity scarcely sullied by the murky water...

Before long my description had bored me into blankness – who needs words when phones and film have made the visual instantly accessible? – and I looked ahead for the bridge which would lead up to the next stage, Ladbroke Grove, the roundabout and the Harrow Road where I would soon find the pillared and porticoed entrance to the cemetery. So far the app would bring me.

You have reached your destination.

Can anyone speak with such certainty? But I was glad to hear it and hoped it was the truth.

After all, I knew Diana lay somewhere nearby, under a turkey oak, her ashes divided into two, half here, half in America with her lover. I had been told that half a century ago and it was no disrespect that this was my first visit. Many people never visit the Queen, nor the President of the United States nor of the Soviet Union for that matter, or China's resident charmer. But it doesn't imply a lack of respect. They may yearn all their lives but lack the right circumstances.

Wherever Di was, in a Catholic heaven or an atheist vacuum, she knew I loved her. I began to walk, casually, to impress the outside world: a woman with flowers, a man jogging. I looked vaguely, without passion, for the turkey oak. Raising my eyes (casually) I saw ahead a vast acreage of stoneware: crosses, figures, angels with wings, women with drapes, pyramids, mausoleums. I saw chestnut trees, cheery trees, prettily in flower, hollies, oaks (common), sycamore... Why had my app deserted me? At least it could have informed me of the vastness I approached, a domain to encompass the deaths of thousands, hundreds of thousands. Why had no one told me that I would need a map to find Di's grave, let alone the Other. My Mother (rhyme).

Moreover, this world ahead of me was girded and crossed and criss-crossed with paths, some narrow, some broad. Which one would I take? Where was the courage to take on such an act of discovery? Did Christopher Columbus hesitate before he headed for the New World? Did Stout Cortez blink nervously when he spotted the Pacific from a peak in Darien? Did Marco Polo, Henry the Navigator, Vasco da Gama, Amerigo Vespucci, Edmund Hillary, Yuri Gagarin...

As I distracted myself with words, I walked slowly forward, continuing for five minutes or so, then turned right. Perhaps Millie had told me the whereabouts of Di's grave. Perhaps Father Louis, R.I.P. 1995, had told me, or even Brad. You never know what the unconscious is up to. I remembered a description too, the white marble stone, the brass-rimmed holder for flowers, even the inscription, *Remember Di Flynn who gave her life for her beliefs 1940–1968.* Beliefs?

So I found Di's grave. And the turkey oak was enormous and had dropped a limb on the grave next door. Thank you, turkey oak, for that bench, although the relations of Thomas Liversedge Fish '*The owner of 400 Public Houses and known as the Gold Fish*' might not have been so pleased.

I sat on the branch and looked at Di's grave, calm and untouched, Portland stone, I estimated, not marble, no flowers in the holder of course. I reflected on her life – on her death. She had met a violent end like her mother, the other. A sniper in that far away city of Hue. Brad believed that if she'd lived, she'd have married him and lived happily ever after in California.

Could that be true? Was there a different plan laid out for her which that sharpshooter had blocked? Maybe. A loving God as Millie believed would never have planned such a cruel end. But then again, was it so cruel? From childhood on, when Brendan came home and told his derring-do stories of war, Di had yearned to be a courageous soldier. There was no reason she shouldn't have run off with Brad the moment he asked her. They loved each other. She chose instead to take a helicopter and stand with her notebook beside young men who had no choice but to risk their lives. She wrote to me about it. Her earlier reports were read by people in different places around the world. So perhaps Hue was a fitting climax to her work and Brad's rosy future would have been downhill all the way. Who knows?

God alone knows. I smiled to myself. It was Millie helping me out.

Despite the long leather coat I was wearing, the branch was beginning to feel uncomfortable. Time to move on from Mr Goldfish. I stood up, stretched my legs, stamped my feet, then looked ahead once more to those jagged waves of stone. Some were fallen into each other's arms, like lovers clasped in anguish, angels, headless or wingless, yet flying still, arches in half like a sickle moon, mausoleums sprung open while others tidily shut, crosses sturdily upright or turned into broken planks. They were not waves but the crests breaking on a great storm-tossed ocean.

I hesitated, almost sat down again. A flurry of questions so befuddled my head that my writer's self noted, 'I can't hear myself think.'

Why did I want to find Julie's grave?

Why did I think she was buried in this cemetery?

If she was buried here, wherever was she among all these sympathy-seeking memorials?

Why had I not thought of this earlier? Done some research? Asked for a map? Many people would know where she was buried.

Why didn't I just run away? But isn't that what I had always done.

I turned round and started for the gate. I only didn't run because I was eighty years old and had never liked running anyway. Did the aforementioned Stout Cortes, Amerigo Vespucci, Christopher Columbus, ever turn tail? I reached the gates, porticoed and pillared, and stopped abruptly.

Another question appeared. Did I expect to understand my mother by standing at her grave? Or was I by this time a respectful witness? Isn't that why people went to graves? I had certainly stood witness at Di's grave.

Noticing a bench, I went over and sat down, although collapsed would be more accurate. Why did thoughts of my mother still have that effect after over fifty years? My heartbeat galloped as if it knew something I didn't and was dashing that way. I tried to think of

Lennie old like me. We loved each other. I wanted to scream it out. Somebody loved me.

I was tired and the sun warmed me in a friendly way and gradually I felt comforted. I shut my eyes.

When I opened them again, there was a man seated at the other end of the bench. He had come so quietly that I hadn't heard his arrival. *Like a ghost*, I thought.

'Alright, are you?'

I considered. I liked his voice, Northern, youthful, although he must have been in his fifties. There seemed no reason not to tell the truth.

'I'm looking for my mother's grave.'

'Been here long, has she?'

'Over half a century.'

'Famous?'

I was taken aback. I looked again at his respectable tweed jacket, his agreeable well shaved face. 'Why do you ask that?'

'If she was famous, I might know the grave. I come here often.'

'I see.' He was a grave-yard star-fucker. 'My sister is definitely here. She's next to a Mr Fish.'

'Ah, that would be Mr Goldfish.' He looked pleased like a man who'd passed a test.

'What sort of famous do you like?'

'Most of them here are historical. You can check on them online.'

'A sort of hobby?'

'I learn a lot. Not many people know that Lord Byron's faithful attendant Giovanni Battista Falcieri (1798–1874), following his master's death, married Disraeli's maid and worked as a messenger for the India office.' He looked up to see my reaction.

'That is interesting.' It was tempting to tell him my mother's name. If she was here, he would surely know her resting place. The two words echoed in my head. *Resting place*. But I couldn't let this man lead me there. I imagined him looking up her history. Or was it possible he knew it already and my part in it?

'I never knew my own mother,' the man said. I thought he must be lonely to talk so long to an elderly stranger. 'I first came, just like you, looking for her grave.'

'Did you find it?'

'No. Never did. I was adopted, which didn't help. But the search gave me a way forward.'

'I see.'

'And now I don't look for her anymore. When all's said and done, I wouldn't know how to react. If you haven't known your mother when you're growing up, you can't suddenly expect to be close. Particularly when she's dead.' He seemed to be waiting for an answer.

'True enough,' I said.

'But she gave me something, so it's okay. You have to be glad about that, don't you?'

'You mean your hobby.'

'That's right.' He gathered steam as if he was saying aloud words usually inside his head. 'You can't go on worrying about things you're never going to have. She wasn't there for me but there'll have been a reason. I just don't know it. If you know what I mean.' He stood up. 'I'll be on my way now. I enjoyed our little chat.' He gave a courteous bow.

'Thank you.' I raised my hand in farewell.

Was it only a writer's frustrated curiosity that had kept Julie forever alive in my imagination? Boxing a shadow until I was an old woman. The sun was even warmer and the purring of a wood pigeon somewhere nearby made me feel sleepy. I shut my eyes again.

The man was right of course. I could never know Julie's whole story. If there was a secret, it would remain hidden from me. After all, I had forgiven her decades ago and thought I had forgiven myself.

Yet now on that wooden bench in the cemetery, in the dream-like state that the stranger's words had helped to create, I felt a quite different sense of inner change, as if, after all these years, I could truly acknowledge Julie as my mother and, by letting her rest in peace, find peace myself.

ACKNOWLEDGEMENTS

Many thanks to all at Unicorn Publishing, particularly Ian Strathcarron, and Ryan Gearing; also, my ever encouraging editor, Lucie Skilton, my energetic publicist, Lauren Tanner, and my no-holds-barred designer, Matt Wilson.

Once again, my friends and family especially Rose, Chloe and Caspar Billington, have seen me through *War Babies* and the difficult times that accompanied its preparation. My husband, Kevin, was there for the writing, but will not see the publication. His advice and enthusiasm over fifty years was all part of his continuous loving support.